# BILLIONAIRE BOSS

## DOMINATING DESIRES
### BOOK FOUR

# MAHI MISTRY

Published by Mahi Mistry
Cover Design by GetCovers
Edited by Jeanie Creech
Proofread by Edresa Ramos
ISBN e-Book: 978-93-5526-832-7
ISBN paperback: 978-93-5627-659-8

# PROLOGUE

## DAMON

I shouldn't have kissed her.

There were so many reasons not to but…

A small moan poured out of her pouty lips, and I swallowed it with a groan, licking her lips, savoring them. She tasted like sweet honey, and I would be damned if I didn't want to know how her other sets of lips tasted like.

Arousal shot through my veins, and I had to force myself to withdraw and glare down at the woman in my arms. My fingers dug into her hips, feeling the warmth of her skin underneath the tight dress that clung to her like a second skin.

"Fuck," she breathed out, lashes blinking up at me. I couldn't see her face because the lights in the club were still dim. I could only hear her and feel her. Pressed against my suit like she was ready to climb into my bed. Ready to climb *me*.

"Kiss me."

I stiffened.

"Again," she demanded, her voice soft and husky.

How long had it been since I shared a bed with another person? Too many years.

*Yet this woman...*

I was about to ask her for her name when everyone around us cheered. I moved back, dragging her lithe frame with me. She was taller than the average woman, her waist small and long hair brushing against my arm that was wrapped around her. I would not let her go so easily.

There was a blackout party in my club. Once you found a partner, the DJ would count down from ten, and the entire club would fall into complete darkness for a few seconds. Then you had to share a kiss with your partner or the person closest to you with their consent. I had guards wearing night vision glasses for a few minutes, making sure everyone was safe. I always made rounds before the blackout party to check with the floor managers, but today I was stopped.

Her musky vanilla perfume was delicious. I wanted to lick her neck and growl in her ears that she must wear it again if we meet next time.

*Next time already, Damon?*

"Wait, I'll get a room—"

I held her elbow and pulled her back to my chest. My lips were still tingling from the kiss we shared, and I wasn't ready to let her go just yet.

"I have a room," I said, my voice husky. "Come with me."

I ignored the small tone of familiarity upon hearing her voice. Maybe she was someone who frequented my club a lot. My arm relaxed at the dip of her waist as she followed me wordlessly. Once we were in the main hallway with much better light, I turned around to get a glimpse of—

"What the fuck are you doing here?" I demanded, a growl emanating from my throat as I glared at the woman—no, the girl—I was so familiar with.

Her eyes widened, blinking at me. She parted her lips, the

lips I had kissed and devoured, but nothing came out. And for the first time since I had known her, Summer Hayes was speechless.

"Why are *you* here?" she demanded, her voice husky from—

My ears turned warm, and I noticed that a few of the patrons were looking at us. I grabbed her wrist and dragged her to my office, slamming the door shut.

It was awfully quiet in my office since it was soundproof. I narrowed my eyes at her and yanked out my tie. She watched me with a hand on her hip, standing by the door and taping her god-awful high heels.

*Fucking hell. This was bad.*

"I don't believe that I'm such a terrible kisser that it got your man-panties in a twist."

I glared at her harder, removing my jacket and draping it over my chair. My entire body was feeling hot all of a sudden.

"It's prom night," I said with as much calm as I could. Which wasn't much, if I was being honest. She was dressed up, her makeup done well with bright colors on her lids, and her cheekbones dusted in glitter that made her face glow. She looked stunning. Too pretty to be alone on prom night. But why was she here? "What the fuck are you doing here, Summer?" *Do Emma and Mia know?*

*Fuck. I just kissed my little sister's best friend.*

Her dark eyes looked away from me, and for the first time since we kissed, I could breathe. "I got bored," she said, her shoulder slumping.

By the tone of her voice, she wasn't bored.

But I didn't care.

"Do Emma and Mia know you are here?"

Her eyes fell on me and I was surprised by the emotions swirling in her dark eyes. "They think I'm home."

My jaw clenched. I didn't like her slouching when she could be at her high school and be the prom queen. "Why?" *What happened? Did someone hurt you? Tell me everything.*

"I already told you, I got bored," she said and straightened up her spine. "I came here because I wanted to get laid."

"No, you're not," I said too quickly. "I... I'm driving you home. Come on."

"No, you're not!" she snapped, taking a step back from me. "I-I can sleep with whomever I want. You're not my dad."

"Thank fuck I'm not," I sneered. "If something happened at the prom, tell me."

Summer blinked at me, swallowing the lump in her throat. I watched her, trying not to get distracted by the sweet perfume.

"Why do you care?" she mumbled.

I ignored the itch to cup her cheek and make her look at me and demand what had happened. From what little I knew about her—from sleepovers at Emma's house to meeting her at the club, to noticing her at cheer practice during my school visits—I knew she was like her name. Bubbly, charming and always fucking happy. It infuriated me, but I didn't care. I also didn't care that something had happened at the prom that she rushed over here without telling the truth to her friends. I didn't care. Not one bit.

"I don't." I clenched my fists. "I don't want Emma to scold me if she finds out about this."

Something dimmed in her eyes as she scoffed and rolled her eyes. "Of course, you don't. Pigs would start flying if you started caring about someone other than yourself. I'll drive myself home."

I didn't show how badly her comment hurt and I brushed it away. I picked up my suit jacket and key fob. "Like hell you are. I'll drop you home—"

"No," she ordered. "I'll get a cab. I don't want to be with you right now."

I buttoned my suit and chuckled darkly. "You stopped me and kissed me like you were in heat and now—"

Soft blush made her golden-brown skin glow. "I would have never kissed you if I had known it was you, Damon. Heck, I wouldn't even kiss you if you were the last person on this earth."

"Feeling's mutual, sweetheart," I replied, and closing the distance between us, I threw her over my shoulder. "I don't trust you to find your way home safely."

"Put me down. Now!" she shrieked, her small fists hitting my back.

The guards looked alarmed, but when they saw my face, they didn't say anything. I carefully held her dress because her flashing my entire sex club was the last thing I needed tonight.

I ignored her and put her in the car, strapping her seat belt and driving her to Hayes' residence. I hated how she kept fumbling with her fingers, tapping her feet, and the sweet perfume that lingered in the car. I was glad that she was silent during the entire ride, but before she left, she glared at me and said, "Forget about the kiss. It never happened."

Summer slammed the door, making my jaw clench. I stared at the empty passenger seat and looked at the vacant road ahead.

As if I could ever forget the kiss or her little moans.

*Why the fuck does it have to be her?*

# PART I

"That's a good girl."

1

# I DARE YOU

## SUMMER

***Two Years Later***

It was a shame that I was going commando for the masquerade party. A shame, indeed.

A lone sigh escaped my lips when I took a sip of bubbly champagne. My eyes averted from the crowd mingling with each other to the huge golden chandelier on the ceiling of the club. Beautiful men and women swayed to the erotic music, masks covering their eyes, nose and cheekbones. Feathers, ribbons, and gems adorned their masks as their pearly white teeth gleamed in the dim lights.

I was wearing a mask too. I had to. No one could know that Summer Hayes skipped the premiere of her show halfway through and went to the nearest sex club in Hollywood just because she was bored.

My hand tightened on the cold flute glass as I looked around, wishing I had free rein to talk and flirt with anyone I wanted. But I knew Heather, my agent, would be disappointed if I didn't make them sign an NDA before taking them to the nearest room.

I swallowed the bubbly alcohol, basking in its burn, and raised my arm to take another flute when I crashed into a wall.

Cold champagne splashed on my dress, goosebumps erupting all over my body. My eyes went wide as I raised my gaze to look at the man I had bumped into, which was most definitely not a wall. If the wall had glaciers like those stormy gray eyes, I'd be freezing.

"I'm sorry," I said, eyeing the tall man looming over me wearing a dark suit. He had a harsh scowl on his face—at least, the bottom half of the face which wasn't covered with a black mask—but he was probably the most handsome man in the club. Which was saying something, since it was full of models, actors and athletes who had nothing better to do on a Friday.

"You should look at where you are going," he said, his voice deep as he ignored the server, who was apologizing profusely. His champagne had stained his shirt, too. Dark eyes flashed at me, zeroing on the alcohol that had splashed on my dress.

There was something familiar about his tall height, broad shoulders, and the pure arrogance and control that emitted from him. I wasn't the only one who had noticed that. Many men and women gave the stranger a lingering look. It was hard to miss him. Even though I was tall, especially in high heels, he easily towered over me.

"You are the one who bumped into me, *Sir*," I said, my voice taunting him by enunciating the last word.

His eyes darkened, my skin erupting in goosebumps. "You should watch that mouth of yours."

"Or what?" I kept my hands on my hips and tilted my head. "You're going to bend me over and spank me?"

His lips twitched, and I noticed him checking my wrists, which were empty besides the white band I had to wear. The current club was similar to the Vixen club in Coral Springs. If you are single, wear a white band. In a relationship? Red band. Relationship but want to play? Black band.

He was wearing a white band, too. His hands were veiny and an expensive watch—Patek Philippe—wrapped around his thick wrist. My throat dried, and I lifted my gaze to his face. He was handsome. Dirty blond hair that almost looked brown, dark eyes, plum lips and a sharp jaw that was covered with delicious five o'clock shadow.

*Wait, delicious?*

I held my breath when he leaned down, his spicy musky cologne wafting in my nose. "I just might, kitten."

*Kitten.* He called me kitten as if he owned me. As if I was his pet.

Anger and—I don't know what—rolled off me as I seethed at him. "I dare you to try it, mister."

His lips quirked up, and I didn't realize we were so close that I could feel the heat radiating from his large body. "I prefer being addressed as *Sir.*" His eyes roved over my face as he continued, "And I know you are being a silly brat trying to push my buttons, but I—"

"I dare you, *Sir,*" I said, my voice firm even though my stomach was churning with nerves and anticipation. He was right. I wanted to poke him and play with him. See what would unfurl from his tailored, expensive suit and how he'd fulfill his threat that was masked as a sexy promise.

He leaned back, his piercing gaze pinning me to the spot. He cocked his head to the side as if he was thinking, processing what I had just said, what I had just *offered.*

Heather would be mad if she found out, but I didn't care. It had been too long since I felt a man's body—a real man's body with strong muscles and stubble—on me. The woman I dated a year ago was pretty and elegant, even in bed, but it had ended with a broken heart, and I hadn't slept with anyone since. Or even kissed anyone. The last time I kissed a man was two years ago at—I was *not* going to think about Damon. *Nope.* Not at all.

*But would I be good at kissing if he kissed me now?*

My thoughts came to an abrupt end when his fingers touched me, tipping my chin to him. My skin burned under his hot touch. "Do you know about RACK?"

I nodded, my mouth dry. "Traffic light safe words, too."

"And what about safe gestures?"

I swallowed, my thighs clenching at his velvety baritone voice. "Two taps or snapping my fingers."

I took a sharp intake of breath when he pulled me closer, his gaze penetrating. "I won't hold back, kitten."

"What if I don't want you to hold back?" I asked, my voice breathy.

My stomach clenched when his eyes lowered to my lips. I licked them, feeling my throat dry as his touch, intense stare, body heat, and delicious male scent turned me on. If I could, I would take him to the corner, tuck the dress of my skirt up and ride him until both of us forgot our names.

"These lips," he rumbled, his thumb rubbing over my bottom lip. "The things I want to do to them."

I didn't care whether we were in public. So close to the stage of the club with people surrounding us, sharing their own naughty whispers. I didn't care one bit when I parted my lips and took his thumb in my warm mouth. Staring at his face from beneath my lashes, I sucked on his thumb, licking the soft pad and hollowing my cheeks.

He emitted a low groan, making me clench my thighs. I released it with a pop, my red lipstick smearing at the base of his knuckle.

"You were saying?" I asked, raising my brows, but I was sure he couldn't see them since my mask covered them.

He pulled back, his sharp jaw clenching. "Do you have any limits?" he asked, his voice deeper and hoarser than before.

I smirked and shook my head. "I am sure I can handle it, big guy."

"Even if I want to fuck your ass?"

My eyes widened. Words died in my mouth at his question. This man was blunt and arrogance rolled off of him in fumes. He didn't care about anyone overhearing us. He wasn't insecure about his desires and demanded answers when asked because I was pinned on the wall with a firm, but gentle hand wrapped around my throat.

"I asked you something, kitten," he purred, his low voice making me shiver. "I don't like to repeat myself. Is anal off limits?"

"Yes," I said in a firm voice. "I haven't prepped for it."

He nodded. "Good girl, I want you to be honest throughout the night."

His praise made my knees shaky. He pulled away and offered his hand to me. "Come on, I am going to punish you before I fuck you."

Before I could accept his hand, a man in a white suit appeared by my side.

"You're mistaken." The stranger with white mask dismissed the man in a dark suit who was frowning at him. "She is mine for the night."

2

# RULES

## DAMON

My hand clenched into a fist, and I glared at the man who was eyeing the woman—*my kitten*—like he owned her. It wasn't her fault. She looked stunning in her navy dress (despite the spilled champagne) with her brown skin glowing under the dim light.

"She's with me," I told him, my voice gentle but firm. "Find someone else."

"I'm not sure if you heard me. I said she's mine for the night."

Before I could say anything, the woman stepped between us, glaring at the man. My eyes dipped down the backless dress to the delicious curve of her ass. It was perfect. I wanted to tug off that dress, spank her, and see it jiggle as I fuck her. I couldn't wait.

The woman started, "On what basis? I didn't sign up for any demos or—"

While it was good to know she could stand her own guard, I had already chosen her for the night.

Glaring at the man, I said, "She has a partner."

I brushed past him and wrapped my hand around her dainty wrist. My eyes snapped at her face, her coffee-colored eyes. I felt the burning electricity shoot through me when I touched her.

*I need her. Now.*

Holding her, I dragged her away from the man, shooting him a look that said *I'd like to see you try to take her from me,* and showed my ID to the guard who was assigned in front of the VIP suites.

I had come to Hollywood because I was invited to check out my ex-competitor's sex club, *Aphrodite*. It was similar to my previous club, Vixen, which I had sold off to another investor who would take much better care of it while I work on Moore Beauty. I wasn't planning to go to *Aphrodite*. I was busy making sure our new product for the brand was converting into profit and that the marketing team was doing their job.

But I needed a break and visited it for an hour, planning to watch the Shibari show and leave.

Looking over my shoulder, I eyed the white feathered mask, the dark, luscious waves that I was dying to cradle in my hand. I wanted her. I'm glad I got lost trying to find a way to the show and bumped into her. My shirt clung to me, and I couldn't wait to take it off—

I paused in the middle of the dimly lit hallway, red lights falling all around us. "I have some rules," I said, turning around to face her.

She rolled her eyes, and I ignored the urge to pin her on the wall and turn her bottom bright red. *Stay calm, Damon.* "Rules are boring, but go on, mister uptight."

*She did not just...*

"I won't remove the mask. I don't enjoy repeating, but I'll say it again—watch that little mouth of yours, kitten," I said, my voice lowering an octave. Her eyes brightened and met me head on instead of looking at the floor and listening to my rules.

I was already famous for being a son and brother to Dorothy Moore and Emma Moore, my little sister. Now the CEO of Moore Beauty, I didn't need her or anyone to spread a rumor that I enjoyed visiting sex clubs in my free time and slept around with strangers.

"I won't be removing it either," she said, touching the side of her mask. I clenched my jaw. It was fair. Keeping this purely for pleasure, but I didn't miss the hint of disappointment of not getting to see her face. From what I could see, she had high cheekbones and carved jaw with full, pillowy lips that were begging to be licked, kissed and fucked.

I turned around and walked to the elevator, swiping the card that the owner had given me with the invitation. I was glad I brought it with me.

"I didn't know you come here often," she remarked.

"I don't."

"Hmm. Figured. You are too... you don't seem like the type who'd enjoy this."

She didn't complete her previous sentence. Her posture was straight, as if she wasn't scared. *Good.*

"Give me your panties," I ordered.

She looked at me, her eyes glinting with mischievousness as she tilted her head at me. "You can remove them on your own, *Sir*," she purred, and I watched her with narrowed eyes when she stepped out, walking towards the double doors of the suite.

*Oh, she's leaving with a red ass alright.*

I prowled towards her, and as soon as we were inside the suite, I grabbed her by the back of her neck and pushed her lithe frame against the closed doors with her back against me.

"You are asking to be punished, kitten," I growled in her

ear, relishing in her surprised gasp when I pinned my weight on her so she couldn't move. Wedging my free hand between us, I tucked up her silk dress.

"You finally noticed, Sir?" she breathed out, wriggling her ass towards me.

I paused my hand and pulled back. I stared at her. "You are a brat."

She turned around, my eyes dropping to her cleavage for a moment before they found her eyes. "Ding ding. Do you want a reward or a treat, Sir?"

I sighed and turned around to see the suite. It was similar to what I had back in Coral Springs. An enormous bed with poster legs, dim lights making the space sensual, a living area with comfortable couches, a bar, and a closet with transparent glass full of condoms, lube and toys.

"I don't play with brats," I said, pouring myself a glass of whiskey.

"You're missing out," she said in a sing-song voice and I shook my head. She seemed familiar, at least her behavior did, but I couldn't pinpoint exactly how. *Why do I feel like I know her?* I turned around, ready to ask if she wanted a drink—

I almost sputtered out my drink looking at her half-naked back. The silk dress was pooling around her perfectly shaped peach ass before she tugged it down. I stared at the golden-brown skin, drinking in her delicious curves, the soft muscles of her calves tensing when she bent, and her bare pussy.

"Turn around," I heard myself say. I swallowed the alcohol, licked my lips, and leaned on the bar's platform.

She was completely naked besides her mask.

"I didn't ask you to remove your heels," I said, watching her like a predator. My cock stirred in my pants, watching her peach-shaped ass, begging me to turn it red.

"You didn't ask me to strip either," she replied with a small smile. "If you are not going to play with a brat, then I'll go find someone who will. Oh, maybe that guy in white suit!"

She bent down to pick up her dress. I let out a small chuckle and sauntered up to her. "I didn't ask you to leave either."

Her chocolate eyes were gleaming underneath the warm lights of the suite. "You said you don't play with brats—"

"What's your safe word?" I interrupted her, watching her as she scrunched the dress in her hands.

"Red."

"And safe gesture?"

Her eyes widened. "I..."

Tilting my head, I waited, counting down the seconds before I could punish her, make her beg for it.

"I'll tap or snap my fingers."

"Good girl." I pushed her on the bed, bending her over until her ass was in the air and gave it a nice, hard spank, making her gasp. I kept my hand on her back, the other caressing the burn as I leaned down to whisper in her ear, "I warned you twice and you didn't listen, so take your punishment like a good little kitten."

3

# PUNISH ME

## SUMMER

**H**oly *shit*.

My body trembled, his warm, firm hand finally holding me and spanking me like I wanted. I had been eyeing his veiny hands—sue me, I love masculine hands—and imagining them wrapping around my neck, sucking on his fingers, and moaning when he fucks me with them. I was at my limit, and finally he touched me.

I arched my back and looked over my shoulder with a small smirk. "Maybe this is what I wanted all along, Sir," I said, my voice soft and sultry. "Punish me."

A small gasp escaped my throat when he wrapped his hand around my hair, tugging it until I was forced to look in the mirror across from us. My hair fell in waves around us, and I shivered at the sight of him fully clothed in his suit and me naked. Light fell over his sharp, handsome face, creating shadows and making him look stern and intimidating. But my eyes were gleaming, seeing his tall and broad body pinning me to the bed, manhandling me.

*Yes. This is what I have been craving all this time.*

Not any fumbling hands from guys, asking to kiss me for the umpteenth time while we were in bed.

*This. Him.* The feel of his hard, muscular body pressing against my back, his harsh, warm breath fanning over my neck.

*"Beg,"* his deep voice commanded. I bit my lip when he squeezed my ass and growled in my ear, "Use that dirty little mouth and beg me to spank you, kitten."

"Please," I breathed out, arching and pushing back against him. I wanted to touch him. Wanted him to touch me everywhere. "Please spank me, Daddy."

I bit my cheek and waited.

"Oh, you bratty little kitten," he whispered softly. "I'm going to teach you a lesson today, and you're going to thank me every time I spank you."

I smirked and looked over my shoulder when he pulled back. "What lesson are you going to teach me, Master?"

My stomach clenched with nerves seeing the impassive expression on his masked face. Instead of lowering his zipper and fucking me like I expected him to, he tilted his head.

"Remember this," he started, loosening his tie and keeping his eyes pinned on me. "When your ass hurts, that little tongue of yours is to blame. Now, be a good girl and keep your wrists together. Or I will, and you won't like it when I do."

My mouth dried up as I followed his instructions. There was something about his tone that made me feel on edge and that I should really heed his orders. My thighs squeezed together when he leaned over me and tied my wrists together with his tie. His hard body, even through the thin shirt, felt warm and inviting when it pressed against my back. I watched his long fingers expertly craft a tie, securing my wrists together. He tugged at it a few times, and when it didn't open, he pulled away. I instantly craved his warmth and the intoxicating smell of his cologne, but I shut up.

I jumped when he spanked my ass. "Nuh uh, keep your legs spread. I like seeing your pretty pussy," he said, his polished shoe tapping my ankle. "Wider, kitten. That's a good girl."

*Fuck. Him.* The pet name was already infuriating, but his praise made me want to be good.

"The lesson I'll be teaching you today is how to behave and be grateful," he said, his voice taunting me. I looked at the mirror and my eyes widened, watching him remove his belt. The sound of the metal buckle made me swallow, and I tightened my grip on the tie that was wrapped around my wrists.

I shivered when he ran his hand across my ass, his voice soft as he said, "I don't like using a belt on my partner because it can hurt and leave bruises." I took a sharp intake of breath when he spanked me with his hand. "But you are a dirty little brat who doesn't know how to be respectful. Calling me master and daddy instead of Sir like I asked you to. I know you are a brat and would enjoy the punishment if I spanked you with my hands, hm?"

I didn't have to agree. I knew he knew it, too.

"That's what I thought. Be a good kitten and take the punishment well. I want you to thank me after every spank, understood?"

I nodded.

A moment later, the leather belt landed on my ass. Pain erupted over my skin, making me groan into the sheets and wanting to soothe it, but he tied my hands. *Fuck.*

"How do you address me, kitten?"

"*Sir.*" I squirmed and said, "Thank you, Sir."

"Good. Do you understand what I just said?"

I glared at him through the reflection and said, "Yes, Sir."

"See? You're a fast learner. Be grateful that I'm being nice and giving you ten spanks." His condescending tone shouldn't have turned me on, but my pussy clenched at hearing his words, and I braced myself when he got into position to swing the belt.

*Thwack.*

My hands clenched the sheets. "T-thank you, Sir."

He didn't reply. *Spank. Spank. Spank.*

"Oh, f-fuck," I cried out, the pain burning my skin as I squeezed my eyes shut and sputtered out a meek, "Thank you, Sir."

*Spank.*

"I can't hear you. Be loud and clear."

*Fuck him.*

"Thank you, Sir."

"Sweetheart, I haven't spanked you yet, but I'm glad you are being a good girl and thanking your Sir for punishing you."

God, he was an ass!

*Spank. Spank. Spank.*

"T-thank you, Sir!" Tears burned my eyes, and it was hard staying upright, but he kept his hand on my hips, making sure I didn't fall on the bed and kept my ass in the air for punishment.

*Spank.*

"Ow, that hurt!" I cried out, a sobbing whimper escaping my throat. "T-thank you, Sir."

"It hurts? *Good.*" He let out a low chuckle. "You look so pretty when you're helpless."

I squeezed my thighs together and gasped when he spread my legs wider. "No, no, we are not done yet—*look at you,*" his voice growled at the end, and I looked in front of me to find him leaning down and staring at my pussy. "You're soaking wet. *Pathetic.* Is that all it takes to tame a bratty kitten, *hm?* A belt to your ass? Such a dirty little slut getting turned on by this."

*Oh fuck. Why did he have to be so mean and hot?* And where had he been all my life? He was perfect, and I wanted more.

"Please Sir," I begged, arching my back and raising my ass even though it was burning.

I sighed when he rubbed my ass, his cool touch soothing me. "Please what, kitten? Spank you more?" I trembled, clenching, and he noticed, squeezing my cheek and making me whimper. "Someone's a bit of a pain slut, hm?"

I bit my lip and braced myself when his touch left me.

*Spank.*

"Thank you, Sir," I exhaled sharply when he landed the last blow. It was definitely harder than before. Both my cheeks were burning, and I wanted to soothe the pain.

"Now, the last one needs to be—"

My head shot up. "Last one? But you spanked me ten times!" I hated I was whining about a punishment, but his spanking had already turned me into a puddle.

"I couldn't hear you one time, so it doesn't count. On your back." He turned me on my back, a small smirk curling on his lips when I winced. Lying on the sheet was like a splash of cold water on my scorching cheeks.

"Open your legs," he said. "I don't have all night to punish you, kitten."

I frowned, spreading my thighs. I swallowed at the sight of him in a suit, holding his leather belt in his hand. I met his eyes and asked, "W-what are you going to do, Sir?"

I knew better than to address him as something else, even playfully. He wasn't a brat tamer, but he tamed the brat in me well with his filthy talk and belt.

He gave me a small smile. "I'm going to spank your pussy."

# 4

# POOR THING

## DAMON

I loved the look of surprise and shock turning into fear and excitement in her eyes. Even though half of her face was masked, her eyes were very expressive.

"It will hurt!" she blurted, but still kept her thighs open.

*Good girl.*

I knew a little spanking with a belt would turn the brat into a tamed kitten. She was lucky it was our first time playing, or I wouldn't bat an eye using a cane to punish her.

"Then why are you getting wet, kitten?" I asked, spreading her wider and groaning at the sight of her bare sex. The scent of her feminine, musky arousal wafted in the air. "Don't move your hands."

I straightened up and noticed her taking a shuddering breath. I flexed my hands, making sure my grip was tight on the looped belt, and spanked her pussy with a light slap. I wanted to punish her. Not hurt her.

With a deep breath, I raised the leather and gently slapped it on her pussy.

She whimpered, her sex clenching as I dropped the belt and made sure she was okay. I took her on my lap and soothed her back, gently tugging off the tie from her bound wrists. I rubbed my thumb over her hands, making sure I hadn't hurt her. Her skin was soft and there was a hint of sweet perfume.

"You took the punishment so well, kitten," I whispered, kissing her forehead as she eyed me through her long lashes. *Remove your mask.* I wanted to see her entire face and kiss it. Kiss her.

My jaw clenched. I never got emotional during my scenes, and yet this woman had waltzed into me and in the span of thirty minutes, I wanted to know everything about her.

*Especially her name.*

"Now can we fuck?" she asked bluntly, making me chuckle at the raw lust in her eyes.

"You just got spanked and now you want to fuck?" I raised my brow, caressing her perky breasts and pinching the nipple. "My dirty little pain slut."

She moaned, arching her back and pressing against me. I pinched her again, noting her reaction, the little scrunch of her brow, her teeth biting into the fullest part of her bottom lip, and her thighs clenching and rubbing together.

I held her wrist when she tried to lower her hand between her legs, and she had the gall to glare at me. Her fiery brown eyes shot daggers at me as I pinned her on the bed, keeping her thighs spread with my knees.

"Don't touch yourself until I tell you to, kitten," I warned her. "I'll be good and let you touch yourself."

"Please," she said, writhing on the bed.

I tsked, "Poor thing. So wet and horny." I let go of her wrist and leaned back. "Touch yourself for me. Don't cum."

Removing my jacket, I made myself comfortable in the armchair and watched her lean on her elbows. My hands flexed, wanting to touch and mark her golden-brown skin with kisses, to trace every inch of her stunning body. With her dark wavy hair, pouty lips and nimble limbs, she looked like a nymph. Instead of forcing her onto her stomach and rutting inside her like a mindless animal, I unbuttoned my shirt sleeves and rolled them over my arms.

My cock pressed against the zipper when she licked her lips and lowered her right hand over her pretty wet cunt. She made sure I was looking at her and touched her swollen clit.

"Go slow," I demanded, my voice hoarse. "If you cum without my permission, your pussy will be red like your ass."

Her eyes gleamed at that, and she rubbed faster. "What if I want that, Sir?"

"Get your pussy spanked?"

She slid her fingers over her slicked lips and nodded.

"Tsk, such a naughty slut wanting her cunt spanked." I leaned back in the chair and crossed my leg. "It depends on how prettily you beg, kitten."

She moaned, her thighs quivering when she rubbed her clit again, wetness dripping out of her. My mouth watered. Her musky feminine scent coated the air, and I wanted nothing but to get on my knees and worship her gorgeous body and her pretty cunt. She looked like a goddess. A sex goddess.

"Fuck," her soft moan went straight to my dick.

"Stop," I ordered. "Finger yourself."

"I'm close," she argued, her voice sultry.

"I want you to edge, kitten," I said with a small smile at the shocked look on her face. "You aren't going to cum until I allow it. Until I make you cum. I'm preparing you for my cock. You know why?"

"Why?" Her voice was barely audible.

I stood up and walked closer to her, breathing in her scent, and cupped her hand that was on her pussy and whispered, "Because I'm going to use this little cunt of yours until

I'm satisfied." I squeezed, relishing her whimper, and slid my hand into my pocket. "Now be a good toy and touch yourself."

Her eyes were half-lidded behind the mask, glazed with lust as she followed my order. I watched her middle finger slide in, eliciting a small sigh from her. My hands clenched inside my pockets, every vein in my body fired with the urge to take her.

"Two fingers," I said, my voice gruff.

She moaned, clenching her walls around her nimble digits, and my eyes snapped to her face. She was close.

"Go on," I said, tilting my head, "Fuck yourself. My cock is much bigger than your fingers, I'm afraid."

"I'm close," she said, gritting her teeth as if she was angry at me, but it came out as a pathetic whine.

"Aw, what's the matter?" I taunted her, relishing in the burn of her glare. "It's frustrating, isn't it, kitten? Bratting and not getting what you want, *hm*?"

She didn't reply. The wet squelch of her pussy made me lean closer and spread her thighs wider as she grabbed sheets with her other hand.

"I love seeing you like this," I groaned at the sight in front of me. "A needy, hot fucking mess."

"P-please," she begged, removing her fingers. I took them in my mouth, moaning at her sweet, musky taste, and licked them clean. "Fuck me. *Now*."

"Not yet, kitten." My eyes flashed at her. "You need to learn to beg better, and once you are nothing but a drippy, needy little mess for me, maybe I will. Now be a good girl and let me eat you out," I said, leaning down until my knees were on the floor, with her pussy in front of me.

5

# BRAT

## SUMMER

"OhmyfuckingGod—" I said, letting out a loud moan at the end when his tongue licked at my swollen clit.

*This man was good.* So fucking good. I was so close to asking his name and his number because no one had ever made me so horny before. Or eaten me out like he was starving and my pussy was his own personal buffet.

"You taste so fucking good, kitten," he groaned against my sex, his warm breath and the reverberations making me clench.

"Suck my clit," I said, my voice breathy.

His stormy gray eyes flashed at me, and I let out a whimper when his palm smacked against my pussy before rubbing it. "You are not in a position to give me orders, kitten." I nodded, but he spanked my pussy again, this time harder, making me groan and pull away. But his hold was firm, and the soft burn of the spank made me wetter. "Don't make me teach you manners again. Be a good slut now."

*Fuck. Me.*

I took a deep breath and met his eyes. "Spank me more, Sir." I rushed to add, *"Please."*

"Good girl." He leaned down and kissed my clit, making me blush. I wish we could remove the mask. Fuck the NDA. I wanted to know who the person was behind the mask. There was something familiar about him, his personality. Like we have met before.

I was pulled back to earth when my sex burned with the spank from his hand. I whimpered when he soothed it by rubbing his fingers over me, sliding my wetness around my clit and watching me with his piercing gaze.

"I love the sounds you make when I spank your pretty cunt, kitten," he whispered, his dirty talk edging me further.

"Please," I urged, my voice breaking when he spanked me again, lighter than before.

"Tell me, who's in charge of this orgasm, kitten?" he growled, leaning over and wrapping his hand around my throat when I was too embarrassed to meet his eyes. "Look at me and tell me."

"Y-you," I said, biting my lip when he slowly rubbed my clit.

"That's right. Not you. It's me," he said, smacking my pussy again, making me groan. "I control this little pussy now. I tell you when and how to cum... or not."

"Please, let me cum," I begged, arching my hips in his hand that kept spanking me and rubbing my clit. Balancing pain with pleasure and keeping me on the edge.

He tsked and leaned back, spreading my thighs and asked, "Do you think you deserve to cum? Showing so little respect and being such a greedy little kitten, hm?"

"I do." I raised my chin.

His brow arched, and I had to bite my lip when he slowly slid a finger inside me. I clenched on it, wishing it was something else.

"Beg more," he said, adding a second finger, making me moan.

"Please, please, please let me cum," I begged, moving my hips and groaning when he fucked me with his fingers. I had to hold on to the sheets when his lips sucked on my clit while curling his fingers in a come-hither motion inside me.

I was just on the edge of my orgasm and squeezed my eyes shut when I felt myself clench.

Just when I could reach the delicious climax, the asshole pulled away. I glared at him when he licked his lips, but my glare turned into wide eyes when I saw him pull out his cock from his pants.

It was big. Bigger than the average Joes I had two years ago. And oddly enough, it was pretty too, with a thick girth, a flushed mushroom head and glistening with pre-cum, and veins around the shaft.

"On your hands and knees, kitten," he said, wrapping his hands around his dick and pumping it slowly.

I met his eyes and said, "I want to put it in my mouth."

He froze, his eyes snapping at me as if it took him a moment to hear what I said. So I kneeled on the bed in front of him and repeated, "I said I want to put your cock in my mouth."

"I heard you the first time," he snapped, his eyes flashing at me as if he was angry at me for offering him a blowjob. Over the years, I had noticed that oral sex for men was much better than offering sex. And whenever I did it, they thanked me, bought me expensive gifts I didn't want, and one time, after my cheerleader practice, Chris had even asked me to marry him after I'd sucked him off in the locker room.

But his reaction was the complete opposite. He was angry.

"Did I say something wrong?" I asked, concern lacing my voice.

"I don't want my cock sucked, kitten," he replied, his voice firm. "If I did, I'd make you deep throat it until you were a pretty mess covered with tears and cum."

My sex clenched hearing his filthy talk. I was surprised when he cupped my jaw and pressed his lips against mine. Warm, soft lips. I was in shock to feel the electric burn when he kissed me, my mouth parting as our tongues danced with each other. It felt familiar. The kiss and his soft touch were so odd compared to his rough hold minutes ago.

I didn't know when my back touched the mattress or when he was rubbing against my entrance, but I knew one thing—that it felt natural. Like it was meant to be.

We both pulled away, breathing hard and staring at each other's eyes through the masks. I glanced at his lips, pink and swollen from the kiss. I blinked, wondering why I was so blunt asking him to do all these kinky things, but I was blushing from one kiss.

*What the fuck is wrong with me?*

"Condom!" I blurted, removing my arms from his neck (when did that happen?) and added, "I am on pills but…"

He stared at me, his face stoic. "Yes," he pulled away slowly. "I am clean, but condom—*yes*."

Even he seemed confused, and I was glad that we were both affected by that kiss.

I licked my lips and watched him open a chest drawer and remove his shirt. My mouth watered at the sight of his muscled, broad back. I shamelessly stared at his abs when he walked back to the bed, removing his boxers and pants along the way.

He wasn't too muscular or too lean. Just the right amount that made me want to climb him on the spot.

"Take a picture, kitten," he deadpanned.

"Can I?" I asked, sounding hopeful.

He shook his head, tearing the foil packet with his teeth

and rolling the condom on his length. I swallowed again at his size and looked at my pussy, which hadn't been fucked for the last two years.

"Be gentle," I said, my voice small.

He frowned and nodded, hovering above me. "Of course, kitten."

"You're big," I breathed out, feeling his tip brushing against my slicked lips. I didn't know why I felt nervous all of a sudden.

He scoffed and cupped my face. "Are you having second thoughts? We can stop and call it a night—"

I wrapped my legs around his torso. "You're not denying me after teasing me all night. Fuck me and make me cum. Sir."

"*Brat.*" He smirked and kissed my nose, making me blush. "I will fuck you, but remember, it's up to me if you cum. I can deny you if I want."

6

# YOU CAN TAKE IT

### DAMON

I had said the filthiest words to her the entire night. Words that were humiliating, degrading with praise, but she blushed at a small peck on her nose. Her breath wavered when I kissed her.

She was strange. Heck, I felt strange too. I wanted to keep kissing her and see if I could make her blush anywhere else.

So I did just that. Ignoring all the warning signs warring in my brain, I leaned down and captured her pouty lips, licking the plump part before pressing my teeth into it. I swallowed her groan and slid my tip inside her sopping pussy.

She whimpered when I pulled away and rubbed her sensitive clit. "Shh, you can take it, kitten," I whispered, slowly inching inside. "Relax for me—*that's it*. There we go."

Her eyes were wide, gleaming with desire, and I wanted to take my time instead of ramming in like a wild beast. I kept my fingers on her clit, teasing her, until she relaxed and I was fully inside her.

"Fuck, you fit me like a glove."

We both groaned, my hands clenching the sheets as her

warm, wet pussy tightened around me. Before I could ask her to relax, she looked at me, lashes fluttering through the mask, and said, "Don't tell me you're going to cum so soon, Sir. It wouldn't bother me, but—"

I choked her, gently pressing the sides of her neck, and growled, "Stop with that fucking attitude before I—" I retreated, slamming inside her and enunciated each word with my harsh thrusts, "Fuck. It. Out. Of you, kitten."

She whimpered and mewled, grabbing my shoulders and digging her nails into my skin with each thrust.

"Be a good fucking girl and take it," I groaned, slamming inside her warm cunt, my balls already full and ready to release. She felt so good.

She whimpered, moaning and arching her perfect tits at me. I squeezed them, pinching the nipple before taking it in my hot mouth and giving her breast a small hickey. I groaned at the feel of her nails raking through my hair when I repeated my actions to her other breast, giving it more attention until her legs started trembling around me.

I pulled away to spread her legs wide and paced my thrusts deeper and harder, slowing down. Her wide eyes met mine, lips parting with pretty gasps as I kept fucking her.

"Look at me when I fill your pretty fucking pussy," I growled, looking down at the erotic sight of our unison. "Look how well your cunt takes my cock, kitten. As if it was made just for me, hm?"

I slammed inside her, her fingers wringing the sheets as she groaned, "Yes, please—*fuck, harder!*"

Pulling out, I ordered her, "On your knees, kitten. Show me your red ass—*thatta girl.*"

I slid in with a wet squelch and tugged her hair so she could see me railing her from behind in the reflection. "See how perfect you look when you obey? Such a good little toy for me."

She cursed, her mask a little askew from the fucking as I lowered my hand to her clit, keeping my pace. "Please, I-I'm close, Sir," she whimpered.

"Tell me this pussy belongs to me," I said, grunting with pleasure when I felt her tighten as I found the perfect sensitive spot. "Tell me I can use it whenever I want, kitten."

"Yes," she gasped, my fingers strumming along her swollen clit. "Your pussy. Use it whenever you want, Sir, plea—*ah!*"

"Such a good fucking girl," I groaned, slamming inside her when I felt her orgasm inch closer. "Cum for me, kitten. Go on—fuck, there we go. *Yes.* Such a good girl, keep cumming. *Fuck.*"

Her long moan turned into a whimper when she came with a loud gush, her walls clamping me and triggering my orgasm. I shot a huge load of cum inside her, feeling the wetness drip down our sweaty body and soaking the bed.

It took me a few good seconds to realize what had happened, and I pulled out. She melted into the sheets with a groan.

"Squirt for me again," I said, turning her on her back and sliding my fingers inside her.

"N-no, I'm sensitive."

I pinned her hands away and said, "Use your safe word or cum for me right now. I want you to squirt in my hands, kitten."

She let out a small whimper, biting her lip when her walls clenched my fingers, which kept curling inside her, rubbing and teasing the G-spot. It didn't take too long to have her squirming and moaning as she came again, her juices covering my hands, forearms and bed sheets.

"That was so fucking sexy," I said in a husky voice, eyeing her parted lips and trembling body. "*You* are so fucking sexy."

I kissed her knee and promised her I'd be right back and

not to move an inch. As soon as I cleaned up in the ensuite washroom, I looked at the masked man in the reflection and swallowed. My stormy gray eyes were clear for the first time in many years, and I had a soft flush to my skin.

Shaking my head, I fixed my mask and went back to the bedroom to give my kitten the aftercare she needed. The aftercare I needed to give her for my sanity. There had been too many times in my previous club that I found a sub breaking down after a rough scene and an abuser leaving them in the room without another look. That's why I had a strict policy to do a thorough background check before allowing anyone to be involved in D/S scenes.

"How are you doing, kitten?" I asked softly, gently cleaning her sex with a warm rag. She protested, but I held on to her ankle, raising my brow. "I made a mess out of your pretty pussy. It's my job to make sure it's clean and okay. Clear?"

She blushed, looking away and mumbled a small 'Yes, Sir.'

"Good girl. Now answer my question."

She hummed, her body quivering when I pulled her on my lap, the ends of her long hair tickling my torso. "I feel fuzzy."

I stroked her back and kneaded the muscles in her legs with my other hand. Her eyes followed my hands. "That's normal. Do you feel like crying?"

Her eyes snapped at me. "No, why?"

"It's pretty natural to cry and let out your emotions after a scene."

She frowned and shifted on my lap, facing me. "I don't feel like crying. Do you? I won't judge."

I chuckled, pulling her closer and kissing her lips. "No, kitten, I don't feel like crying."

"Good." Her eyes fell on my lips before she cleared her throat. "I didn't know I could do that."

"Do what?"

"You know…" She nodded at the puddle on the bed sheet. "Squirt."

I smirked, lowering my hand to squeeze her butt. "I'm honored to be the first person to make you squirt." I cupped her face and made her look at me. "Are you sure you're feeling okay, love? I said a lot of degrading and humiliating things to you, and I don't want you to take them seriously."

She nodded, her eyes earnest. "I… It's weird, but I didn't feel anything except desire when you said those words. But if someone else had said that, I'd have felt differently."

I frowned. "You've never played in a scene before or been called slut or toy?"

She swallowed and looked away. "Scene. This was my first time sleeping with a dominant."

I noticed she didn't answer my second question, so I didn't push it.

"I'm grateful. Now you know what it's like to be with a dominant. If they don't offer aftercare, punch them in their balls and walk away. Better yet, call me."

"Okay, dad." She rolled her eyes with a cheeky smile. "Does that mean I get your number?"

I eyed her and swooped her into my arms, making our way to the washroom. "Let's clean up first."

# 7

# ON MY LAP

## SUMMER

I had all but melted into his arms during the bath, which was both calming and awkward. Calming because he kept reassuring me with sweet words, softly caressing my skin and bathing me. Awkward because we were both naked except for the mask. He let me take my time once he was sure I was okay and removed it to wash my face with cold water.

It seemed so unreal. The entire night. *Him.*

Staring at my reflection in the mirror, I exhaled. "He is wild," I mumbled, blushing and touching the hickeys on my neck, breasts and hips. He even bit my ass and left a tiny hickey over it. My nipples hardened at the memory of his lips, teeth and hands touching me everywhere, manhandling me like I was made for his pleasure.

I wondered who he was beneath the mask when I tied mine back to my head, making sure it was perfect. *Could he be a famous actor?* Nah, I'd recognize his voice. But he sounded awfully familiar. Maybe a model. He has sharp cheekbones and jawline. Not to mention *that* body.

Wrapping a towel around my body, I stepped out of the

washroom to find him sitting on the edge of the bed, his piercing gray eyes on me.

"On my lap, kitten," he said, a hint of dominance in his tone.

"I thought the scene was over," I said, biting back my smile and walking towards him, getting rid of the towel. I didn't care, even though my pussy was sore and it would be much harder to walk tomorrow.

"It is, but I don't want you to feel uncomfortable tomorrow whenever you sit," he said, draping me over his lap, my ass facing him. I took a sharp intake of breath when something cold landed on my ass, and he started massaging it into my skin. "And I wanted another reason to touch your perfect body."

I sighed, closing my eyes and relaxing into his gentle touch. No one had ever massaged me before, especially after rough sex, and the thought made me sad and grateful that he wasn't a douchebag. I ignored the urge to ask him for his name or get his number because I knew relationships were impossible for me.

*Wait... relationship? Hold your horses, Summer! Yes, he has a good dick which he knows how to use, but that doesn't mean he has a good heart.*

I shook away those thoughts and let out a groan when he kneaded my shoulders after spreading me out on the clean sheets. I swear he seemed unreal.

"Your muscles are so tight. It's not healthy," he commented, his half naked body radiating heat from staying so close.

"I've been bu—*fuck, that feels so good*—busy," I sighed, squirming at how good he was making me feel.

"Is that why you came here today?" he asked, turning me on my back, his eyes dropping on my breasts and massaging them.

I bit my lip, shamelessly drinking in his gorgeous body. "Yes. I wasn't planning to… I never do this."

"Do what, kitten? Let a stranger edge you, spank your pretty pussy and fuck you?" He was so smug that I rolled my eyes at him.

He laid down beside me, and, meeting his eyes through the mask, I said, "*This*. Have a one-night stand."

He kept staring at me, his fingers mindlessly caressing my body, as if he didn't want to stop touching me. After a moment, he asked, "Do you want it to be a one—"

Before he could finish, my stomach grumbled. *Loudly*. My eyes widened, and I blurted, "I'm so sorry."

He chuckled and kissed my belly. "I should apologize. Let's get you fed. What do you want to eat?"

He called the main lobby and ordered pizza and tiramisu. He was definitely a man after my heart.

"I thought this was a sex club and didn't take food orders," I said, leaning against the headboard.

"They don't," he said, roving his gaze over me. "I am their special guest."

"Special, hm?" I teased and looked around to find my dress was missing. It was worth more than my monthly rent, so I'd need it. "Uh, where's my dress?"

"I sent it to the dry cleaner with my shirt. Don't worry, it'll be here in an hour if you need to leave."

"I don't," I blurted and remembered the press and sighed. "I might have to. But thanks for getting it cleaned. I'll pay—"

"Hush, kitten," he said, leaning close to me. "I wrecked your pretty body the entire night. It's the least I could do."

I smiled and asked, "There must be a way I can repay your generosity, Sir."

He eyed me and said, "There is."

"What?"

"Give me your name. Your number," he said, my smile

freezing. "I know I was the one who didn't want to remove the mask and stay anonymous, but... I want to know who you are."

I stared at him, thinking about all the worst-case scenarios of telling him my name and giving him my number. "I'm sorry, but I can't," I said, looking down at my lap and fidgeting with my fingers. "It's not that I don't want to, but... *I can't.*"

He ran a hand through his hair—the one I was tugging on when he ate me out—and sighed, "It's alright. You don't need to apologize. I understand."

Thankfully, I was saved from the conversation by a knock on the door. I shamelessly eyed his perfect butt in boxers when he got up to get the food. It was a little awkward to stuff my face with pizza naked and talk about our hobbies without revealing too much.

He had a little sister, who he adored, no parents, and ran a successful business. On weekends, he liked to stay in, read, or volunteer to help at an animal shelter.

Yes, he was the perfect man anyone could ask for, and I had the worst luck to meet him when I couldn't tell him who I was.

I told him I was really close with my friends and family, but they didn't live in LA and how I was lucky and grateful enough to be accepted for my small audition. I didn't tell him more because the upcoming series was quite famous and getting a lot of global traction.

"You must be someone famous if you want to remain anonymous," he asked after we both cleaned up after eating an entire pizza. "Model, actress, opera singer?"

"I wish." I let out a soft chuckle and shook my head. "I cannot sing unless yelling Taylor Swift's songs in the shower counts." I pursed my lips and met his soft eyes. It made me feel warm when he stared at me like that, really listening to what I had to say. No man had ever paid attention to me like that. It felt wonderful and addictive.

And I wanted more.

"My manager would be mad if she found out I slept with someone without having them sign an NDA," I said the truth. "But I'm really glad I met you tonight, Mister Uptight."

He scoffed, "You think I'm uptight?"

I nodded seriously. "You are very strict—*What are you doing?*"

He pinned me on my back, hovering above me. My thighs clenched. "Showing you how… *flexible* I am, kitten. Although I should apologize first."

I swallowed. "Apologize for what?"

Seeing the devilish smirk on his face, *I knew*.

"You will be very, very sore tomorrow," he purred, leaning down and capturing my lips in a heated kiss.

8

# GRUMPY OLD MAN

## SUMMER

I woke up with an aching body. My bleary eyes blinked at the sleeping person beside me and unconsciously, a small smile tugged at my lips. Even asleep, he hadn't removed his mask. I rolled over and tried to stretch without wincing. My entire body felt sore.

After our late-night pizza, we fucked till morning until I passed out. I remember that at one point, we were on the floor. I don't know how that happened.

Taking a deep breath, I sat up and checked my cell phone. It was almost four in the morning, and my agent was blowing up my phone with texts in all caps.

*Damn, twelve missed calls?*

I peeked over my shoulder to find him asleep and quietly got dressed. I didn't enjoy doing the walk of shame, especially when there was no shame. But I had to leave, or I was sure my agent would get arrested for homicide. *My* murder.

Smoothing my dress, I longingly looked at the naked man on the bed. Without thinking twice, I grabbed a notepad from the coffee table and wrote my personal number.

***'If you want to play with a brat again.'***

I scribbled an 'S' in the end and left the suite with my heart pounding between my ribs.

The party had almost ended, but a few of the patrons lingered at the bar and tables. Some of them gave me suggestive looks, but I was sore and I didn't think my pussy would get wet without a certain man with piercing gray eyes. At least for a while.

As soon as I got in my Uber, I took off the damn mask and sighed, rubbing my face. Thankfully, the driver was a sweet old man and didn't talk for the entire ride. I got a ding on my phone and opened the group chat of me, Emma, Mia, and her sweet neighbor, Ivy.

Mia had attached a selfie of her with a very grumpy James, her boyfriend, glaring at the camera. I chuckled at the Mickey Mouse red headband with huge ear flaps he was wearing, and at Mia wearing a similar headband in pink with a huge grin on her face and flush on her cheeks, with Disney Land on their background. They looked adorable.

**'Grumpy old man discovers Disney Land and frowns,'** read Mia's caption.

Emma replied with a selfie. Cillian had a sheet mask on his face with a stoic expression as Emma kissed his cheek, and it looked like there were very few clothes involved. **'Grumpy old man loves his white rice sheet masks,'** read her caption.

**Summer: I wish I had a grumpy old sugar daddy as a boyfriend. You guys are slaying! xx**

**Emma: ty love! Cillian asked about your premiere. How was it?**

**Summer: I skipped it we will talk about it when we meet**

**Mia: uh-oh, do u wanna call? James is sleeping rn but I'm here if u want to vent xo**

Emma sent tea emojis, making me smile and my heart

sunk. I missed them so fucking much. I missed our sleep-overs and movie nights, studying all day in the library and pulling all-nighters during exams, and spending days at the salon gossiping with the sweet old owner and getting our nails done. I missed Mia's father Clyde's cooking, who made the best tacos I have ever had, and, oddly enough, Damon, Emma's older brother. Yes, he never once smiled in my presence or gave me another look, but I missed his grumpy, emotionless face.

My lips tingled at the memory of our kiss at his club when I had skipped my prom night. *Did he wonder about it too? I don't think so. He must have men and women begging to kiss him... or do other things.*

I snapped out of my head when the car stopped. I thanked the driver and walked to the set of the show. Colt, one of my co-stars, invited me to his trailer, and I'd rather talk with him than go back to my place where I knew my agent would be. I didn't feel like facing her without having three shots of espresso and a warm shower first.

Shower that Colt's trailer had.

* * *

"Please fix your bra, Miss Hayes."

I groaned, supporting my heavy head in my hand. The throbbing increased, and I searched around the leather seat to find a bottle of water. Thankfully, one was pushed in my hand, and I grumbled out a small thanks before downing four large gulps.

"Bra, please. Miss Hayes," my agent, Heather, said in a stern voice and I blinked at her, my vision blurry.

*Fuck.* I thought. *I fucked it up really badly this time.*

I pushed the strap up and straightened my tank top. I looked out of the car window and winced at the shit storm that would go on in a few minutes. As predicted, both my private cell phone and Heather's phone started blowing up. Ring after ring and bell notification sound of my social media.

I ran a hand through my hair and leaned back in the seat. *This is the end of Summer Hayes.*

"Are they canceling me?" I asked glumly, chugging more water and staring lifelessly at the window. It would be dawn in a few hours. "Are they kicking me out of the show?"

Heather was silent for a few seconds, which felt like minutes, and I sighed. I knew the answer to both questions. "What is canceling?" she asked.

I snickered. Of course. She was twenty-eight, only six years older than me, and yet she didn't know what cancel culture was. I would have explained it to her like the last time she asked me what 'Gotta Zayn' meant when paparazzi appeared while I was buying a taco from a food truck, or the time when I said 'it's goat' to the premiere dress of the show.

"It means I might get boycotted. Shunned. Ostracized by my fans because of..." I waved my hand around. "I wish I could post a fake crying apology video and be done with it."

"You can't," she said, her voice monotone. For the past three years, we have worked together. I have never heard her happy or sad. Only angry, frustrated or disappointed. I was the reason for all of that. "Your video is already trending on Twitter and celebrity meme pages have created a meme template and—"

"I get it." My headache worsened. "They don't even know the truth and they're blaming me..." I sighed, shaking my head. "I should have never signed the stupid ass contract."

Don't get me wrong. I was grateful and privileged enough to drop out of my art degree when I was selected for the manic pixie dream girl role. I had practiced before the audition and surprised my friends Mia and Emma, who were both still at university. They were happy for me, but they had warned me to be careful since it was Los Angeles.

The new adult romantic mini-series had done really well on one of the famous entertainment platforms. My character gave relationship advice to the main characters because she had a tragic past and would never find her own partner. Everyone loved my character and so did I. There were rumors of my character being the major role for the next season, but production was being sneaky.

And now... after that video, I could say goodbye to my role. To my short-lived acting career. I'd need to freshen up my resume and look for an actual nine-to-five job. The thought itself made me want to open the door of the car and roll out onto the highway.

"What were you doing there, anyway?" Heather asked me after a while. The weather was gloomy, and there was already traffic on the main highway. "I thought you didn't like orgy."

"I don't!" I defended myself. "Colt invited me to his trailer, and I went. We were drinking, I may have gotten a bit drunk, and talking about the next season one moment, and the next I was passing out and they were—" I furiously stabbed my index finger into the circle I made with my other index and thumb. "I woke up hearing a camera shutter click and opened the door."

I wished I could go back in time and never open that door.

The paparazzi had made his way into the trailer and found me with the two main male characters of the show. They were the love interests of the love triangle. Yes, they played around with each other in private, but I was so drunk and tired that I didn't remember what they had done. But I had changed into a tiny tank top (my dress smelled like sex) and shorts, with my hair mussed up since I was asleep.

Anyone would think I had a threesome with them since they were both half naked under the sheets. And no one would 'cancel' them since they were handsome white men.

"Okay. That's fair, but you didn't need to punch him."

I grimaced. I had punched the paparazzi because he was trying to push his way into the bedroom, and I was sleepy, drunk, and had a headache. I couldn't take it anymore. He had invaded our privacy, and I couldn't help myself from throwing a mean punch.

"Yeah, about that. Is he going to sue?" I asked and shook my head. "Don't tell me. I need to eat, shower, and sleep for a week straight before you tell me what I have to do next."

I needed to call Emma and Mia, too. They would believe me. They had to.

Someone called me again, and I tossed my phone to Heather. I wasn't sober enough to have a professional talk, or drunk enough to nod through it.

"It says Mom."

I snatched it from her hand and picked up the phone. *You never miss your mother's call.* Even if you are on a casting call, in the loo, or death row. "Mom!" I said with fake excitement. My own beaming voice made my headache worse. "How are you? Why'd you call?"

For a long time, I didn't hear a reply. My stomach twisted with nerves, and I pressed my phone closer, avoiding Heather's stare. "Mom? Is everything okay?"

"We made a mistake, Summer," I heard her sniffling, and I straightened up. "I...I need your help."

"What happened?" I demanded. "Did you get hurt? Dad? I told you not to fix the garage by yourself. I was going to come next we—"

"We are fine! But our... your..."

"Mom, what is it?"

"It's your…" She sighed and my blood ran cold when she said, "It's my sister."

My hand clenched. "What about her?"

"She came to our house today."

"I thought she was in Canada," I said, my voice harsh. "What did she want this time? More money? A car? Our home?"

"Sweet. I think you should visit us as soon as you can."

I slumped. Mom never called me anything other than my name. *Summer.* She named me Summer because I was always smiling and laughing and rarely cried as a child.

"I'll be there, okay? Don't worry, I'll take care of everything."

"I love you, Summer."

"Love you too, Mom."

I ended the call and covered my face. How could I take care of it when my life was hanging by a thread?

"You know we can't leave without a press release and control this entire shit show, right?"

"Yes, I know." I clenched my jaw and let out a long sigh. "I need you to book a ticket for someone."

"Who?"

I looked out of the window and said, "My biological mom."

9

# I DON'T KNOW HER

## DAMON

I glared at the replies and resisted the urge to slam the iPad on the desk and instead took a deep breath, holding the tablet gently.

"What the fuck is this?" I asked, glaring at our marketing agent who brought me the latest news of my late mother's beauty brand, *Moore*, and how the new promotion was going down the hill.

I had invested over a million dollars, and it was going down the drain.

"I don't think we are marketing the product well, Mr. Grant."

I stood up, the chair creaking and rolling back as I glared at her. "You don't think I can see that?! Remind me, Janice," I said, keeping my palms on the desk and looming over her. She cowered, trying to hide behind her long bangs. "How much did I invest in this green lipstick? And it's ads, marketing, PR, hm?"

"It's Jane."

My left eye twitched. "I don't give a fuck about your name. I paid you—this whole weird marketing idea of frog—

50

and I don't see a single fucking cent of profit."

She was trembling, making me want to ball my fists. I hated working as the CEO of Moore cosmetics. After Dorothy's death, Emma owned the brand, but she was busy studying and smooching off with her old boyfriend that she didn't have time to handle a multibillion-dollar beauty brand. In the end, I had to accept the CEO job and hand over my Vixen club to someone else.

I would rather work in that sex club, holed up in my tiny office than step into the pink and glitter world of cosmetics where everything smelled like chocolates and candies. Even the fifty-dollar foot scrub we sold came in different flavors.

*Who the fuck needs different flavors for foot scrub?*

"I don't see the results I paid for," I said in a calm tone as much as I could muster. But in the end, I was sure I scared her by the look of terror on her face. "I'll ask Rahul to send me a list of our marketing team and who came up with this stupid fucking idea. Even a five year old has a better marketing strategy than this."

I called Rahul, who was in his late twenties and the only person I'd trust with my calendar and schedule. I ignored his cackling when I asked him for the list of people in the marketing team and ended the call. Yes, he had warned me, but I was stupid enough to sell green lipstick.

"What the fuck are you still doing here, Jade?" I demanded, fixing my cufflinks as I sat down on my chair.

She swallowed. "Someone's calling you, Dick."

I stared at her. "What the fuck did you just say?" I was about to stand up when she turned on her heels and ran out of my office.

I glared at the empty spot and moved my gaze to my phone. It was Emma, but before I could pick it up, it went to voicemail. I sighed and leaned back in my chair. As soon as I closed my eyes, my head went straight to Thursday night. My cock bulged at the thought of the kitten.

Picking up my phone, I saw the text I had sent her,

**Me: It was upsetting to wake up alone, but I hope we can have a repeat soon—D**

She hadn't replied, but it was only Monday. And, okay. I admit it. I suck at flirting through texts. But at least it's better than sending her an unsolicited picture of my dick.

*Or did she recognize it was me? Should I resend the message with 'Sir' in the end?* I started typing and stopped.

What the fuck was I doing acting like a fucking teenager? I didn't even react this way when I *was* a teenager. *Jesus fucking Christ.* I didn't have time to think about her when I had to get the sales on track.

I wondered why Emma called, since she rarely ever called me, so I dialed her number, expecting her to announce that she was in Los Angeles.

"I'm busy," I said as a way of greeting, my tone soft. No matter our past, she was my little sister. The only person I considered as my family. And after what had happened in her high school, I was sure as hell not trusting her life in someone else's hands, even though that person was a veteran with years of military training under his belt. "I can't pick you up or your old boyfriend from the airport."

"Cillian's not *that* old. And we are not in LA," she replied, her voice sweet. "And hello to you, too. I missed you."

"He is older than me by five years, Em," I sighed and leaned back in the chair, pinching the bridge of my nose. "I wish I could have dinner with you."

"Awww, I knew you missed me, too."

If someone had told me that Emma would ever talk to me like this, I'd have laughed and paid them a grand. But I was so glad we had bonded over our relationship. That I was not as fucked up as my father.

I cracked a small smile. "You know you can move here if you want to. I have a condo furnished and ready for you."

I heard a gruff voice, and I knew Cillian was close to her. I rolled my eyes. Despite their age difference, they were inseparable, and I'd be a shithead if I didn't think he was good for Emma.

"I told you before. I like it here in Coral Springs. But anyway, I called you because I need a favor."

I straightened up. Emma Moore, my twenty-two-year-old sister and a billionaire, was the last person on the planet who needed a favor from me. "What is it?"

"Do you know Summer?"

"*No*," I lied. "I don't know her." My hand tightened on the phone.

Just hearing her name ignited a flash of memories in my head that I had tried my best to forget. The taste of her brown skin, soft dark curls, pillowy lips I could kiss—

*No. I wasn't going there.*

"You're such a terrible liar, Damon," Emma snickered and continued, her voice serious, "She... *well*, something happened and I need you to be there for her for a night."

"No," I blurted. I wasn't going anywhere ten feet near that woman.

"You didn't even hear me—"

"I said no, Emma. I'm busy. I'm working on this marketing—"

"Please, Damon," her voice turned soft. "She needs someone with her for that dinner. *Please*."

I swallowed the lump in my throat. I couldn't say no to her when she asked me for it. She wouldn't have asked me if it wasn't serious.

"What do I have to do?"

"Great! I knew you would agree. Just be at the address I sent you at seven sharp. Tonight. Thanks, bye-bye!"

Emma ended the call before I could open my mouth to argue.

She knew me too well.

I glared at the photo of her in a messy bun. I took it when she was grumpy, eating cereal from a bowl.

Checking the address, I slumped in my chair and shook my head.

I knew Emma was evil, but I didn't know she was this malicious.

I shouldn't have trusted my sister. *Fuck.*

# PART II

"Let me play with you and your body."

# 10

# SIMP

## DAMON

I checked the time on the watch and sighed, staring at the roof of my car. Why the fuck do I have to support her gathering when she was the reason for her own fucking mess?

*Emma. You're doing a favor for Emma. Nothing else.*

Grumbling underneath my breath, I let the valet open my car door and gave him a hefty tip before staring up at the enormous building. The evening air was chilly as I buttoned my suit and clenched my jaw. I hated social gatherings. I hated her.

The last time we were together, it had ended up with me kissing her, scolding her, and driving her cute, pouty ass home.

*No, fuck, Damon! Stop thinking about her ass.*

I walked towards the revolving doors and paused when the woman in a deep red dress went in at the same time from the other side.

"You can go ahead," I said, shamelessly staring at her ass. Her high heels made it look perkier, and the dress was stuck to her like a second skin, accentuating her curves.

"Oh, thank you!" She smiled and raised her head, her smile freezing. "It's *you*!"

Summer enunciated *you* like she was addressing maggots.

I rolled my eyes at her. "Trust me, I don't want to breathe the same air as you, but here we are."

On the flip side, I was gagging at the thought of eye-fucking her moments ago. If I had known the sexy woman in red was my little sister's best friend…. *Oh God.*

Shaking my head, I tried to walk in at the same time she did, and the security shot us both a strange look. I seethed at her, pushing the glass door, but the little shit wouldn't budge. *This woman would be the end of me.*

I gave up and walked back so she could walk in. I followed suit when she flashed me a winning grin. If I was someone else, it would take me a millisecond to fall in love seeing her gorgeous smile with a little dimple below her lip and her shining eyes.

But I was Damon, and I hated seeing her grin. She looked like trouble and dressed like one.

"Don't ruin this for me," she said, brushing her dark waves over her shoulders. It was surprising to see it without any wild highlights like pink or blue. She always did something crazy with her hair and despite the school rules, kept her hair dyed. It infuriated me that I noticed it. It was even more infuriating that I remembered her ruthless prank, which ended up with me in blue hair and a failed interview.

*Remember, you don't care about her.*

"You ruined it for yourself," I said in a harsh tone, staring down at her even though she was in heels. "Don't blame it on me if you ruin this party to better your name, Summer Hayes."

She stared at me unblinkingly, as if my tone or glare didn't affect her. I hated it didn't, and she wasn't the least bit intimidated. "You haven't changed at all. Such a pity to have a handsome face and a shitty personality. See you later, *Chad*."

*She did not just...*

I shot her and her perky ass daggers as she swayed her hips, walking away. Grinding my teeth, I followed her. She was asking to be bent over my lap and have her ass—*no. Nuh-uh.* I'm not going there. *She is off-limits.*

From what I had read, a paparazzi guy entered her co-star's trailer and found two men naked and her in tiny clothes. To make matters worse, she had punched the guy, and he had sued the ass off her, but her lawyers must be good, because the pap had vanished. But the video clip was still trending everywhere, and she was now a famous meme. It was worse than the previous Oscars.

I didn't care that she had threesomes with her co-stars, or orgies. I just had to appear at the charity dinner for the homeless, sign some checks, and get the fuck out.

Not to mention, it would look good for Moore Beauty. That's all I cared about.

Buttoning my suit, I walked into the main hall and ignored all the camera flashes and flirty smiles coming my way. I didn't care. They would write a two-thousand-word essay about how rude I was at the charity or a fake rumor about sleeping with the competitor's daughter just for more sales. It was all bullshit. I had seen my mother and how fame got to her head.

"If I looked like her, I'd have threesomes every day."

"I know right, like she's so lucky!"

I ignored the women talking about Summer that way when she said her small speech about helping the community she lived in and giving back. I was sure it was all written by her manager, anyway.

Thank God they were serving dinner straight after the speech. I was about to sit on the far side of the hall at an empty table, but one of the employees with an earpiece and lots of notes grabbed me and sat me down on the table full of famous models, actors and actresses.

I didn't mind them.

*What I did mind was...*

"Simp," Summer muttered underneath her breath, making a face at me when I had to sit beside her.

"What the fuck does that mean?" I asked her in a not so soft tone.

"Oh, you must be a millennial." The woman sitting beside her giggled and said, "Simp is a slang for men who are... um... obsessed with a certain woman or women."

I scoffed and looked at Summer from head to toe, grabbing the nearest champagne flute and said in the blandest tone I could muster, "You're not my type."

She batted her long lashes at me as I took a huge sip of the bubbly alcohol. "That's a lie, and we both know it, Damon."

My hand clenched underneath the table, hearing her say my name. "How?"

Summer leaned closer, her musky vanilla perfume making me want to pull away because it was so damn exotic and addictive. *Why the fuck did they have to put the chairs so close to each other?* My knee kept bumping against her leg and it was infuriating. "If I wasn't your type, you wouldn't kiss me like you wanted to devour me in public," she whispered, her sultry voice making me want to snap.

"That kiss was a stupid mistake." I took a deep breath, and looking straight at her, I said, "And I wouldn't touch you with a ten-feet rod even if I wanted to. You're nothing but trouble. This evening proves it."

Her cheeks flushed with embarrassment and it surprised me. "It's not what it looked like." She shook her head and looked away from me. "You wouldn't believe me, anyway."

*What's not to believe?* Pictures of hickeys on her neck were already out.

She ignored me for the rest of the dinner, talking and laughing with the other people at the table. It was oddly alarming to see her charming everyone around her, even though they were probably strangers.

I would have been the happiest person in the room because she didn't talk to me. Except an actress in her forties kept giving me sly looks, lowering the neck of her dress to show off her ample cleavage, and flirting with me.

I had enough when she licked the cream from the dessert spoon very suggestively. I was about to stand up and go to the washroom when Summer laughed loudly. Her hand, that was holding an almost full flute, bumped against my thigh when I stood, and another moment I felt the cold alcohol drench my pants.

All laughter stopped and Summer turned to look at me, her chocolate eyes widening as she looked at my crotch and tried to stifle a laugh.

*This little shit is begging to be spanked.*

11

# SISTER'S BEST FRIEND

## DAMON

I sat down, feeling the cold seep from my slacks to my skin. Thank fuck she spilled it on my thighs instead of crotch.

"I'm so sorry," Summer said, her voice high-pitched as she took a clean napkin and went on her knees to dab it over my thigh. "I wasn't looking and it just… *happened.*"

She looked up at me, her big, doe-brown eyes making me clench my teeth. She didn't know how fucking sinful she looked on her knees with that dress on. Patting dry my soaked slacks as if she truly wanted to help me, she kept blubbering about how it was an honest mistake, her hands going everywhere over my thigh.

Thankfully, everyone had moved on from the minor incident. I leaned down and held her warm hand on my thigh. *"Don't."* I bit out the word as if I was cursing, pulling away her hand, standing up.

I went to the washroom and glared at the bulge. *Are you fucking serious?* I cursed, running a hand through my hair and splashing some cold water on my face to cool down.

I despised her and yet my body reacted like a fucking teenager whenever she was around.

*Why the fuck did she have to kneel on the fucking ground and pat me dry?* I hope she didn't do that to everyone she spilled something on.

"Fucking hell, Summer," I swore underneath my breath and calmed myself enough to step out of the washroom. There was no saving the cream slacks I was wearing, so I had to leave early after signing some checks.

I saw the little abomination walking into a hall, and I followed her to talk to her. *About what?* I had to scold her. Maybe get a rise out of her pretty body instead of her infamous grin.

She walked into a room, leaving the door open, and I looked around the empty hall before following her. "Summer."

She looked over her shoulder and sighed, as if she was glad to see me. *What the hell is she on?* "Oh, it's you. Come on in. Can you wait for a bit? The underwire of this bra is poking the shit out of my underboob," she said, walking into what looked like an open closet.

"I didn't need to know all that," I said to myself as I looked around the small room. With two couches, a mini fridge and a television.

I sat down on the couch and took a glance at her body as she tried to fix something in her bra, in nothing but her innerwear, the dress spilling around her heels. I had seen her in a bikini hundreds of times whenever she stayed over at Emma's and I was there. So, it wasn't a surprise to see her feel comfortable enough to be half-naked in my presence.

But I wasn't expecting *that*.

Those hickeys. On her cleavage and stomach. I didn't know when I stood up and walked closer until I could see her perfect ass in nude underwear. The ass that I had spanked and bit last week.

It was *her*.

The woman… the brat I slept with.

*What the fuck?*

"Oh, hi, can you help me zip this up?" She smiled at me, looking so innocent, her voice soft, as if she didn't realize that it was me who had edged and fucked her hard.

I said nothing when she turned around. My hand was shaking, but I clenched it and helped her with the zipper, her hair falling on her back as she thanked me.

*If she's the same woman, then were the rumors true? Did she have a threesome? Did I not fuck her hard enough?*

I closed my eyes shut. I should know better than to trust those rumors.

"I'm sorry for the spill. I would offer to dry clean it, and I don't think any of these dresses would fit you for the rest of the night."

"No."

"Yeah. Thought so. I'll pay for the dry cleaning, don't worry," she shrugged and was about to walk away when I held her arm.

"Do you always go around spilling things on people?" I asked, angry at her.

*Why did she have to be the one person I felt comfortable with after years of not having sex?*

"What do you mean?" She frowned at me. "Of course not! I just… people just walk into me sometimes." *Of course, they did.* It wasn't because she was a fucking klutz.

"Where did you get those hickeys from?" I asked, my voice deep and low.

Her cheeks slashed with color, and she pulled away from my touch. "It's none of your business."

"So you slept with your co-stars."

"Shut up, Damon," Summer snapped, shaking her head at me. "I didn't, but you'll believe the worst of me, anyway. I don't have time for this right now."

She was about to leave, but I asked her again, "Then tell me the truth."

Summer looked over her shoulder and said, "I had a one-night stand."

"Of course, you did." I clenched my jaw. "Was he good to you?" *Was I enough?*

"Yes, he was way better than you and your kiss," she said, walking away, her heels clacking against the marble.

I closed my eyes and pinched the bridge of my nose. *"Fuck."*

I signed some checks and thanked the organizers with a fake smile before ignoring the actress who kept flirting with me, slipping a key for her hotel room in my pocket. I stared at Summer for the last time, our eyes meeting briefly before I rushed out of the damn hall.

Tugging at my tie, I breathed in the humid air. I needed to make sure my eyes weren't playing things on me.

The entire drive to my penthouse, I kept thinking how it couldn't be her. She was Summer after all. We had hate at first sight. At least, I did, seeing the grinning girl in braces making cookies with my sister and making her laugh. It had been years since I saw Emma laugh like that, and I was young and stupidly jealous that she was fine living with Mom, who never ever cared about me while I suffered alone with Dad and Drake.

I was in college and I hated how bitter her cookies were when Summer made me eat them. Despite my rude comment about her cookies, she just laughed and told me she'd make them better next time.

It couldn't be her.

I didn't want it to be *her*.

As soon as I reached my place, I checked my tablet and Googled her name. Ignoring the feeling of how I was acting like a stalker, I checked her Instagram and the pictures of her at the premiere of her upcoming show, *Hate Love.*

*How did I not recognize it was her?* Of course, I couldn't. Her hair was longer, and the last time I had seen her was the night of her prom when we kissed. I only recognized her today because of her face. And it was covered with a damn mask. Only if we had removed them…

Even her dress. She wore the same blue colored dress in her premiere photo.

*Fuck.*

I slept with my sister's best friend.

I slumped on the couch, which was also my bed-slash-desk. It was multipurpose, and I was glad it had lasted me for over two years even though I thrifted it for less than forty dollars.

My feet ached from wearing heels all night, and I tried to rub away the soreness. The event to improve my name and drown out the rumors was successful with little to no accidents.

Except *that* jerk getting mad over a tiny spill.

But I gotta admit, even though he was a huge grump, his thighs were strong. I remembered the dark gleam in his eyes when I was trying to help him pat it dry. He was definitely a weirdo for getting angry at me. Even when I suggested having it dry cleaned.

My private phone rang. A video call from my girlfriends. I smiled and accepted it, making sure my background was the plain wall.

"Hi my loves!" I beamed at seeing their smiling faces. "I miss you guys so much."

Mia grinned, her green eyes shining. "I miss you too, Summer! It's no fun without you here."

"Mhmm, so you better book a ticket to Coral Springs as soon as… everything clears out," Emma said, pointing out the big elephant in the room.

I groaned. "I wish I could sue the paparazzi. But Heather is being a big meanie and told me it's unreasonable!"

"James said he knows a few people who can threaten him to drop the lawsuit…," Mia trailed off when she saw our faces. I mean, I can accept it coming from Cillian since he has done some shady work, but *James*? The man who always wears an expensive three-piece suit and glares at anyone who infuriates him through his glasses? *Nuh-uh.* "Why are you staring at me like that?"

"We are just concerned, M," Emma replied and looked at me. She looked like she was in her room. "Heather is right. You can't sue him because you punched him. If you hadn't, we could have sued the shit out of him for trespassing and filming you and your partners."

"They are not my partners. They were fooling around, and I was tired and a bit tipsy so I was passed out."

Mia sympathized with me, but Emma looked at me suspiciously. She was the mother hen of our group, so I knew she wouldn't believe me. But I didn't want to tell them about the one-night stand I had at a sex club of all places. If I did, Emma would ask Damon about it just to make sure the person I slept with had a good background history and no crime records. *Yes.* She would go that far to protect me and keep me safe. Especially after what happened to her in high school.

"Also, did I mention your brother is a huge piece of ass?" I complained, suddenly feeling riled up. "He had the audacity to show up at the same time as the host a.k.a. me."

Mia and Emma nodded, so I huffed and continued my

rant. "I don't know how you two are related. He is so grumpy and frown-y and he's always, *'I don't give a fuck about you'*, *'Move out of my way before I murder you with my eyes',"* I tried to mimic his deep voice pitching mine low. "He probably doesn't even know how to smile. Do you have his baby album? I'm sure you do, and I'm even surer that Dorothy— may she rest in peace— photoshopped the smile on his baby pictures, because I don't trust that that human or creature or whatever he is, can actually smile. His face muscles are glued in a permanent scowl. Do you know how much of an ass he was with me at the event?"

Emma pursed her lips and shook her head. Mia said, "No, go on."

I took a deep breath and settled deeper in my couch-slash-bed-slash-desk and continued, *"Right!* So, he didn't let me go through the revolving door. He pretends to be a gentleman, but he's *so* not. I pushed my way through the door, and then he had the audacity to accuse me of having a threesome or an orgy with my cast. Not only that, he kept flirting with my good friend who's wayyyyy too old for him. Like *too* old. Like a century old or something." I shrugged, picking a loose thread on the couch. "I mean, I don't care if he wants to hit up a cougar, but I should tell you right now, Em. She's way too good for him. She deserves better."

Emma nodded. Mia looked like she was snuggled up in her bed with a silly grin on her face.

"You guys know how clumsy I am so—"

*"Uh-oh,"* Emma and Mia said in unison, making me pout.

"I didn't do it on purpose! I was laughing at some weird joke my friends told, and I just busted out laughing. I just… didn't realize I was holding the champagne flute, and I may or may not have flung it on Damon's pants."

They both looked at me through my tiny phone screen

and a second later laughed out loud, clutching their stomachs. Their giggles made me frown.

"Guys, it wasn't on purpose. As much as I loathe him, I'd *never* do that."

"Did he scold you or threatened to sue you?" Emma asked in between her laugh while Mia was turning red from laughing.

*Wow. Such good and supportive friends I have.*

"Surprisingly, neither. I helped him pat it dry, and he seemed angry because I am Summer Hayes and I shouldn't touch a single hair on his body because he's above me, a God among mortals." I rolled my eyes and sighed. "At least he helped me zip up my dress without any complaint or taunt when I had to fix the underwire of the bra. I offered to get it dry-cleaned but..." *Then he started shitting about the man I slept with.* I shouldn't have changed in front of him. I didn't think Damon was the type of person to stare and didn't realize I hadn't applied concealer on my stomach or butt where *that* man had given me hickeys.

*I'm such an idiot.*

"But?" Mia prodded.

"*Nothing*," I said too quickly. "I left and then I didn't see him for the rest of the night. He signed over two million dollars' check, so thank him for me. I'm sure he went to a sex club with mirrors everywhere so he can look at himself all the time. I bet he moans his name instead of his partner's when he cu—"

"*Ooookay!*" Emma said, interrupting me. "I really don't want you to finish that sentence. I will talk to him and—*why are you trending on Twitter again?*"

"Oh no," I said and quickly opened Twitter to see that my name was trending. *Again.*

*Don't people have better things to do than be nosy?*

I found various clips and videos of me accidentally

throwing champagne on Damon and him just glaring at me. Lots of captions said I moved on fast, that it was a sure way to seduce a billionaire and I can find another way to ruin his pants.

"Oh my god, they're trashing you," Mia said in a sad voice, her puppy eyes making me feel marginally better.

Emma was smiling. "At least, this looks funny. Let me send it to Damon."

"My manager is going to kill me."

"Don't worry about it," Emma rolled her eyes, brushing her golden blond hair. "Just ignore it. I'm sure this will help boost your show. Did they talk about you being the main character in the next season?"

I shook my head. "Not yet." *I hope I am.* I'd need the money and any brand deals that come with it.

"Aw, I'm sure something good will come out of it," Mia said with a small smile. She was always optimistic about it and I trusted her.

"I have to go on a date with Cillian, so bye-bye. We'll talk soon," Emma said, giving us flying kisses and looking at me. "You know we are always here if you want to vent?"

"I know. I love you guys," I said with sincerity. She smiled and left the call, leaving me with a very thoughtful face of Mia staring at me. "What?"

*Fuck. Did she find out how and where I live?*

"Nothing. I was just wondering," she said and tilted her head, tapping her chin with her index finger. "You sure talk about Damon a lot, considering you hate him."

My stomach warmed, and I said, "I mean, *duh!*"

She kept staring and humming.

"Stop hanging out with James so much. You're being suspicious like him." *And he's always suspicious.*

"I heard that!" I grinned, hearing James yell in the background, making Mia chuckle. "And you're the one with bad rep, Summer, not me," James said, popping up on the screen, standing beside Mia.

"Anyway," Mia pushed his face away and smiled at me, "call me whenever you want. I'm not sure I can relate, but I can try to understand how hard it is to live in a different city without your friends and family."

My eyes watered at her gentle words, and I wished I could hug her and tell her everything about it, but I didn't want to stress her. So, I smiled and replied, "I appreciate it, love. Goodnight!"

I dropped the phone when it turned black and stared up at the flaky ceiling, a tear leaking out of the corner of my eye.

Just a few more days. Or weeks.

*I can do it.*

I am Summer fucking Hayes.

13

## H-O-T

SUMMER

I chugged a large gulp of cheap wine and stared at the articles and their atrocious headlines. 'Twenty-two-year-old *Hate-Love* Star Flirting With the Dashing CEO of Moore Beauty: Do You Think Sugar Daddy Damon Is *H-O-T*? Read More!'

*Gross.*

Even if he paid me a grand to be in his presence, I wouldn't accept it. I'd need at least fifty to sixty grand in this economy.

I wonder what his face would look like when he finds out about the rumors. I snickered, drinking more wine. His nose would flare, and he'd snap or bark at anyone closest to him before calling me.

*I hope he doesn't.*

Slumping on the couch, I scrolled through more articles until I opened my emails and stopped at the one that said, 'Confidential.' I sat up straighter.

*Are the producers going to keep me in the second season of Hate-Love? Will I be the main character?*

My hopes and dreams died as soon as I opened it. It was

from *Moore*. Of course, Damon had to ruin it. The email stated something about being an ambassador, and they even CC'd my manager.

"Who wants to be an ambassador at this age?" I grumbled, my words slurring from all the alcohol I had been ingesting for the past hour.

I was feeling lonely after calling my girlfriends and felt lonelier after a cold shower (hot water only comes in the morning), so I opened the cheap wine that I had purchased to celebrate something and decided that me getting canceled came close.

I was about to turn-off my phone and throw it away, but I noticed the zeroes in the amount I'd get paid. "What the fuck?" I gasped. "How rich is this guy?"

That's what Heather meant when she texted me in all caps to fill out the form. I opened it and even though I was drunk, I could at least type out the draft why I was the perfect fit. I can ask Heather to edit it in the morning and send it.

The extra money from doing makeup and skincare shoots would definitely help me get out of the shit hole I was living in quicker.

Sipping some wine, I cracked my neck and started typing, moving my thumbs quickly.

I'd rather die than see anyone take my position.

I could ask Emma, since it was her company before she asked Damon to help her, but it didn't feel right to ask her. I wanted to prove to myself that I am talented and that I can be the face of Moore Beauty.

* * *

I WOKE UP WITH A START, SLAMMING ON THE ALARM CLOCK TO make it stop ringing. My head hurt, and the constant beep of the evilest electronic device to exist made the headache worse. I forced my heavy lids open and checked the time, groaning as I twisted out of the comforter.

The clock showed it was nine-fifteen.

"No," I moaned, stripping out of my clothes and rushing to the small shower. I had less than twenty minutes before Heather arrived and either scolded me or gave me a stink eye for being late for one interview in ages that wasn't related to any shady rumors or incidents.

I hated the thought of Damon being there, but beggars can't be choosers.

Brushing my teeth, washing my curls, and doing my makeup took most of the time. I threw on the first blouse that caught my eye and paired it with a pencil skirt and heels. I didn't have time for breakfast even though I was starving, but I didn't forget my meds. I'd need them if I was going to survive the interview.

"See? I'm on time," I said, panting after stomping downstairs from my apartment in high heels. I buckled the seat belt and ignored Heather's confused look. "Drive. I don't want to give him a chance to tease me."

"Summer, your top—"

I nodded, "Yes, I thrifted it. I need to check my form and send it."

Her dark eyes finally looked at the road as she started driving. I only accepted a driver if we were going to fancy events, and most of the time, she drove me around in the agency car or I took cabs.

"You still haven't sent the form?" she asked, disappointment lacing her tone. "I told you how important it is."

I checked the web browser on my phone to find the draft and opened the inbox when I couldn't find it. "I remember writing the draft—*oh*." My eyes widened seeing the confirmation email from Moore. I had already sent it.

I checked the time, and my phone fell in my lap. I sent it the night before when I was shitfaced.

"What did you do?" Heather asked, glancing at me with narrowed eyes.

"Nothing." I took a deep breath and smoothed my skirt. "I already sent the form." And it may or may not be full of grammatical errors and some weird stuff because I was desperate-for-money drunk and had no shame.

"Let's hope they're more lenient towards the rumors."

I rolled my eyes. "You clearly haven't met Damon."

"I wish I had." She gave me a hard look before taking a turn. "It would have saved us from the paparazzi waiting at the building."

I winced. "We should probably go from the back." Then I added, crossing my arms like a petulant kid, "I didn't do anything. And neither did he. The paparazzi would start the rumors that I'm pregnant if they could. They're shit and we both know it."

"ARE YOU PREGNANT?!"

"What the fuck?" I asked, worried at her bulging eyes. "Of course, I'm not! *Jesus*. That was a joke."

She sighed and ran a hand through her short, blunt, straight hair. "You're going to kill me one day, Summer." She muttered underneath her breath, "I swear to God, she's my last client."

I closed my eyes and leaned back on the seat. I still had a mild headache, but it was better than before. I wished we could make a stop at Dunkin' Donuts and get some donuts and coffee, but time was of the essence.

Thankfully, we reached our destination in time and went through the back, so there were no cameras or reporters waiting to spread more rumors.

"Summer, you really should check your—" Heather started when we stepped into the elevator.

"I'm sorry, I'm just trying to remember what I wrote in the form," I said, squeezing my eyes closed and forcing my brain to remember everything from last night.

"But your blouse is—"

"*Fuck*. I can't remember." I cursed and shook my head as the doors opened and we stepped into the enormous building that belonged to my best friend and an asshole. It smelled like candy–chocolate that had a luxurious afternote. I tried not to gawk at the beautiful women walking gracefully in heels or the handsome men in suits. Huge banners of their new product were placed against the walls with large screens playing ads. There was a freaking chandelier in the front lobby.

*Who the fuck has a chandelier in the office building? Moore Beauty, that's who.*

"Good morning!" I jumped hearing the bubbly voice of the receptionist as she smiled and did a double take at me. *Yeah, I get that a lot.*

"Hi, we are here for the ambassador program…," Heather said, trailing off and giving me a look.

*What, woman?*

The receptionist, named Layla, said, "Of course! Boss is waiting for you, Ms. Summer. Although… um… I don't know if I should say it, but your top is—"

I grinned, "I thrifted it. If you want the address of the store, let me know. Which floor did you say it was?"

"*Uh…*" Layla and Heather shared a look. "It's the top floor. Second elevator from the hall. It's private, so you can… you know."

"Thank you!" I said and walked towards the elevator, my heels clacking against the marble floor.

"Heather, why aren't you coming with me?" I asked when she didn't follow.

"You should have a discussion in private before I can

agree and disagree on some terms," she said. "I'll join you as soon as you're done."

I prepared myself in the car and smiled at the confused look of the assistant who escorted me to the devil's office once I stepped out of the private elevator. Why were they looking at me like that? I had checked my makeup, and it was perfect. Even my curls were shining.

"Mr. Damon is closing an interview," he said, pushing his glasses over his nose. He looked cute. "Would you like some tea? Coffee? Snacks?"

"Can I have a decaf with six espresso shots with two pumps of sweetener?" *Pretty please?*

He raised his brow a little and nodded. "Right away, miss."

"Thank you! I like your glasses…" I checked the name tag on his suit and added, "Rahul."

He smiled. "Thank you."

We both turned our heads to Damon's office door when someone squealed before the door opened. I took in a sharp breath when I saw a beautiful woman with long legs walking out of his office. She was sobbing, her perfect makeup staying in place as she cried out, "I hate you! I hope you die with blue balls!" over her shoulder before stumbling away on her heels.

"Should we help her?" I mumbled, touching my chest and trying to calm my pounding heartbeat. I knew Damon was as ruthless in his business as he was in real life, but I didn't know he made pretty girls cry.

"It's okay. That's the third interview of the day, and it's nothing new," Rahul replied. "Come on, it's your turn."

I braced myself when he knocked on the door with a shiny label that read, *CEO Damon Grant.*

"Enter," came a brusque reply.

I clenched my hand in a fist and stepped in.

# NO REGRETS

## DAMON

I scrolled through the tabloid, my jaw clenching at the pictures of me and Summer. I had already sued the photographer and the reporter with defamation, and even though they took the article down, she was trending on all the social media.

*Of course, they didn't target me because I'm a rich, white man, but they were calling her slurs here and there and I hated it.*

Someone knocked on the door and entered before I could reply.

"I'm here to be the ambassador of Moore," the woman said, keeping her hand on her hips as she strutted in.

Rahul, my assistant, winced at me. "I'm sorry. I told her not to enter, but she didn't listen."

The woman in the mini dress rolled her eyes and made herself comfortable sitting across from me. "Oh, whatever. I have everything you need for the Moore Beauty."

I nodded at Rahul and kept my tablet aside and once he left, I leaned back on the chair and asked, "And what is that, Miss…?"

"Elaine," she said with a smile, and stood up. I eyed her face as she walked around my desk, swiveling my chair towards her. "But you can call me anything you want."

I raised my brow when she touched my arm and whispered, "I have the perfect face and body, Mr. Damon."

Before she could lower her long nails to my crotch, I stopped her. "If you touch me again, I will make sure there's no future for your face or body, Miss Elaine." I stood up and glared at her. "Now get the fuck out of my office before I call security."

She shivered but moved her dark hair over her shoulder and said, "I'm just trying to—"

"Don't try," I cut her off and nodded at the door. "Get out."

"Let me just give you a taste of what I can do for the company and you." She kept up with her sultry voice, leaning closer so I could see through her cleavage.

I pinched the bridge of my nose. "I'm sorry for whoever taught you that sexual favors will get you things on a silver platter, but in my company they won't." Tears sprung in her eyes, and I offered her a tissue that was on my desk. "Please leave before I ask security to take you out of this building."

"You're such a piece of shit!" she squealed. "I hope you rot in hell!"

I hummed and sat down in my chair once she left, screaming more threats. It wasn't new. Before her, a guy who was a famous influencer with a vast audience offered me a blowjob for nothing in return. His words, and I quote, 'You're just hot. It'll be a shame to not have your cock sucked by me.' When I told him no and to get out, he was shocked that someone denied him.

I sighed when someone knocked on the door. *Please let it be a sane person who actually wants the job.*

"Come in," I said when Rahul opened the door, his smile wavering, looking at my face. "What?"

He looked at my shoulder and said, "Ms. Summer has arrived."

*Thank fuck.* Even though she wasn't sane, she would never offer to have sex with me for the job.

My cock tightened. I hated to admit it, but the idea of her begging for the position bent over my desk was deliciously hot.

"Bring her up."

"But I thought we could start—"

I raised my brow, and he closed his mouth. "I want to have a little chat with her. Alone."

He nodded, leaving my office. I sighed and leaned back, going through her application. I wish I hadn't checked it in the morning. I could have pretended to dismiss her application, but I got curious. I read how she wanted more inclusivity when it came to makeup and skincare. More models who are people of color, plus size models, LGBTQ, disabled. She must have been drunk since she rambled on about Taylor Swift, and her grammar was off. But her thoughts made sense.

Moore Beauty had diverse models in their branding and ads, but the marketing team never included anything else. *I* didn't think about anything else. We had already launched a weird product with no audience when we had millions, billions of them.

And despite our differences, and the small part where we had sex and she didn't know it was me, I wanted her to be a part of the brand. Represent it.

Other models and actresses were still responding, talking to their managers and agents, but Summer was the first one who responded without her manager. She could have easily asked Emma, and my sister would have trusted me to accept her, but she didn't.

My heart pounded in my ears when I heard the soft voices outside the office. When someone knocked, I took a deep breath and straightened up.

"Enter."

I took her in when she entered the office, my mouth going dry looking at her. Her hair was still damp, and I had to clench my hand in a fist to stop myself from remembering how soft and ticklish her hair felt over my skin. Her brown skin was glowing and *fuck*—those legs. Long and toned in the tight pencil skirt and high heels.

*Fuck me.* She looked like she was a woman on a mission.

Her chocolate eyes moved around the office, and I wondered how it'd feel to see it for the first time. Two couches with a coffee table. A floor-to-ceiling bookshelf full of books, makeup products and our magazines. A door leading to a private bathroom. And lastly, the vast mahogany desk.

"Good morning," Summer said, eyeing me like I was a rock.

"Your top is inside out," I said as a greeting.

She stopped mid-walk, her eyes widening as she looked down and saw the seams of her white blouse. She cursed underneath her breath.

"It's a new trend," she replied.

I gave her a look and pointed to the door. "Go change."

"Thanks," she said dryly, hurrying into the washroom and slamming the door behind her.

*Did no one tell her about her top this entire time?*

I shook my head and drank some cold water to calm down. *I have to forget that night. If I don't, I'm not sure I'd be able to work with her, let alone have a conversation without remembering how pretty she looked with her legs—*

*No. Have some self-control.*

"Sorry about that," she said, stepping out of the washroom and sitting on the chair across from me. "So... I take it you read everything I wrote?"

*"Everything."*

"Even the bit about—"

*"Taylor Swift?* Yes." I leaned back in the chair and, crossing my arms, I looked at her. "I want to hire you."

She eyed me suspiciously and slowly said, "Okay."

She really didn't know it was me.

"Do you know what you'll have to do?"

"Photoshoots for the products, billboards, ads, magazines?" she asked and continued speaking, her chin high and shoulders relaxed. "I'll be honest. I haven't done any photoshoots for any brand, so you'd be better off hiring someone else who has experience."

"But?"

"But I would like to be a part of my friend's company and bring inclusivity. I know this isn't in the agreement, but I'd like to have some of my own rules."

I stared at her, wondering what the hell happened to the girl with a clumsy grin and the urge to bring chaos wherever she went. Now a woman with such grace. No wonder they hired her for the role of a smart friend of the main character. It is the way of how she spoke, and few people in this day and age spoke after listening. It was charming.

"Okay, we can discuss the agreement once we talk with your manager."

She smiled, her eyes shining, and I clenched my fist before continuing, "You know we will have to travel too, right?"

"Travel?"

I nodded. "I am not paying you millions to sit and look

pretty in front of the camera, even though that's a part of it. But we want more pictures in different places."

Others would have been excited to travel for free, but she looked worried, a small frown on her face. "W-will it take too long? Traveling?"

I narrowed my eyes and leaned on the desk, clasping my hands together. "I didn't see any movie or show shooting in your schedule for the next year."

She pursed her lips. "Tell me. I'd like to be home soon."

I raised my brow. I didn't expect that. She always seemed like a free bird and never thought how she'd feel alone in a city full of fame and cameras. "No, it won't take too long. I can ask our marketing and photography team to see if we can schedule something in Coral Springs." I'd get to spend some time with Emma too.

"Okay, thanks."

"Before we continue, I want to know something," I said, standing up from the chair. "Do you regret your one-night stand?"

I couldn't breathe as the silence echoed in the office. I wanted to know if she did or did not. If she said yes, then I'd forget about it and never tell her or let her find out it was me she slept with. If she said no... Well, that'd definitely complicate a lot of things.

"Why are you asking that?" she asked, staring up at me even while sitting down. "It's none of your business."

"Tell me, Summer."

She tilted her head. I rarely called her by her name, and she knew I was serious and not playing around or teasing her.

I was so grateful for the desk that separated us.

"I don't regret it," she answered calmly. I sighed, closing my eyes. *Fuck.* "Even though it's still none of your business and extremely creepy to ask me about it during an in—"

I opened my eyes and glared at her. Leaning close, I said, "It is my fucking business, *kitten*."

Her eyes widened and lips parted. I was sure she stopped breathing as I walked around the desk to get closer to her.

"And I'm proud to know you don't regret that night. Since you'll be working for me, kitten."

# 15

# YOU'RE NOT MY TYPE

## SUMMER

I was grateful for the plush chair my butt was stuck to. Because if I were standing, I'd have fainted.

"It can't be you!" I said, my voice high pitched. Clearly, I was having a mental breakdown.

He didn't seem pleased either. *Fuck, fuck, fuck.* He spanked me. Teased me, made me cum better than my battery-operated friends, *and* he was caring. Damon and caring didn't belong in the same sentence and *yet...*

I chuckled, fanning my flustered cheeks and neck. I felt so hot all of a sudden. "I get it. Emma and Mia, you can come out." I grinned at Damon and stood up. "That's a really great prank, by the way. Your acting is so good. I almost believed it—"

"I gave you those hickeys," Damon said, his voice low and velvety that made my stomach clench with nerves. "The ones on your pretty tits. Your stomach, hips, and, if I remember, one on your perfect as—"

"Okay!" I threw my hands in front of me and turned away from him, pacing around and shaking my head. Even without the coffee, I felt wired and jittery. I had taken my meds, and they weren't working. "I don't believe it."

"I don't care if you believe it or not, but it happened."

I glared at him. *How dare he sound so casual about it?* As if it didn't matter to him that we did more than just share a kiss.

A horrified thought came to my head, and I cupped my mouth, staring at him with wide eyes. He narrowed his eyes at me. "What?"

"I..." I didn't know what to say. I couldn't even ask Google what to do when you find out that your soon-to-be-boss-slash-best-friend's-older-brother was the hot one-night stand you had. "Did you know?"

"Know what?" he asked, his voice snappy as he walked closer.

I took a step back, and I was trapped against the doors of the office. He was so close I could smell his musky cologne. I needed to get out of its range before I slapped him or kissed him.

*Save me, Rahul!*

"Did you know it was me that night?" I asked, swallowing the lump in my throat and looking at the marble floor. His shiny shoes and my heels were awfully close. "Were you playing with me? Did you just want to get in my pants?" *Like all the boys I dated when I was young? So you can tell your rich friends you had sex with Summer Hayes, cheerleader and now a Hollywood star, and brag about it? Call me a whore?*

"What the fuck, Summer?" His voice made me snap out of my head, and I looked at him, saw the disgust on his face. "I know you think so low of me, but I wouldn't have slept with you, let alone touch you, if I knew it was you that night."

*Ouch. But thank God.*

"I wouldn't sleep with you either. You're not my type."

Damon stared me down, his gaze roving from my head to toe. "Didn't seem like it that night. You were all over me."

My face burned, and I clenched my hands into fists. "So were you. Giving me a hickey on my ass? Really?"

He smirked—*oh, that devilish little cocky smirk*. What I wouldn't do to punch it off his face. Sliding his hands in his pockets, he tilted his head and asked, "How's your ass, by the way? It was quite a spanking. Are your cheeks bruised? I can help you if you want, kitten."

Before I could maul that sly smile, someone knocked on the door, making me jump. I sighed in relief when he moved away, and Rahul entered the room with an enormous glass of coffee. I thanked him, begging him with my eyes not to leave me alone, but it went over his head as the devil over my shoulder ordered him to leave.

"So if—"

I stopped him, raising my palm. "I can't have this conversation without coffee."

He stared at me as if I was from another planet when I drank four large gulps. "Gen Z and their addiction with caffeine," he muttered, loud enough for me to hear.

"It's decaf, you grumpy boomer," I said proudly and continued, "How did you know it was me?"

"Call me boomer again and see what happens." Damon's stormy gray eyes were piercing. I licked my lips and strangely, I wanted to call him boomer again and see what happens. "I found out during the charity event. When you paraded half-naked, and I saw your hickeys."

I drank more decaf. "*Hm*," was my intelligent reply. I wanted to ask him why he didn't send me any message, but I was too proud to ask him that. It might not have been as memorable for him as it was for me, since he didn't care to reach out. He was a sex club owner, after all. He must have partners, rotating them weekly so he doesn't get bored.

"If that's all, I'd like to make you an offer."

I paused and looked at him. Chuckling, I shook my head.

"Are you for real, Damon? Why… I don't want to work with you."

He frowned, dark eyes pinning me on the spot. I was stupid. *How the hell didn't I recognize him that night? He's so grumpy, with soft dirty-blonde hair and the most intense gray eyes I've ever seen.*

"Why not?"

I pointed at the air between us. "We had sex. Multiple times. And… you are Emma's brother."

"Half-brother."

"You're…" I shook my head and turned around. "I'm leaving."

"Why does it matter that we had sex?" he asked, following me. My pace quickened to leave his office, but I was wearing heels, dammit. I just needed to get away from him and his steely eyes. "Lots of people use sex to get the position I'm offering you on a silver platter."

I let out a humorless chuckle and turned around to face him. "If you just wanted a blowie, please go ahead and ask me right now so you feel better about handing me the check," I said with a saccharine smile.

"Sweetheart, if I wanted to, you'd beg for my cock," he purred, my hand tightening on the glass I was holding. *Don't waste the decaf on him, Summer.* "And you know what I meant. I don't want to kiss you, let alone have sex with you, so just accept the damn offer!"

"I don't know what you meant, Mr. Grant," I said, keeping my voice soft. "All I heard is how you abuse your power of authority and sexually harass women to give you a blowjob—"

"Don't say another word."

I steeled myself. "I have met enough jerks like you in just two years, and I will not stand here and let you or any other white man berate me or anyone else. Go shove that offer up your ass, asshole."

I thought twice about dumping the coffee on him, but I didn't have enough money to dry clean his expensive suit that was worth my monthly rent. Instead, I settled for turning around and walking away with an extra sway in my hips.

But before I could open the door, his hand stopped it, and I took a sharp intake of breath when I felt his body behind me.

*Fuck. Me.*

I should have dumped the coffee on him.

16

# HER BOYFRIEND

## SUMMER

I stiffened, clenching my hands in a fist.

"You are so fucking infuriating," he whispered, his harsh, warm breath fanning over my neck, making my heart stutter.

"Feeling's mutual," I said, turning around and glaring at him. "Let me leave."

His stormy dark eyes met mine, and I hated the way he looked at me, making butterflies flutter in my stomach. Maybe I was delusional, and they were actually moths warning me to get away from him.

"I apologize for accentuating that white men in power demanding sex or as you said and I quote, 'blowie' for a position, but... I'm not one of them." His jaw clenched, and I eyed his high cheekbones and sharp jaw peppered with the right amount of stubble. He took a step back and I could finally breathe something that was not his musky cologne. "I am sorry if it made you uncomfortable. We have strict HR policies, and I want you to work here."

It was odd.

*He* was odd! How can he make me so angry and then stare

at me with such sincerity a moment later, apologizing for his words and actions?! All while looking like an Abercrombie model.

Still… I had had enough instances of men in power, especially in Hollywood, that I felt wary. I knew he never did that, didn't even think about it, but working with him for a long period felt intimate.

I swallowed and looked at his Adam's apple. "I can't work with you, Damon."

"Why not?" he demanded, his voice stern.

I had forgotten just how stubborn he was.

"I-I have my own reasons," I said, keeping my chin high. *One of the main reasons being you're one of the best sexual partners I've ever had, and I'm still not over my teenage crush for you, and it might disrupt our professional relationship.*

"Tell me. I'm willing to make a few arrangements," he said, sliding his hands in his pockets.

"Why are you being so stubborn about it?" I asked. "We had sex. Rough sex with a D/S kink and… and you're Emma's brother!"

"That didn't stop you from kissing me on your prom day."

I narrowed my eyes at him. "I don't want to argue about what happened in the past."

"Then forget about it," he said harshly, his words cold, making me stiff. "We are both adults, and we can have a professional relationship… without thinking or talking about how much we enjoyed that night."

I knew he was going to say something else. He was holding himself back.

"Say it," I said, crossing my arms. "Whatever you were going to say."

He stared at me for a moment, thinking if he should say it or not, but I was also a stubborn piece of ass.

"Are you sure?" he asked, and I nodded. He moved closer

and, averting his eyes from my lips to my eyes, he whispered, "I was going to say that we don't have to talk about how much you loved getting your pretty pussy spanked and how gorgeous you looked making a mess on my cock."

My thighs clenched, and I blinked hazily at him, his pupils dilated, with a slight flush to his cheeks. *Damn him!*

"I... I-I can't," I said, my voice barely audible as I pushed him away and walked out of his office. The cool air felt like a splash of cold water on my skin. I ignored the assistant's narrowed eyes and walked to the elevator. My skin felt clammy, and my head was buzzing.

Did Rahul give me a decaf or something else? Because I was feeling jittery and—*Shit!* The paycheck.

I internally cried and blamed myself for having the luck of sleeping with Damon out of all the people.

"Heather, I need to walk. I'll call you later," I ended the call before she could ask for any answers and left the Moore building feeling anxious and unsure about my future. Thankfully, there were no paparazzi around.

*How will I help mom and dad? What about* her? I felt confused and conflicted.

Eyeing the tall buildings and bustling people, I hugged myself. It was a dream to work and live in Los Angeles, but the beaches, movies and even some people didn't feel like home. The air was always humid or warm. I didn't have my friends with me or my family.

I missed home.

I was passing through a busy deli when I heard someone call my name.

"Summer?" I froze, hearing *that* voice. "Summer fucking Hayes, is that you? Oh, wow!"

I took a deep breath and forced a small smile as I turned around to meet one of the douchiest guys on the earth, my ex-boyfriend, Garrett.

Unfortunately, I was unlucky and clumsy at the worst time and my heel got stuck in the groove on the ground, making me wobbly and ready to high-five the granite with my face.

Before I could curse, a pair of strong arms wrapped around my waist and held me up. My eyes widened to find stormy gray eyes staring at me with concern before moving to my feet.

I stayed speechless when he kneeled and pulled out my high heel from the groove and held my foot, gently sliding it back into the shoe. He muttered something underneath his breath, and I clutched his shoulder when Garrett came closer, a pretty blonde in his arms.

"Long time no see, huh?" he asked with a cocky grin on his face that I wished I could punch. "Hearing a lot about you in the press."

To make matters worse, he was unfortunately a celebrity journalist for one of the most famous magazines. I'd read his online articles, and one blog from him could ruin a celebrity's life. He had already ended the career of aspiring models, actors- or actresses-to-be before their big break. He was ruthless.

"Yeah, hello," I said, my voice sounding distant.

"This is my girlfriend, Julian. Julian... this is Summer. My ex from high school. You remember I told you about dating a cheerleader? That's *her*." He said *her* like he was proud of dating me for a week, fooling around with me in a locker room, spreading disgusting rumors, and ruining my prom.

No wonder he was the most hated celebrity journalist today.

I smiled at his girlfriend, who looked too pretty and too kind to be with an asshole like him, and shook her hand. "I'm Summer Hayes, and this...," I trailed off, looking at Damon who was glaring at Garrett and his mopey brown hair. I looked between them and realized the stark difference. Even Julian was eyeing him. *Of course, she is!* Garrett was cute as long as he didn't open his mouth, but Damon? He looked like a freaking Greek God compared to him with his tall height and tailored, expensive suit with a Patek Philippe on his wrist.

"This is my boyfriend, Damon," I said with a small smile, hauling him closer and wrapping my hand through his arm.

His face snapped at me and he said, "I am not—"

I tipped on my toes and whispered, "I'll do anything. Please play along."

Damon's eyes gleamed, and with the most charming smile, he wrapped his hand around my waist, pulling me closer and said, "I'm her boyfriend, Damon Grant."

I licked my lips, staring at his small dimple with jealousy. He never smiled at me like that. Hell, I didn't even know he had a dimple! How dare he?

"Oh… nice to meet you," Garrett mumbled, frowning at us. "Aren't you a lesbian?"

I rolled my eyes and before I could speak, Damon said, "She's bisexual. Aren't you, kitten?"

*He remembers?*

My cheeks flushed, and I pinched his butt, making him exhale sharply. "I am," I said, squealing in the end before covering it up with a cough when he pinched my butt in return.

I glared at him while smiling, promising to smother him in his sleep with a pillow.

"Aren't you, like, the CEO of that famous makeup brand?" Julian asked, twirling her hair and eyeing Damon's crotch shamelessly.

I wished I could cover it because I felt violated.

Gaarret's eyes lit up. "Yeah! You flirted with him at that event to make up for the org—"

"It was the other way around, Gale," Damon replied.

"It's Garrett," he replied, fuming. I pursed my lips to stop myself from laughing at his flustered face.

"We have to go. I'm taking her on a special date to celebrate our one-month anniversary," Damon said, kissing me on the temple as I whispered, *'I'm going to kill you,'* and he kissed my cheek whispering, *'I'd like to see you try, kitten,'* before looking back at the couple in front of us. "It was *not* nice meeting you, and I hope you have the day you deserve."

We turned around, Damon's hand lowering to my butt, giving it a small squeeze as we walked away.

That was *so* intentional.

"You're an asshole, you know that?" I said, letting him touch me for a few more moments so it looked real.

The mischievous twinkle in his gray eyes was my answer.

17

# BECAUSE I CAN

## DAMON

Walking with her lithe body pressed against my side was definitely strange. And somehow comforting at the same time. I looked at her, her soft curls framing her sharp face, and noted the splatter of freckles on her nose and cheeks.

She was pretty. Very pretty. Like the girl next door who always had a smile on her face.

"Do I have something on my face?" she asked, frowning at me.

I was glad she wasn't questioning why I hadn't moved my arm from her waist.

"Yes," I lied and stopped her. People walked past us without a care in the world. The smell of crispy fries and salty breeze hung in the air. I touched her cheek, staring at her brown eyes that were glowing with golden hues in the setting sun and—*fuck, why did she have to be so fucking beautiful?* "Better," I said, tucking her hair over her ear and stepping back, clenching my hand behind my back because it felt shaky.

She rubbed her cheek and pouted. "You're a weirdo."

I scoffed, following her and glaring at the old man who checked out her ass. He walked away quickly, and I wrapped my arm around her waist again.

"Says the girl who has that douchebag with a porn-stache as her friend."

"He's not my friend," she snapped. "He's my ex."

I made a face, and she covered hers, seeing me. "That's worse, Summer."

"I know," she groaned and stopped again. "Where are we going, anyway?"

"Somewhere private," I said, checking the time on my watch and looking at her feet. Without thinking, I grabbed her hand and dragged her to the nearest shoe store. "Come with me."

"I don't need shoes. Why are we here? Do you need shoes?" she asked, her voice small and angry as the staff smiled at us.

I eyed the various sneakers and pointed to three pairs, making her sit down. "Try them on."

"But I don't need them."

"Yes, you do." I glared at her, crossing my arms. "Try. Them. On."

She didn't argue, but huffed and rolled her eyes at me. I clenched my jaw when she tried to hide her wince, removing her heel and trying on a sneaker. When I helped her with it, I noticed a small sore on her foot. I didn't like that she had to walk in such high heels and be in constant pain.

I won't lie. I loved to see her in pain. But only when it was me who gave her that pain with a hint of pleasure.

"Walk in them. Are they comfortable?" I asked, my voice stern, and the staff were eyeing us. Of course, they knew Summer. Her face was plastered on most of the billboards and magazines for her latest show. I glared at them until they looked away.

"Yeah, they are good, but I really don't understand what we are doing here. This isn't even something private. Is this some—"

"*Shh.*" She was taking them off already, but I stopped her. "Keep them on."

I ignored her protest when I took the heels, noting her size, and asked one employee for a carry bag.

"What are you doing? Why are you paying for the shoes?" She sounded furious when I gave a black card to pay for her three pairs of shoes.

"Because I can."

"I never asked you to."

Before I could argue with her, the employee handed me my card and three bags with her shoes and heels. "Let your boyfriend pay for them, ma'am. By the way, I love the trailer for *Hate Love*. I can't wait for it to air! Do you mind giving me an autograph?"

Neither of us denied being a couple, and I noticed how Summer's eyes lit up as she talked with her fan, signing an autograph and even taking a picture with her.

"I'll pay you back," Summer said as soon as we stepped out of the store.

I didn't reply and led her to the restaurant where I had made a reservation before following Summer out of the office. She walked much better than before, and I was sure her feet would thank me in the future.

The restaurant was in a little alley so very few people frequented it. As soon as you stepped inside, the warm and cozy interior with dark colors welcomed you along with a delicious scent of spices and smoked food.

"I didn't know this was a restaurant," Summer said,

looking around the small place with a soft smile. She thanked our server and looked at the menu.

"I'm sorry." My throat constricted saying the words, and I glared at the clean table before continuing, "I was trying to push you, and what I said before you left wasn't professional, and if you work for me, it won't happen again."

She didn't reply and when I met her eyes, she was staring at me with narrowed eyes. "Wasn't professional? It wasn't appropriate, Damon."

"I thought you liked my dirty talk, kitten."

Her cheeks flushed, and she looked around before leaning close and whispered, "Can you stop calling me that?"

I pointed at the menu. "I recommend their baked ziti."

Thankfully, she didn't bring it up again for the remainder of our lunch, and we ate our food talking about Emma, Mia, Moore Beauty and her job.

"Enough with small talk, I want—" the ringtone of her phone interrupted me. Her hand tightened on the phone and she stood up.

"I've got to take this."

I watched her walk out of the restaurant and talk to someone on the phone.

"She's pretty." I looked at the old lady, Nina, the owner of the restaurant.

"Yes."

"You've never brought a girl here." She smiled at me. "Is she your lady?"

I looked at her silhouette from the glass door and nodded. "Yeah, well. I'm trying."

Nina patted my shoulder. "Go talk to her. She looks like she needs someone, son."

I stood up and smiled at her, picking our empty plates. Summer had devoured the ziti as if it was her last meal.

"Let me know if you need help with the dishes, Nina," I

said, placing the plates in the kitchen where her son and daughter smiled at me.

"Yes, yes, I will. You always cleaned the dishes well," she replied.

I nodded, remembering the days where I had nowhere to go, no way to survive on my own, and that sweet old lady took me in and let me help her with her small restaurant.

Leaning down, I kissed her cheek and said, "Call me whenever you need something. I'll see you soon."

I said my goodbyes and when I stepped out of the restaurant, Summer was still on her call, looking more anxious than I had ever seen her. Her smile and laugh looked forced. She was pacing around, and she didn't even notice me.

Staying quiet, I heard someone on the other side talking about money and saw how her spine straightened. "I already processed it. What do you mean it's not enough?" Her tone was sharp and angry. "Why are you like this? I told you I don't have mon—*no*. Don't you dare go begging Mom or I'll sue you."

I felt like I was in between something serious, so I walked away, waiting for her and wondering about her words. *Was she in trouble with someone?* If she was, Emma would tell me or help her on her own. By the way she talked, it seemed like it was troubling her. And she definitely said something about money.

I pulled out my phone, and he picked up on the third ring. "What is it?"

"I need a file on someone."

"Who?"

I looked over my shoulder to see the frown on Summer's face as she ran a hand through her hair, ending the call. "Someone famous."

"What did you do?" Rahul's voice was accusing.

I rolled my eyes. "I did nothing. We might hire her as our

ambassador, so I need all the details. From her parents to her living situation, her bills. Everything."

"Sheesh. Sounds serious. Who is it anyway?"

"Summer Hayes."

"Oh, fuck."

1 8

## DEAL

SUMMER

My hand was shaking with anger and shame when I ended the call. My biological mom, Carol, needed more funds for her boyfriend, who was an alcoholic. My parents had already paid her for her house with the money I sent them for their savings, and now she wanted more.

"Everything okay?"

I looked at Damon, his gray eyes closed off and I prayed he heard nothing. "Y-yeah, everything is fine," I forced a smile and looked at the small restaurant. "I thought we were going to talk in private?"

He stared at me for a moment. Without the heels, I reached his shoulders, and I didn't like that he could look down on me. "Right this way," he said, turning around, and I followed him.

*He is acting weird today.*

I needed to ask Emma about him and if he had suffered any injury to his head.

I recalled the sleepovers I had at Emma's house and how I'd stumble into him at night when I wanted water. He was very tall and lanky with the same dark glare. He even helped me with cereal when I couldn't reach the cabinet and told me it was full of sugar and it's unhealthy when I ate a mouthful in front of him. That was before he moved to his university, and when he came back, he looked bigger with muscles, and his glare darker than ever.

That was when I accidentally dyed his hair blue, and he threatened to sue silly teenager me.

"Where are we going?" I asked, suspicious of his electric car. He opened the door on the back and I sat down gingerly, eyeing the closed separator between the driver and us.

Damon didn't reply when the driver started the car. He looked at me, and I was taken aback by the intensity of his gaze. "Did you enjoy the night you spent with me?" he asked, his voice leveled.

My thighs clenched, and I licked my lips, remembering how possessive his hold was. He was definitely like one of the heroes from the romance books I devoured.

"You mean the night where I thought you were a stranger? Yes. I liked that."

"*Brat*," he said, rolling his eyes and fixing his tie. He leaned back on the seats and said, "I'd like to offer you something."

"Unless it's a million dollars, no thanks," I joked.

"Deal."

"What?" I snapped my head at him. But he looked serious. *Damnit, he always looked serious.* "You're joking and I was kidding."

Even though a million dollars would solve all of my problems and more.

"Do you remember what you said that night, kitten?" he asked, his voice low and husky.

My cheeks warmed. "I said many things. What are you talking about, Damon?"

He leaned closer, his large frame and the musky cologne

making all the coherent thoughts in my head evaporate. I knew there was a driver in the front, but I didn't care. I wanted to climb him and have a quickie.

"You told me your pretty pussy belongs to me," he whispered, his filthy words making me clench and cream my panties. "That I can use it whenever I want. Do you remember or do you need a reminder?"

I clutched my handbag and narrowed my eyes at him. "What are you doing, Damon?"

He eyed me, roving his stormy eyes over my figure and shamelessly staring at my chest before meeting my eyes. "I'm offering you a million dollars to let me use you whenever and however I want, kitten."

My eyes widened and lips parted. A million dollars for… *sex?*

"I-I don't understand." I scoffed. "Are you asking me to be your whore? Jesus, stop the car. I want to get away from you."

"I know you like consensual non-consent," he said calmly, as if we were having a small talk. "I read your kinks at *Aphrodite*. I know you like having different role-plays and being forced through punishments because you're a brat. Am I wrong?"

"Doesn't mean you can ask me to—"

"I'll pay you for your job. Not sex, Summer. But I'd be disappointed to find someone else when we have great chemistry. In bed."

I stared at him. My best friend's older brother, who was an asshole, and my soon-to-be boss if I accept his offer. Yes, I enjoyed thinking about being forced into a scene when I had all the power to stop it with a safe word or a gesture. Reading and hearing hot romance books was wonderful, but they also offered new kinks.

The thought of it with him… his hard body pressing me against the seat of the car, tugging my skirt up and taking me with my hands pinned. He'd be rough and spank me or choke me if I tried to fight it. I knew he would enjoy every single second of it as much as I would. But I also knew he'd stop as soon as I said the safe word.

"I know your dirty little head is thinking about it right now, kitten," Damon said, his husky voice pulling me out of my fantasy, my face hot. "For six months. Let me play with you and your body."

"What do you want in return?" I asked, crossing my arms and trying to be brave and make a fair deal with the devil. "I know you're not nice enough to just give me a million dollars just for being an ambassador or… or rough sex."

He chuckled. It was dark and delicious. "Sweetheart, call it what it is. Consensual non-consent. Rape fantasy." I shivered. "I will be your fake boyfriend and pretend to be your doting and loving partner in public. But behind the closed doors, you'll be my good little slut."

It was wrong. And humiliating. It shouldn't have turned me on, but dammit, it did. And he knew I was turned on. Just by his words—no, not words. His promise. Damon Grant didn't just say things unless he meant it. And he meant what he said…

"I… I need to talk to Heather or—"

He could tell I was struggling and dropped a file on my lap. He was way too close for my sanity. "Don't tell Heather. She is your agent. Look at it and tell me if you need to make any changes."

I was gaping at the contract and eyed him. "You knew I would say yes?"

"It was a ninety-to-ten percent chance."

"Why ten percent?"

"Because you hate me," he replied with a small smirk that made me wish I could slap it away.

"I'd still hate you if we do *this*."

"I figured," he said, his voice soft. Before I could ask him what was going on in his head, he continued in his cocky voice, "It was drafted by a lawyer, so don't worry about the NDA or anything. Even if you hate it or something happens, I won't sue you."

"Yeah, sure," I snorted, reading the terms and conditions. "Like the time you threatened to sue me because you accidentally used the blue conditioner."

*Damn him.* Everything read professional, and it was all about being an ambassador for his brand. Nothing seemed fishy, and the zeroes made me want to sign it right away.

"Don't blame me for your actions. My hair was blue for an entire month, and I failed a very important interview because of you." He sounded mad and when I eyed him, he was tugging at his tie. He looked cute when he was mad. *Wait what?* "Why the fuck would you add blue dye to a conditioner, anyway?"

I bit my cheek. "I wanted to prank Emma. I'm surprised you didn't suspect anything since you caught me adding the dye to the conditioner."

I remembered it like the next day. I had sneaked into the bathroom and squealed when Damon had entered, shirtless and sweaty. He looked grumpy and left as soon as he saw me. I finished my job quickly with warm cheeks. He scolded me that I should have locked the door, and I apologized before he slammed it closed. Then he showered and used the dyed conditioner.

"I remember telling you to close the door." He frowned and looked at me. "Drake used to walk in without knocking, and I didn't want him anywhere close to Emma. Or you."

I froze, hearing his name from Damon's lips. His sibling and Emma's half-brother, Drake, had stalked her, kidnapped her and would've assaulted her if Cillian hadn't stopped him. I remembered how terrifying it was for Emma and how glad

I was to find out he was murdered by his fellow inmates. Damon looked like he took it the hardest, even though he didn't show it.

He was distant when he left for his university and never saw Emma as his sister and treated her like a stranger. But after their mother passed away and the whole stalking incident, they were back to normal. I was glad he made up with her, but I was still upset because it took him so long to realize that it hurt Emma.

"I didn't know he was always a creep."

"Yeah," he said, his voice distant. Clearing his throat, he looked at me and the file. "Any thoughts on our fake and sexual relationship?"

19

# COME TO ME

### DAMON

Her dark eyes slid from me to her lap, re-reading the terms and conditions that I had asked my assistant and lawyer to draft before her call ended. There are certain benefits of being rich. Like people prioritizing your demands and finishing it quicker than usual when bargained with the right amount.

That's why anything can be bought.

*Even Summer Hayes.*

After all, it's a forbidden offer she can't refuse.

Her blouse heaved with each deep breath she took. Asshole or not, I had a point. And she liked it by the looks of it.

I leaned closer, offering her a fountain pen that was worth more than the car we were in and whispered against the shell of her ear, "I'm offering you everything you want on a silver platter, kitten."

She swallowed, my eyes falling to her lips as she licked them. They were plump and perfect. I could kiss them for hours. "I need time."

My hand clenched. "How many hours?"

"I don't trust you." She closed the file and looked at me. "Not yet."

There was a pinch in my heart, but I didn't show it. I wanted her to trust me. Without trust, there was nothing between us.

I leaned back and asked, "What do you want me to do for you to trust me, Summer?"

She bit her lip, thinking, and looking away. I couldn't bear it. The sexual tension was suffocating, and all I wanted to do was haul her pretty ass on my lap and kiss her.

"Come to my place," I blurted without thinking. Ever since I stumbled into her, I had been saying and doing lots of things without thinking.

"Why?"

"We can do anything you want."

Her brows raised and a twinkle of mischief gleamed in her eyes. "Anything? Just so I can trust you?"

"Yes."

She tucked a lock behind her ear and slowly nodded. "Okay, fine. I'll come with you."

I informed the driver and turned to her. "There will be more pictures of us online."

"I figured Garett will write an article about us." She winced. "Heather is going to kill me."

I frowned. "You're really scared of this Heather. Who is she?"

Summer shrugged. "She is the only agent I trust. She gave me the idea to host the charity event after the whole orgy debacle."

I scoffed. "Doing that right after that makes you look more guilty than anything." Her face dulled, and I continued, "You should have accepted an interview or posted a statement about what had happened. If anyone posts rumors, slap a defamation lawsuit on them."

"It's not that easy."

I titled my head. "You can have my PR and lawyers at your feet. Don't ask that silly agent of yours for ideas. Come to me."

Summer didn't argue for the first time and looked ahead, the file still in her lap. If she signed it, I'd love to do all the filthy things that have been churning in my head. We'd be professionals during our work, even with the fake relationship, but behind the closed doors, I'd make her beg and crawl.

"Oh, fuck, it's raining," she said, looking out of the window.

The rain pattered loudly on the roof of the car as the driver weaved through the traffic to the silent road to my house.

I thanked the driver for giving me an open umbrella and asked him to leave early. Summer didn't wait and was already bouncing out of the car, grinning up at the stormy sky like a kid.

"You'll get drenched," I warned her, but she looked so happy that I stayed still, watching her splash around. My heart warmed at the sight of her flushed cheeks and bright eyes.

I snapped out of my thoughts when she called me over to a small alley across the gate of my house. It was dark with barely any light, and I found flashes of tiny gleaming green eyes. Summer was kneeling on the ground, cooing at the bundle of dark fur in her hands.

Her hair was wet, her white blouse was soaked, and I wanted to scold her that she'd get cold, but I couldn't utter a thing when she looked up at me with the biggest puppy eyes ever and a black cat purring in her arms.

"No," I said.

"But—"

"I said no, Summer," I said, ignoring the tiny meows of the scrawny cat.

"He was alone in this tiny box." Her voice seemed sad as she pointed to the said box.

I leaned down, offering the shade of an umbrella to both of them, and looked at the grubby cloth in the box. My nose flared.

*How dare someone leave a cat like this?*

"Put him back in the box. I can keep him for a day," I said, not too happy about the situation I was in.

Summer beamed, "Yay! I knew you had a heart in there somewhere." She looked down at the cat and said, "I'm keeping him close. His fur is wet, so he needs warmth. Don't you, little gremlin?"

I ignored her cooing and draped my suit jacket over her dainty shoulders, making our way to the building. The security guard looked alarmed but didn't utter a word as we brought the black cat inside my place.

Summer kept him in the tiny box on the coffee table as she inspected her surroundings. The dark-colored sofas facing the large screen TV which I barely used. She hugged herself, looking at the floor-to-ceiling glass doors that led to the backyard and pool as silence hung around us. Even the cat seemed quiet.

"It's pretty," she commented, looking over her shoulder. Her cheeks were flushed from the rain. *You are prettier.* "I'm surprised you have photo frames."

I walked closer to the box and watched the cat peer outside, his tiny nose sniffing his new surroundings. He looked old and scrawny.

"I'm surprised you're single and living alone in this huge ass mansion."

"It's smaller than your house back home," I replied. "Go take a shower. You stink."

She faced me after seeing all the photo frames. "Of course, you're single with that mouth."

I tilted my head. "Last time I checked, you loved how this mouth sucked on your clit making you squirt."

Her cheeks flushed more, but instead of backing off, she raised her chin and said, "That was one time."

Roving my gaze over her soaked clothes that were stuck to her like second skin, I said in a lower tone, "I can give you a repeat if you want me to."

Summer stared at me with wide eyes, her lips parting as I walked closer to her. Temperature increased in the room, and the air felt heavier when she took a step back, bumping into the wall. Trapped and nowhere to go.

My eyes trailed over the water droplet sliding over her slender neck as I leaned closer and licked it. Her hot breath fanned over my skin as I held her waist, tugging the blouse from the tight skirt.

"I can eat your pretty pussy right here, kitten," I whispered, my voice hoarse. "I want to make a mess out of you."

"*Oh,*" she whimpered, her hands curling into a fist as she grabbed my shirt when I removed her blouse and cupped her perfect breasts in my hands. I kissed her dark little nipples through the bra until she was panting, and I pinched and played with them until she was moving her hips for more friction.

"Oh, fuck," she moaned when I bit her neck. "Let's get this to—"

She was interrupted by the tiny mewl of the cat, and we both froze before pulling away.

*Fuck.* We had a stray cat to take care of.

Summer didn't meet my eyes as she grabbed my suit jacket and kept it around her. I turned away and cleared my throat.

I pointed her to the guest room and said, "Go take a warm shower with the cat. Keep him close. I'll be right back."

"Where are you going?" she asked, still dripping water on the marble floor.

"To the pet store. He looks scrawny." I swallowed and looked away. I needed to force away my hard-on. I couldn't even stay alone with her without pouncing on her like a wild animal. I needed more self-control. Clearing my throat again, I said, "*Go*. Shower now."

Before I left the house, I heard Summer say, "For someone who is always grumpy and hates everyone, you are sometimes sweet."

My jaw clenched, and I left the place with a tight grip on the umbrella.

# CAT MOM

## SUMMER

I hummed and kept one eye on the cat as I looked around the guest room. It was bigger than the apartment I was renting, and it had heated floors.

"Do you want to take a bath with me?" I asked the cat, and he meowed loudly, rubbing his tiny body against my leg. He was very friendly, so he was definitely used to humans. I hated the thought of someone dumping him in an alley just because he was old.

"Okay!" I picked him up. "Let's have a bath together."

Stripping out of my soaked clothes, I started the water while playing with the cat. Despite being abandoned in the rain, he was very playful and energetic. I had already toweled him dry, but he'd need a proper bath with cat body wash. How anyone could abandon this cute little creature was beyond my thinking.

"You're like Damon." I chuckled when he started play-fighting me, nibbling on my finger before running away. "Grumpy and cute."

I sighed in the bath, keeping an eye on the cat, who was kneading a towel and staring at me with his beady little yellow eyes. I had always wanted a pet, but my parents always disagreed and when I could adopt one, I had to move to Los Angeles.

Taking a warm bath was so relaxing that I started to doze off, but my phone's constant vibration woke me up. I sat up, checking the messages from Heather about how we needed to talk and why I wasn't in my apartment, and I better not be mooching with Damon Grant.

**Heather: He's bad news, Summer.**

My heart thudded. I knew he was bad news, hell—it was all over his face. But I didn't have a choice. If I could get a million dollars just to work with him and play-pretend as his girlfriend while we have hot, kinky sex behind closed doors, I was all in.

I would be stupid not to accept it.

There were already articles about me. The most current one read, *'Hot Bachelor Daddy Damon Has Found Love in Holly-wood's Famous Actress Who Had an Orgy? Read the Juiciest Gossip Now!'* I rolled my eyes when I saw it was none other than Garrett who had written the stupid article. He must have rushed to his laptop and posted the article as soon as he saw me with Damon.

Good thing he hadn't changed much since high school.

I kept my phone on the floor before standing up from the bath. I dried off silently, careful not to wake up the kitten. I wondered what I'd tell Emma and Mia. I was more worried about their opinion than anything else. *Will Emma know I'm with her brother just for some money? Will Mia find out that I'm just pretending?*

Shaking my head, I started my paranormal romance audiobook. It had a reverse harem trope with four vampire lords and one human girl. The plot was thrilling, and it kept me on the edge of my seat. I hummed and applied body lotion.

"I'm back." I heard Damon outside the bathroom. "Is the cat okay?"

I made sure the robe was tight and stepped out with the cat wrapped in a towel. Damon was holding a paper bag, and his shirt was drenched from the rain. "He played with me and then fell asle—"

"'*Stop squirming, little lamb, and pull out my cock.*'" I froze. The hot audiobook narrator continued in his breathy voice, "*I demanded, pulling her close by her hair.*"

Damon raised his brow, and I quickly blurted, "Alexa, play Despacito."

But of course, I had an iPhone, and the audiobook kept going, the voice actor whispering, "*Mhmm, good girl. Now touch it—fuck, yes.*'"

I pursed my lips hearing the groan, and Damon crossed his arms when I went back into the bathroom and stopped the audiobook. I finally took a breath and slowly walked out, even though I wanted to die from embarrassment.

"You heard nothing," I whispered, not meeting his eyes.

"'*Stop squirming and pull out my cock,*'" Damon said, and I snapped my head at him. He was smirking. Leaning closer, he whispered in my ear, "I heard everything, kitten."

My cheeks went hot, and I turned away, grabbing the paper bag from him and asked if he bought everything. Thankfully, the devil took pity on me and we both fed the cat wet food in a cute pet bowl. Together, we set up a small nook in the guest room for the cat with warm blankets Damon bought. As soon as we placed the litter box, the cat went in and used it.

"How about Void?" I said, smiling at his fluffy tail when he sniffed his surroundings.

"Void? For what?"

"His name. He is like a little void."

"We are not keeping him," Damon said, and I frowned.

"Why not?"

He glared at me. "We don't have time to foster a cat, Summer. Who will take care of him while we are working?"

I pouted, staring at the little bundle of black fur. "I can take him with me—"

"No." He was so fucking stubborn. He shot me another glare before leaving me alone with the cat.

I petted Void, loving the way he purred, and whispered, "Ignore the ugly, scowling man, okay? You're not going anywhere. I promise."

I jumped when Damon said, "Wear this."

I eyed him as he walked away, closing the door behind him, and wondered if he heard me or not. Removing the robe, I wore the tee shirt he offered. It was very soft and reached my thighs. I loved how it smelled a little like him and detergent. Unfortunately, the sweats were too long, and I had to roll them up from the bottom.

"How do I look?" I asked Void, and he meowed loudly in reply, running towards me. "Yeah? Great? Why, thank you, Void!"

When I stepped out of the room, I found Damon glaring. *Wow, what a surprise.* "Do you ever stop glaring at people?" I asked, crossing my arms.

I had forgotten I wasn't wearing a bra, and for a second, his eyes flitted over my chest before looking at my eyes again. "No," he replied and added, "Stop coddling him and getting so close. We will drop him at the shelter tomorrow morning."

"We can't!" I said and swallowed. "If you don't want Void, I'll take him in."

"Oh, really? And how will you look after him?"

I didn't have an answer, but I said, "I will hire a cat sitter."

"Summer, stop being stubborn. We will both have busy schedules starting tomorrow, and we can't look after a cat."

He was right, and I hated that. But I didn't want him alone in the shelter. "I'll take him to the vet tomorrow morning and adopt him," I said, my word final. I didn't want Void to be an orphan. He had found me and trusted me enough to take care of him in the rain. I wouldn't break his trust.

Damon was rummaging in the kitchen, and he looked over his shoulder and said, "You can't take care of him—"

"Yes, I can," I said, my voice firm. "He is not a kitten, so he won't get adopted easily, and Halloween is coming up. I don't want bad people to hurt him when he can be safe with me."

"You're so fucking stubborn," he muttered and turned around. "Fine. We'll talk about it later. Reheat the pizzas, I'll go take a shower."

I grinned and wrapped my arms around him. "Thank you, thank you, thank you! I promise I'll be the best cat mom."

"I… *uh*. Yes," he said, patting my back.

*Oh shoot.* I'm hugging Damon.

I quickly pulled away, seeing color flash on his cheekbones as he cleared his throat and looked away. *Is he blushing?*

*No, only humans can blush.*

"I'll go reheat the pizzas," I said, watching him walk to his room. I smiled, looking at the pizzas while Void rubbed his body over my legs.

Maybe Damon has a heart after all.

21

# FILTHY LITTLE KITTEN

## DAMON

I groaned. Warm water sluiced down my back as I squeezed my cock. Summer's pretty face flashed in my head, and even though I hated the thought of masturbating to her like a crazy hormonal teenager, I didn't regret it. How stunning she looked with her trembling legs as she squirted over my hand and cock, making a mess for me.

"Fuck," I moaned, keeping my eyes shut as filthy images and fantasies flashed through my mind.

Summer bent over my office desk. Kneeling over the rough carpet in the living room. On her stomach, with her pretty ass and pussy exposed. Begging me not to take her as we played out our dirty little fantasy. She'd try to crawl away from me, but I'd take her like an animal until we both came.

*'Don't cum in me,'* she'd beg, but I knew we both wanted it, so I'd shoot my seed in her, breed her, and once we are done, fuck my cum in her with my fingers just to make sure I did my job perfectly.

My balls tightened as I fucked my fist repeatedly before coming into my hands. Her name fell off my lips, and when I opened my eyes, guilt washed over me as the water washed away my sins. I sighed, leaning on the cold tile.

*What the fuck am I doing? Rubbing one out while she's out there taking care of a cat?*

I swallowed and stepped out of the shower. I needed to have more self-control. Especially if she signs the contract and I own her. At least for six months.

I had plans for her tonight, but the black cat was a welcome distraction. A small smile tugged at my lips, thinking back to her beaming smile when I agreed to keep the cat.

Maybe we can co-parent the cat.

"Did you reheat the pizzas...?" I trailed off seeing our food in the kitchen, but Summer and the cat were nowhere in sight. Frowning, I looked around and found them in the living room.

Passed out.

I watched her sprawled out on the soft rug with the cat nestled against her arm. They were snuggling. I took a quick picture and kept my index finger on my lips when Void looked at me with his bleary eyes. I tucked both of them into a blanket and sat on the couch.

"You didn't even dry your hair?" I whispered, touching her soft locks that were still damp. "If you get sick, don't blame it on me."

My phone pinged with a message and I leaned back on the couch. Rahul had sent me the document I had asked him to get. I opened it, eyeing the woman dead asleep in the living room with a stray cat.

After a while, I tried to calm down and glared at her. *Why the fuck didn't she tell anyone? Not even Emma or Mia?* She could have told them. She should have.

No matter. I will make her sign the contract even if she hates me. I will take care of her and her worries.

* * *

"GOOD MORNING, SUNSHINE," I DEADPANNED WHEN SUMMER moaned as she woke up from the rug. The cat looked up from the couch, stretched, and walked away with his tail high.

I had already worked out in my house gym, showered and got dressed for the day while she didn't move an inch. Even when the cat started kneading her stomach and left her when he didn't get any pets.

"What time is it?" she grumbled, yawning and rubbing her eyes. My tee shirt, which she was wearing, drooped over her shoulder, making my eyes zero in on her décolletage. I glanced away and served sunny-side up eggs with bacon and a glass of orange juice.

"It's nine in the morning." I placed the plates on the island and asked, "Do you want coffee?"

"Do you have decaf?" she asked mid-yawn. "Did I sleep here all night?" She stretched her limbs while I tried not to stare at her hard nipples that were poking through the tee.

"No, I don't have decaf, and yes you did," I answered, checking the cat's bowl. He had devoured the wet food I had given him early in the morning, and now he was trotting around the house like he owned it.

"No wonder I feel like my back's going to break," she groaned and slumped on the stool. "Why didn't you wake me up or take me to bed?"

I stared at her as I leaned over the island. "You slept like a log, kitten. I didn't want to touch you while you were sleeping."

She hummed, and looking me in the eye, said, "What if I was into it?"

I raised my brow. "You are into somnophilia?"

Her cheeks flushed, and it was the prettiest shade ever, making her freckles stand out. "Maybe."

"Filthy little kitten," I whispered and flicked her forehead. "Finish your breakfast. We have a long day ahead."

"Yes, Sir," she replied, shoving bacon in her mouth and moaning exaggeratedly.

*Brat.*

"Oh, shoot." Summer stood up without finishing her breakfast, and I frowned, watching her look for something in her purse.

"Your phone is charging on the nightstand," I said, but she still kept looking. "What is it?"

"My meds." She was frowning. "I need my meds."

I swallowed and clenched the fork. "What meds?"

Her eyes met mine, and she sighed, shaking her head. "Forget it. I'll ask Heather to bring it."

I narrowed my eyes at her and said, "If I'm going to fuck you and use you however I want, I need to know if you have any medical conditions, Summer."

Her eyes became hard, and she clenched her jaw. "I have ADHD. I need adderall to focus and have a normal day without spiraling and making impulsive decisions."

I kept my fork down. That explained a lot. Her candle-making phase, her grades never being consistent, her stubbornness and being impulsive enough to have a one-night stand on the day of her show's premier.

"I can get it for you," I said, noting how she looked anywhere but at me. *Is she embarrassed about being neurodivergent? Or telling me she has ADHD?* "I can get your meds from your house."

"*No*," she said, her eyes wide. Her reply was too quick. "It's okay. I'll ask Heather to bring it."

I nodded. "When did you get diagnosed?"

She played around with the food and said, "After graduation. I didn't want to go to college or university, and not having a routine like school made me... weird. So, after counseling with five different psychiatrists and being told I had anxiety and depression, I finally talked to Aiden—"

"Aiden?" I clenched my jaw.

"Yeah, Ivy's husband. He referred me to his friend, and now I'm on meds."

I didn't know how hard it was for her to find one doctor who would listen to her, so I reached out and held her hand. Squeezing her palm, I said, "Thank you for telling me, Summer." Her eyes were glistening, so I let go of her hand, already missing its warmth, and cleared my throat. "I'll send you my STD test results... if you end up signing the contract."

"Y-yeah, sure!" she said, her voice high pitched. "I got tested after... you know. So... yeah."

I nodded and finished my food and ordered her to go shower. I cleaned the kitchen and loaded up the dishwasher as the cat stared at me sitting on the island.

"Do you want something?" I asked, crossing my arms and staring down at him.

But his face was so relaxed and intimidatingly cute that he might as well be staring me down.

"No?" I asked and finally relented to give him pets on the head. "Will you be good today? My friend is coming to watch over you while we are out. Is that okay?"

He meowed as if he didn't completely agree with me, but he'd let it go. I should probably cat-safe my house and get him some toys and cat trees. Growing up, pets were out of the question with two selfish parents and one sick sibling. Drake always joked about killing animals, and I was scared that he might hurt an innocent animal if I adopted one.

"Don't worry," I said, staring into his huge pupils. "I won't abandon you."

I had to pull back my hand when my phone rang. Speak of the devil. My smile dropped as I picked it up.

"What do you want?"

"You banging that chick? Your sister's friend, really?" he laughed, the sound void of any emotions. My jaw clenched when he continued, "Do me a favor and ask her how much she wants for offering me her—"

"I dare you to say another word, father," I said. "You want another paycheck? Don't say a word about my girlfriend."

"Girlfriend?" He chortled, coughing in between. "Yeah, right. How much are you paying her to like you, son? You do realize that you're nothing but a worthless piece of shit. You couldn't even protect your own mother, sister, or your brother. You're nothing, Damon. Remember that."

"Is that all?" I asked, gritting my teeth.

"Oh, no no. That's not all. I will meet you soon so we can discuss my wife's company and her assets. I know she left something for me."

An image of his hand hitting mom's cheek flashed through my head. They were always fighting. He was a big-time producer who slept around, and she was the superstar who had finally realized that her husband was abusive and finally left him. I could hear baby Emma's cries like it was only yesterday while Drake smoked in the kitchen when he was twelve. No one scolded him or soothed Emma. I was the one rocking her cradle when mom took her and never looked back.

"Dorothy didn't leave anything to you," I said in a stern voice. "Everything belongs to Emma as it should. You should be lucky that I'm not locking you up in a shitty retirement home, father." I took a deep breath and added in a bitter voice, "If you dare to reach out to Summer, I will kill you."

I ended the call and closed my eyes.

I needed a drink.

22

# MY BOYFRIEND

## SUMMER

When I got out of the shower, a set of clothes, including my undergarments, were placed on the bed. The navy dress looked brand new, and so did the sandals. Not everyone knew I had ADHD, and I kept it that way since people's reactions were always polarizing. My parents, Emma and Mia accepted it very well, but some of my co-stars and the producer of the show thought it was an excuse I used for being lazy when it was just an executive dysfunction.

I never told my partners about it. Especially since my ex-girlfriend started stealing adderall from me when I got diagnosed. But Damon took it well. I wasn't expecting him to hold my hand and thank me.

*He is surprising.*

My heart pounded in my ears when I donned the dress. Its expensive material hugged my body. It fell right on my thighs and looked between professional and casual. If I'm going to have a pretend-billionaire boyfriend-slash-boss, I might as well accept being spoiled.

"I'm surprised that you know my bra size, but I didn't need—*are you okay?*" I asked, walking up to Damon.

He was pacing around with a frown between his brows. He was frowning most of the time, but it looked like something had affected him. When his stormy eyes snapped at me, I straightened up and tucked a lock of hair behind my ear. Damon didn't have any hair styling tools except a hair dryer, so I had used a claw clip from my purse and clipped my hair in place.

"What?" I asked when he kept staring and didn't reply. My cheeks heated when he shamelessly checked me out.

"That dress looks good on you," he said, his voice low.

"I wanted to ask," I started, taking in a deep breath when he faced me, face cold and emotionless. "I wanted to ask why didn't you text me after… that night."

His brows scrunched. "I did."

"You didn't. I never got a text—"

I held my breath when he came closer. He showed me the text he had sent on his phone. He had sent a text the next morning. But to a wrong number.

"That's not my number, Damon," I said, pursing my lips. He glared at his phone and I knew who was to blame. "I'm sorry, I was sleepy so I might have misplaced a number or two."

"Silly brat," he murmured, his hand lifting towards my face, to cup my cheek, but we were interrupted by a furious knocking on the door.

"Who is that?" I asked, watching Void's ears perk up at the door. He stared at it curiously.

Damon opened the door and my lips parted when Heather stormed in, followed by Rahul, Damon's assistant.

"What the hell are you doing here?" Heather demanded, glaring at my dress, sandals, and the cat. Void narrowed his eyes at her.

"I'm so sorry. She threatened me if I didn't let her—*oh my god, look at you!* You're so adorable! Can I pet him?" Rahul said and rushed to Void, who was on the couch, and gently petted his head.

"Why is there a cat here?" Heather asked and crossed her arms, looking between me and Damon when he stepped beside me. "I want to know what is happening between you two right now."

"He is my boyfriend," I said, blood rushing to my cheeks. "And my boss. If I sign the contract."

"I don't care if you are her manager, but don't make a habit of storming inside my house again," Damon said coldly, staring her down.

Thankfully, Heather wasn't afraid of him and narrowed her eyes back. "You kidnapped my client from your office, and the next thing I know there are rumors of you two dating," she turned to me. I stared at her ear when she said, "I expected a message or at least a call when you disappeared."

"You're so fluffy! I love your face and *aw*, look at this—you're purring," Rahul cooed, and he looked like he was about to shed tears through his glasses when Void indulged him further by rolling on his back.

"We were busy," Damon replied, wrapping an arm around my waist. "Do you always invade all your clients' privacy like this? You need a better manager, babe."

I pursed my lips as Heather gaped at him, and that was my cue. "How about you wait for me at the office, yeah?" I forced a smile at Damon, glaring at him, and took Heather's hand. "Drive with me."

"Wait here," Damon ordered and glared at Heather. "Explain everything about Void to Rahul. He will look after him and get him checked at the vet. I'll go arrange the cars."

"It's okay, I have a ca—"

"Summer is my girlfriend." Damon interrupted Heather. "She is not going to sit in anyone's car."

My eyes were wide, staring at his broad back when he walked out of the house. I had to pinch myself to make sure it was real, and I wasn't in a dream… or a nightmare.

"He needs therapy," Heather mumbled underneath her breath, and I shot her a disapproving look before going up to Void, who was basking in Rahul's attention.

"You're really good with cats," I said, smiling at them. "Void loves you."

Rahul blushed, pushing his glasses upon his nose. "We had six cats growing up and I always wanted to adopt cats when I arrived here, but Damon has a busy schedule and so do I. I'd love to be his only pet sitter, isn't that right, you little panther?"

I giggled and showed him Void's bowl, litter box, and how much we fed him when we brought him home. I had already made a list of veterinary clinics nearby when Damon went to shower last night, and I sent it to Rahul.

I kissed Void on his head and bid him farewell as Heather and I made our way to the driveway. As promised, a sleek, electric car was waiting for us, but Damon was nowhere in sight. I blushed furiously when we sat in the backseat, a separator between us and the driver. He didn't have to do that but he had promised he was going to be a doting partner in public… in exchange for me being his dirty little slut when we are alone. Duality of a man.

"Now that we are away from that controlling ass," Heather started, making me sigh, "I want to ask if he is threatening you."

"What? No!"

"Blackmail? I can help you, Summer. Just tell me what's going on and our agency can sue him," Heather said, her voice sincere and concerned.

I shook my head. "It's nothing like that. I... we are actually dating."

She stared at me with her narrowed eyes.

I shrugged, slipping into my acting mode and lied smoothly, "It's not that hard to believe. He is my best friend's older brother, and I always had a silly, teenager crush on him growing up." That wasn't the lie, at least. "We talked a lot yesterday and one thing led to another."

"You mean you fucked?"

I spluttered, "Of course, not!" *I mean, we had a raunchy one-night stand.* "And even if we did, it's none of your business."

Heather sighed and pinched the bridge of her nose. "It is my business because people are still talking about the damn orgy thing."

"Which never happened," I said, clenching my jaw. "I am dating Damon Grant, and if people have a problem with it, they can come and talk it out with me."

"You know those rumors about Drake, right?" Heather asked, her voice low. The car took a sharp break before moving again.

"They are not rumors, they are facts. He was a piece of shit, but Damon is not," I said, not knowing why I had the sudden urge to defend him. Even though he was evil and grumpy, he never gave me the creeps like Drake. "He took in a stray cat, Heather. He could have ignored the poor cat and wooed me into sleeping with him, but he didn't. He... He can be nice sometimes."

"Nice? Damon Grant? Love, I'm not sure what he made you drink, but don't fall for his pretty face. He is the man who made hundreds of women and men cry working for Moore. Not to mention, his dating history is zero. Null. Especially with that face. It's creepy."

That was true. Damon had never dated, or Emma would

know and gossip about it with us. He didn't seem like someone who was secretly bisexual, so he really didn't date anyone. Before me. And even then, what we had was a pretend relationship.

"I know, but I'll sign the contract today," I said, my chin high. "He can even help me clear up the rumors before the first episode releases."

She sighed when we reached Moore Beauty's building. "I don't know why, but this doesn't feel right, Summer. You guys didn't even kiss or seem intimate."

I didn't know what to say, so I blurted, "O-okay, I gotta go."

I rushed to the building elevator and hoped I could get some space alone so I could think.

"Mr. Damon asked you in his office, ma'am," the receptionist from yesterday said with a small smile. I thanked her and ignored the hushed whispers.

Of course, the devil wanted me in his office right away.

# PART III

"You can't run from this, kitten."

## 23

# DON'T FALL IN LOVE

## DAMON

"Yes, clear the floor," I ordered, hanging up the phone, and fixing my tie and cufflinks. I had heard everything I wanted to know in the car while I was driving it, making sure they couldn't see my face.

I have to teach Summer to check who drives the car she's in and not to trust anyone so blindly. Even me. Heather seemed more like her parent, scolding and being persistent, than her manager. I needed to beware of her because Summer trusted her.

"Damon?" Her sweet voice came from the hallway as she knocked on my office door.

"Come in, Summer," I said, standing up from my chair and sliding my hands in my pockets.

She looked stunning in the dress. Its fluttery hem begged to be tugged up. But I behaved like a gentleman and let her sit on the chair as I leaned on the desk, hands in my pockets.

"Do you have your medication with you?" I asked.

She nodded. "Heather brought it from my home."

"Good, eat this and take your med," I said, pushing the egg roll I had ordered for her.

"Right now?" she asked, a small smile on her lips. When I nodded, she continued, "Are you going to sit there and scowl at me as I eat this?"

"Yes." I crossed my arms. "I want to make sure the actress I hired doesn't faint and sue me."

"Meanie." She narrowed her eyes at me even though she had a smile playing on her lips.

I sent her my test result and checked hers while she was eating. We both were clean. I just needed her answer.

Summer took her medication, and when she walked out of the private bathroom, I leaned back in my chair, preparing myself.

"Have you decided if you want to work for me?" I asked, even though I already knew the answer. I had heard it from her mouth while I drove them to this building.

"And be your fake girlfriend?" she asked, her brown eyes gleaming as she sat down across from me.

"Mhmm, and my filthy kitten whenever I tell you." I smirked.

Her cheeks flushed as she pulled out the file of the contract that she had kept in her handbag. I waited patiently, my hands itching to touch her.

"Before you sign," I said, offering her the fountain pen. "I have two more conditions."

"What are they?"

"Don't fall in love with me," I said seriously. Because love didn't exist for people like me, and she deserved someone better. And I didn't want to disappoint her.

Instead of agreeing with me, she laughed so loud that a snort came out of her cute nose. I stared at her, her wide grin as she laughed and laughed before wiping the tears from her eyes.

"Are you for real?" She sniffed, grabbing tissues and dabbing her eyes.

I made a face and said, "Yes. Don't fall in love with me. What's so funny about it?"

She chuckled, shaking her head. "No, it's just that… you sounded really cringe and like some hero of a romantic book or movie when you said that. I wish I could have recorded that, dammit."

"I'm serious, Summer."

She waved her hand like she didn't care and said, "What else, Mister-I-Am-Serious?"

I sighed. "I was going to ask if you can go commando whenever I'm around—"

"*Not.* Happening," she said, her pupils dilating. "I'll pretend I didn't hear that. And F-Y-I, I won't fall in love with you, but you definitely will."

I hummed, letting her believe whatever she wanted as she scrawled her signature on the dotted line.

"There. Done," she announced, sitting back in the chair and looking at it.

"*Good,*" I answered, putting the file away, and leaning over her chair. "Now one more question."

"What?"

"Do you want to talk about kinks and boundaries before or after I fuck you on my desk?"

Her eyes went wide. "Right now?"

I nodded, waiting for her response.

"Before? I–I need to know what we will do so I can prepare myself. Although…"

I tilted my head. "Although?"

She bit her lip, my eyes falling on them, and she released it. "I like spontaneous sex."

"Don't worry, I will keep you on your toes, kitten." I smirked and sat on the other chair. "Be frank and tell me your boundaries and limits. If we are going to have consensual non-consensual scenes, I need to know everything."

Summer nodded and thankfully, she wasn't flustered telling me about her limits. They were all similar to mine. No golden showers, blood play, or too much degradation or humiliation. There were certain words that she didn't like, and I kept a mental note of that. She definitely loved praise kink more.

"And anal?" I asked. "I know you agreed to it that day, but you weren't ready. Has it changed?"

She pursed her lips and looked away. She looked weary. "I... don't know. I have only tried it once, and it wasn't a great experience."

I clenched my jaw. "Let me guess, he didn't use enough lube and rushed it?"

Her silence was my answer.

I leaned close and looking into her eyes, I said, "I am not that boy, Summer. You have the power to say the safe word and I will stop whenever you want, okay?" She nodded slowly, her eyes wide. "Good girl. Trust me to take care of you, and if there's a chance you want to try it, we will go slow."

"Mhmm." She was blushing, her pupils dilated. I noticed her clenching her thighs together, so I kept my hands on them, lifting her dress to reveal her inner thighs.

"There's one more thing," I whispered. "I don't want you to play with my cock unless I have given you explicit consent beforehand."

"Oh... that's okay," she said, definitely confused why I'd do that.

I didn't want to dim the conversation and tell her I was sexually abused by my piece of shit brother.

"Do you have any more questions?" I asked, stroking her soft skin.

"No, I want you to fuck me right now," she breathed out, spreading her legs.

I chuckled and pulled away. "Not so soon, kitten." I ignored her pout and went around my desk to get something from the drawer. I opened the box and pulled out the gold and diamond bracelet. "This is for you. I want you to wear this whenever you consent to being forced or used. If you are not wearing this, I'll take it as a sign that you want normal, vanilla sex. Understood?"

She nodded, admiring the jewelry. "It's beautiful."

"I'm glad you like it."

Summer extended her arm and said, "Help me with it."

So I did. Gently locking it around her dainty wrist. It looked perfect on her, and I loved the way her eyes gleamed looking at it. I couldn't wait to spoil her more. She deserved to be spoiled.

"Do you have something else for me, Sir?" Summer asked cheekily.

"Yes, I do." I leaned back on the desk and said, "Give me your panties before you go to your first shoot."

Her eyes went wide. "What? We have a shoot right now?"

"Yes, you have a product shoot in a few minutes, but don't worry, Layla will explain everything to you."

"I don't think—"

"I wasn't asking, kitten."

Her eyes gleamed with mischief—I knew she wouldn't listen to me because she was a brat—and stood up. I held my breath when she leaned closer, pressing her hands on my chest as she whispered in my ear, "If you want my panties, Sir, come and take them."

Summer turned around and left my office with a trail of her sweet vanilla perfume. I smirked and straightened up, checking the time on my watch.

She would regret her words, but knowing her, she'd probably enjoy the consequences.

2 4

# DIRTY GIRL

## SUMMER

The product shoot was way simpler than what I had in mind. I had to change into various dresses and either smile at the camera or apply the lipstick. The entire studio smelled like candy and sharp perfume, but the photographers and everyone around me were nice and encouraging.

When Damon came to watch the shoot, everyone became quiet. I was still wet from before, and I wanted to tease him and see how he would snap. But I kept my professionalism as we took a video ad for their latest product, which I had never heard of before.

"Has anyone used this before?" I asked the makeup team, but they shook their heads.

*Then why are we selling it?*

I slumped in my chair and asked the makeup artist to leave. I could remove makeup on my own.

"How was your first shoot?" I looked at the mirror and saw Damon standing by the door, his arms crossed.

"It was good," I said honestly, dabbing micellar water on the cotton pad before lifting it to my face. "Can I be honest?"

"Go ahead," he said, coming over and sitting beside me.

I wiped the makeup from my forehead and said, "I don't think this lipstick thing-y is worth spending your marketing budget over. No one uses it."

He sighed. "I figured that."

"How about sending PR packages to influencers?"

"We already did that. Instagram, YouTube, TikTok."

"OnlyFans?" I joked, but then continued, "Oh, you can send it to them, too, right?"

"Maybe," he said, looking at me with narrowed eyes as I continued to wipe off the makeup. "You missed a spot."

He took the cotton pad and, gently holding my face, wiped the corner of my temple. I stared at his gray eyes with bits of blue in them and how his dirty blonde hair seemed like dark brown in different lightning. He was very handsome.

Damon handed it back to me once he was done, and I asked, "Is Void okay? Has Rahul called you?"

"Yes, Void is okay. Vet said he could be over ten years old, and his previous owners could have abandoned him because he's a senior cat."

"Motherfuckers," I grumbled, cleaning up my face.

"I agree. He got dewormed, and I asked the vet to microchip him. They're now back home."

"I'm glad he is okay." I smiled and remembered something. "I think you're too grumpy."

"What?" Damon didn't see this coming and scowled, making me chuckle.

"Everyone was bubbly and talkative before you came, but as soon as they saw you, they went quiet. I think you should do something about it."

"I didn't even do anything." He sighed and asked me, "What do you have in mind, Miss Summer?"

I hummed, removing the pins from my hair and letting

my locks down. "I think you should do an event for your employees, like a team building event with free food."

His scowl turned deeper.

I pointed it out, "See? Stop doing that."

Damon grabbed my hand and tugged me on his lap, making me freeze as I looked around to see if anyone was looking at us.

"That's just how I look, and no one's looking, kitten," he whispered, his hands roving over my body. "Do you think I'd let you go with what you said this morning?"

I shook my head. "I was waiting for you to snap and take me."

"Dirty girl," he purred, grabbing my chin and pressing his lips against mine.

I melted in his arms, squirming on his lap when he deepened the kiss, moving his hand in my hair and pulling me closer. I moaned, feeling his bulge. He was so hot that I could feel his hard chest through the fabric of our clothes. I needed him.

"More," I whispered in between the kisses. "I need more, Damon."

But we continued kissing and touching each other everywhere. I hadn't made out on a couch with a guy since high school, and it felt naughty and fun at the same time. Especially when people were around us and anyone could enter the makeup room and find us.

We finally pulled away to breathe, staring into each other's eyes. His cheeks were flushed and his lips were pink and swollen.

He tapped my butt and said, "Get dressed and meet me in my office."

I nodded and got off his lap. I gave him one last glance before going to the small changing room and changing back into my dress. I could feel how wet I was, and I wished I had brought another pair of panties with me. I'd need extra pairs for the next six months.

When I was making my way to his office, someone grabbed my hand and cupped my mouth. I panicked, trying to move away from them, but their hold tightened.

"You can't run from this, kitten," the deep voice threatened. Relief and anticipation coursed through my body.

My heartbeat increased when Damon took me into a storage room and pressed me behind the closed door, keeping his hand on my mouth. It was dark and musty, barely enough space for the two of us. It was erotic and scary.

"Stay quiet," he ordered, but I tried to scream as soon as he let go of his hold on my mouth. "Bad fucking girl."

I clenched my thighs when he wrapped a hand around my neck, shoving my dress up. When I tried to resist it, he tightened his hold on my neck.

"Shh, stop being such a fucking tease," he crooned, overpowering me. "I know you've been eyeing me for days. Wearing tight little clothes and testing my patience."

I played right into the role, shaking my head when he inched his hand over my thighs. "N-no, I don't know what you're talking about, Sir."

Dark stormy eyes glared at me, and I gasped when he cupped my pussy through my panties and squeezed. "Liar. I can feel how wet your cunt is. I know it's wet for me."

"No, please stop," I stammered, but he didn't let go. I remembered I could safe-word out of it anytime I wanted, but I also wanted to see what he'd do next.

"Shut the fuck up," he growled, tearing my panties and rubbing the lace in his hands. It looked so tiny, and my arousal grew further when he inhaled my scent. "Look at these little red panties. All soaked. Did you wear these thinking about showing them off to me, hm? To your boss?"

I shook my head, knowing he had picked them out for me.

"I didn't!" I tried to push him away, but he was too strong, touching my pussy and rubbing my clit. "No. I don't want this."

"Yes, you fucking do," he whispered. "I pay you enough to have a taste of this tight little pussy. Tell me, whose pussy is this?"

"Mine," I said, biting back my moan when he slid two fingers inside me. I almost whined when he pulled away.

"Wrong answer." He spanked my pussy, making me cry out. I got wetter on the second spank. "I'll ask again because I'm nice, and you better answer correctly. Whose pussy is this?"

"Y-yours," I whispered, staring into his gray eyes that gleamed with evil.

"Such a good girl," he said, cupping my sex like he owned it. "It's my pussy and I can take it however I want."

25

# ARROGANT BOSS

## DAMON

Her body shivered at hearing my filthy words. She looked scared, but her dark chocolaty eyes gave away her true feelings. They were gleaming with desire and lust. Even though she begged and said no, she was rubbing herself on my hand.

Fuck. I needed to fuck her now.

"Open up my zipper," I said, giving her a little space. "Be a good kitten and take my cock out."

Her eyes widened and lips parted, watching me through her lashes. Her fingers fumbled as she removed the buckle of my belt and unzipped my pants. I unknotted my tie and kept glaring at her.

"Please... I don't—"

"Shh, take my cock out and rub it," I said, keeping my voice soft as she trembled, pulling out my semi and stroking it as if she wanted to be anywhere but here.

I chuckled and wrapped my hands around hers, stroking myself with a clenched jaw. "Do I have to train you how to touch a dick, kitten? Judging by your looks and how you dress, I thought you'd know everything."

Summer tried to move back, but I held her hand, stroking myself with her warm palm. "I-I don't sleep around!"

"No, of course you don't," I crooned, leaning closer and kissing her cheek even though she tried to move her head. "You're a good girl. But if I made you an office slut, you wouldn't mind, would you?"

Her eyes were a dark pool of desire. I knew she hadn't listed gangbang or polyamory in her limits or boundaries, and from what I had gathered, she loved reading books where the heroine was shared between a group of men.

"Yeah?" I groaned when she squeezed me. "You want that. And even if you don't, it's okay. I will tie you up on my desk so everyone can take any hole they want. Fuck you like my dirty little slut, yeah?"

She shook her head, shocked and surprised. I used my tie to tie up her wrists.

"Lift your dress," I demanded, knowing how embarrassing and humiliating it was for her to be exposed in front of me.

She wasn't like the Summer from that night. She was open and willing for anything, but today, in the dark storage room, she was just an innocent employee getting corrupted by her dirty boss.

"You are asking for a punishment, girl," I said, my voice husky and deep. She finally moved, lifting her dress for me.

"Hmm," I hummed in appreciation at the sight of her shaved pussy. I touched her clit, loving how sensitive she was to my touch. "I like your pretty cunt like this. Bet you shaved it for your boss, hm?"

"No," she said, her fingers tightening on the dress. "Please let me go. I-I can give you money but p–please..."

I let out a dark chuckle and turned her around, pushing her lithe frame against the door and using my weight to press against her. "I'm not letting you go, kitten. Your body is mine. If I want to whore it out to my colleagues, then you'll be a good fucking girl and let them use you."

"Please, no!" she cried out, shaking her head when I rubbed my cock over her wet slit. I moved her hair over one shoulder and grabbed her breast, pinching and rolling the hard nipple as I slid in the tip.

She was so fucking tight and warm.

"You can take it," I whispered against the shell of her ear when she squirmed and writhed. "Relax, girl. That's it. There we go," I groaned, and she whimpered when I slid all the way inside her, feeling her warm walls clench me.

"P-please stop."

I held her neck and slammed inside her. "Shh, you can take it like a good fucking girl."

She tried her best to hate it every time I fucked her. Rolling my hips and thrusting inside her.

"You look so fucking sexy like this. Do you know that, kitten?" I groaned, my balls tightening with the need to explode, but it was too soon. I wanted to make her cum first. "Pinned against the door with your hands tied and fucked by your boss."

I chuckled when she tried to move away, but I wrapped my hand around her hair and tugged, making her gasp and look at me.

"You're such a dirty fucking girl," I growled in her ear. "Look at me when I fill your pretty pussy. Looked so pretty and smiling in the office, but now look at you," I crooned, making my thrusts deeper and harder. "Being such a good little toy for me."

"Please stop," she begged, squeezing her eyes shut when I made my thrusts rougher.

"No," I said, rolling my fingers around her swollen clit. "You're such a good fucking girl, taking your boss's cock in your tight little cunt."

She whimpered when I rubbed her faster. I knew she was close when her walls clamped me, her body tightening as I used her. She came in a couple of thrusts, moaning and crying out against her tied wrists.

Her pussy spasmed around me, triggering my orgasm as I came inside her, shooting my seed inside her warm walls.

"Fuck," I groaned, emptying my balls and keeping my head on her shoulder.

We both were panting and catching our breaths. I kissed her neck before pulling out slowly and turning her around.

I cupped her face and made her look at me. Her eyes were glistening and her hair looked ruffled. Her lips were swollen, cheeks flushed.

"Are you okay?" I asked, wanting to know if I had gone overboard.

Summed blinked at me and nodded. We both looked down between her legs and my hand clenched, seeing my cum slid down from her pussy to her inner thigh. My eyes widened when she trailed her index finger over it and raised it to her lips.

I cursed when she took her glistening finger in her mouth and sucked, staring at me.

"You're going to be the death of me," I said before kissing her, tasting her lips and groaning.

"It was perfect," she said between our kisses. She was smiling, and I wished I could take a picture, because she looked like she was fucked well and happy. "Arrogant boss must be easy to role-play for you."

I pinched her butt before straightening my clothes and staring at her. "Maybe. We can try something else next time."

"Next time?"

"Yes. But filthier."

She pursed her lips, trying to hide her smile, and looked

at her hands and the knot that kept them together. "Can you…*uh…*?"

I pinned her tied wrists against the door and leaned closer, licking her neck, kissing it. "I love seeing you tied up for me, kitten," I whispered and looked at her flustered face. "I wish I could keep you tied up for me."

"For what?"

"For fucking, obviously," I said, removing the knot with one pull and rubbing her wrists. "I could use you whenever I want. Like my personal fuck toy."

Her eyes lit up, and I had to hold myself back from taking her away to my office and fucking her again. She looked so fucking perfect; she didn't know how much she affected me.

"I…"

I patted her hair and fixed her dress while she stumbled for words. "We should get out of here."

She nodded and opened the door.

I followed her out and I wished we could have hidden in the storage room because my sister and her older, tatted and huge boyfriend were waiting for me in my office.

# FAKE RELATIONSHIP

## SUMMER

I winced seeing my best friend's golden hair, and scrambled back, grabbing Damon's hand. "What do we do?" I whispered, hoping they wouldn't know we just had steamy, kinky sex in the storage room.

Damon's stare was leveled, and he calmly said, "You should clean up while I handle them."

"Do I look that bad?" I frowned, patting down my hair.

"You look perfect, but..." He tilted his head and looked at my thighs. "As much as I love having my cum slide out of your pussy, it won't look appropriate in front of my sister and her boyfriend."

I blushed furiously and pinched his arm. "You didn't have to word it that way, asshole."

I ignored his burning stare when I walked into the closest washroom and cleaned up. And it was a lot. My cheeks were flaming by the time I was done, and I had to take deep breaths to calm myself.

I didn't think Damon would be so rough and say those filthy things. I wasn't sure if he meant them, but I knew he'd never share me with others without my consent. But the fantasy of him not caring about it and letting others use me for his pleasure made my stomach flutter.

There was definitely something wrong with me.

I prepared myself before entering Damon's office, and as soon as I did, I wished I could turn back and walk out. The air was tense and heavy. Emma and Cillian were on one couch while Damon sat across from them showing no emotion on his face. He didn't even look like he had sex minutes ago.

"Hi, Emma!" I beamed, forcing a sincere smile. "Hi, Cillian."

The dark-haired man gave me a nod before moving his eyes to Damon, and they did their silent eye-staring macho contest. Emma, on the other hand, stared at me with her cold blue eyes.

"Hello, Summer," she started, her voice soft and sharp when I made my way towards them. "Imagine my surprise when I found out that you are dating my brother from a tabloid."

"Haha, that sounds very shocking," I said, sitting beside Damon on the couch. "How come you both are here?"

Cillian, as usual, didn't reply. He was a man of few words. Emma narrowed her eyes at me and said, "I was going to surprise you, but you both managed to surprise me instead."

I closed my eyes. I didn't want to lie to her, but I couldn't tell her I needed the financial aid or that her brother's dick was fucking fabulous.

"It's not real, Em," Damon said, saving me.

I nodded. "It's just for PR."

"PR?" she asked, looking between us. "So, it's a fake relationship?"

"Yes." Damon and I said in unison.

Cillian eyed us both, making me look anywhere but at

him. He was wearing a tight tee shirt that showed off his tattoos and muscles.

"I know it sounds crazy, and your brother would be the last person I'd date—"

"Feeling's mutual, sweetheart," Damon interrupted.

I glared at him and continued, "But he needed a famous ambassador for Moore, and I needed someone with a relatively good image to clean up *my* image."

"So, what? Is this a contract-based relationship?"

"Yes," Damon replied.

I rolled my eyes and said, "I thought I was having a stroke because we agreed on something."

Emma stayed silent and looked at Cillian, squeezing his hand. "What do you think?"

He looked at her, and even though a stranger would think he was scowling, he was not. I had seen them together for years, and not once had Cillian ever scowled at her. He looked like a big puppy whenever Emma was around. They were so in love and adorable and so gross I wished I could barf.

"I think they are adults, and we should let them do whatever they want, Doll," Cillian said, eyeing us suspiciously. It would be hard to lie to someone who was an ex military veteran.

But I was also an actress.

"The thing is…" I trailed off and looked at Damon. "Should I tell them?"

He looked confused but nodded. I smiled and said, "Garrett bumped into me."

Emma's face changed in an instant, and she looked furious. "What the fuck did that asshole do?"

"N-nothing bad, but he saw me with Damon. And he published the article, so we ran along with it," I confessed, telling a white lie and hoping it would cover up the big elephant in the room.

That we both smelled like each other's perfume and Damon's hair was ruffled more than usual.

"Who's this Garrett?" Cillian asked.

"My douchey ex-boyfriend who loved to spread rumors about me in high school, and now he gets paid for it," I said with a grin.

"Do you want me to get rid of him?" Cillian asked casually, and my heart dropped.

"If she wants someone gone, I can do that too," Damon replied, glaring at Cillian.

I sometimes wondered if these men were okay. I shared a look with Emma. She squeezed his hand and looked at both of us. "I'm sorry I jumped to conclusions. I know you'd tell me if anything happened between you two, but the thought is so hilarious because you were venting about how much you hate Da—"

"Emma," I forced a smile, glaring at her. "We get it."

"Yeah." She cleared her throat. "So, anyway, I also came here because we wanted to tell you something."

Damon's eyes hardened and glaring at Cillian, he said coldly, "Don't tell me you got my sister pregnant."

Cillian smirked. "What if I did?"

Damon stood up. "What the fuck?"

Emma rubbed her forehead and gave her boyfriend a look. "Damon, he's sterile."

Cillian's smirk widened while Damon became angrier.

"Guys, can we tame down some of that testosterone and hear what Emma has to say?" I asked, tugging Damon's hand until he sat down.

"Thank you, Summer." She smiled at me and showed me the pretty bracelet on her wrist. "Cillian gave this to me last week."

"Oh, it's really pretty!"

Damon grunted.

Emma continued, smiling brightly and looking at Cillian, who had a small smile on his lips. "In Korean tradition, they don't always give a ring to propose, but they give any expensive jewelry, and Cillian gifted me this."

I looked at them and gasped, covering my mouth. "Oh my god, Emma!"

I stood up and hugged her as both of our eyes glistened with tears. "I'm so happy for you!" I squealed and hugged her tighter. "I've always rooted for you both."

"Shush, you only did that so you could ship me with my bodyguard."

I pulled back and grinned at her. "You know it. But hey, it looks like you guys got your happily ever after!"

"There's no happily ever after when you have to do taxes," Cillian grumbled, but at least he sounded happy.

"Congratulations," Damon said, his voice emotionless, but if I looked closely enough, I could see some happiness gleaming in his gray eyes.

"Thank you, Damon," Emma said, accepting a hug from her brother.

I wiped a tear, seeing them and how happy my best friend looked. She deserved someone like Cillian, who would scowl at everyone but her and protect her.

"Summer," Emma whispered as the men chatted in one-word sentences. "Who gave you that hickey?"

"A what?" I asked, my eyes wide as I touched my neck.

*What the fuck, Damon?* You had one job!

2 7

# GREEDY GIRL

## DAMON

I noticed Summer fumbling with her hands as my driver drove us to her place. She had said little after Emma and Cillian left. She wanted to spend time with Void, but she was being stubborn and denied my offer to move in with me.

"What did you talk with Emma about?" I asked, not enjoying the tension between us. "Did she suspect anything?"

"No, but she asked me who gave me this hickey," she deadpanned, showing me her neck.

"That was an accident," I said truthfully. I don't even know when I did that.

"Sure," she said. "I told her I got a burn from curling iron, and she let it go."

I hummed in reply. They invited both of us for dinner, but Summer had plans, and I couldn't force her to join us, even though I'd love to have someone else suffer through the googly eyes of Emma and Cillian.

"Are you sure you don't want to move in with me?" I asked when we reached her fake address. I knew Heather lived there, and she'd walk to her actual home. I knew how well and where she lived. That building was a complete disaster, and it wasn't safe for her. But I didn't want to prod too much.

*Unless...*

"No, that's alright." She gave me a forced smile and paused. I stared at her, waiting, and I was taken aback when she leaned close and kissed my cheek. My skin burned, and I touched it as she said, "Thank you. For today."

I nodded numbly and watched her leave. *She kissed my cheek.*

I cleared my throat and blinked through the brain fog. I called Rahul and asked, "I need to buy a property."

"Dude, what the hell?"

"It's a rental building and the living conditions are not good for the tenants," I said, tugging at my tie. If Summer didn't want to live with me, then fine, I'd make her move.

"How fast can I buy it and evict them to a better place?" I asked, hearing Void's tiny *meow* in the background. Oddly enough, I couldn't wait to reach home and spend time with the cat.

"Give me some more details and I'll see what I can do," Rahul replied, typing something in his laptop.

I gave him the details on the place and ended the call and wondered how she'd react.

* * *

UNFORTUNATELY, SHE DIDN'T TAKE IT WELL. ALL THE OTHER tenants were thankful to move to a better place, but she wasn't. I didn't enjoy seeing her sad or mull over her living conditions and decided to go out with her. As nemeses who worked with each other and occasionally dipped their toes in kinky sex. Nothing else. Obviously.

I don't date.

I had to rely on Google to give me suggestions for good date places, but I cringed at hotels, bars, or something as stupid as going to the beach. Who the fuck goes to the beach on a date? You get sand every-fucking-where and if the sun is too bright, you smell like sticky sun screen, and if the weather isn't good, it's too fucking windy and ruins everything.

I finally decided on something and reserved our tickets, hoping she'd like it.

After a couple of weeks of busy schedule, I had invited her to our marketing meeting because her ideas were better.

We hadn't been able to have sex because we always got interrupted by Void at my place or some employees at the office. It was definitely taking a toll on me. I had gone decades without sex, and I was fine, but after Summer, I didn't think I'd survive two weeks without it.

I was definitely pussy drunk for her.

I faked a yawn when the marketing manager kept rambling on and on about statistics. I was at my limit when none of them let Summer finish. I was so close to firing them.

"Dave," I said, knowing his name was something else. "Let Summer finish."

"Oh, of course, but I just think that this—"

I leaned on the desk and said, "Don't think out loud. I pay you to bring me customers, not ramble about some fucking graph." The entire conference hall went quiet, and I looked at Summer, who was sitting in the back, way too far from me and said, "Speak."

She swallowed and spoke the same things she had told me that day in the makeup room. People were listening to her, nodding along and taking notes about bringing more inclu-sivity to our PR packages.

"I think you had a candle shop, too, right?" one girl spoke up. "I saw your shop and how pretty the candles look."

Summer flushed and talked with her.

I tilted my head and asked, "How about a candle collection with Summer?"

"What?" Everyone raised the question, but the girl was a fan of Summer and started pouring ideas.

I leaned back in the chair, letting them brainstorm, and watched her work with the team. My work here was done.

Once everyone left the conference room, Summer stayed back. Most of them wanted to take pictures with her ever since the fourth episode of her show was released. Her character had saved the main hero from drowning after some dramatic scene and everyone on the internet was talking about how good her acting was.

If I ignored the dramatics of the show, her acting shone the most, and I knew she had worked hard to be where she was.

"You didn't have to do that, you know?" she said, walking over to me.

I trailed my eyes from her heels to her tight pencil skirt and blouse. "Do what?" I asked, standing up and caging her in my arms with her back against the conference table.

She played with my tie and said, "I know you asked that girl to speak about my candle-making phase."

"I didn't ask her anything, Summer," I said, lifting her on the table. "I don't even know her name."

She peered at me through her lashes. "Are you lying?"

"No, kitten," I whispered, kissing her cheek. "I didn't like how that guy kept interrupting you."

"I'm used to it."

"What do you mean?" I frowned. "You shouldn't get used to assholes talking down on you."

She raised her brow, and I rolled my eyes. "I'm serious."

"I sometimes take time to process what's being said, so it's not rare for people to think I'm stupid," she said, looking away.

"You're not stupid," I said sincerely. "And trust me, I'd know. I have met many dumb people, but you're not one of them."

Summer chuckled, "Thanks."

I knew she was feeling shy and embarrassed about it, but I wanted to know more. "Is it the ADHD?"

She hummed, playing with my tie, and said, "I always related to a Hamilton quote. *'He looked at me like I was stupid. I'm not stupid.'*" She swallowed and continued, "It gets overwhelming sometimes."

"Overwhelming?"

"Yeah. Like imagine you're drowning and someone hands you a body."

I cupped her face and said, "Do you feel overwhelmed with me?"

"Sometimes."

"In a good way or bad way?"

She smiled, and I was relieved to see it was a sincere smile. "Definitely good."

I nodded and noted the bracelet on her wrist and pushed her down on the table. "I'm going to make you overwhelmed with orgasm, so be quiet," I whispered, tugging up her pencil skirt and groaning to find her pussy bare. "No panties? Dirty fucking girl."

She giggled. "I removed them before the meeting."

"Greedy girl," I growled before I kneeled on the carpet and spread her legs wide and dove in.

Her pussy smelled so fucking good. Her clit stood out as I licked it before moving my attention to her thighs and leaving hickeys. Her soft sighs and moans made my cock bulge against the zipper. But I wanted to treat her. And me.

"Be quiet, kitten," I warned her, kissing her slicked lips and groaning at her sweet, musky taste. "Your moans belong to me."

"F-fuck," she gasped when I slid two fingers inside her. Her warm walls clenched me as I slowly rubbed the sensitive spot. "Please, Damon."

I chuckled, spanking her pussy and loving the way her body trembled. "No, that's not the right way to beg, kitten."

Her fingers curled in my hair and meeting my eyes, she whispered, "Please, Sir."

I hummed, kissing her clit, and stretched her lips with my other hand so I could kiss and lick every inch of her pretty pussy. "You're so fucking delicious," I groaned, closing my eyes and savoring her taste as I kept her right on the edge. "I could eat you out for days."

"I'm close," she cried out, her fingers tightening on my hair. Her legs trembled and her back arched as I fucked her with my fingers, curling them and sucking her clit in my mouth.

"Hold it," I demanded, pulling away as she tethered on the edge of the orgasm. "Don't cum yet."

# GENTLEMAN

## SUMMER

I whimpered, moving my hips and trying to grind myself on his handsome face.

But Damon was a sadist, and he held the reins of my orgasms. Even though we didn't have sex for the past two weeks, he always found some time to make me cum either by his fingers, his mouth, or ordering me to masturbate while we were alone in his office and he was on a virtual call.

"Please," I begged, almost tasting the orgasm on my tongue.

He ignored me and made out with my pussy. He was French kissing it as if it was his last day on the earth.

"Fuck, Summer, so good," he whispered in between eating me out and holding my thighs wide so I wouldn't close them.

"Cum for me, good girl," he whispered, sucking my clit in his hot mouth and rubbing my G-spot with his fingers. He knew how to make me cum so well.

I squeezed my eyes shut, but before I could fall over the edge of orgasm, someone knocked on the door. We both snapped out of it, and I let out a small groan when he pulled away.

"We are continuing this," Damon said, a strange expression on his face as I sat up and smoothed my skirt down.

I wore my heels, pouting because my clit was still pulsing. "Can I just rub one out in the washroom?" I whispered.

"Absolutely not." He glared at me. "Do I need to remind you it's my pussy, and it comes when I tell her to?"

"Mean." I rolled my eyes even though I secretly loved the dynamics we had, because I knew he'd make me cum way better than I could with my fingers.

The employee who had knocked and cockblocked us had forgotten their glasses.

Once they left, Damon had asked me to go out with him, and I couldn't ignore his advances to take me to his place anymore.

I was apartment-slash-house hunting for days since the new owner was evicting us. They had offered a new apartment, but I couldn't pay the rent when I didn't know shit about my next job. I had used my savings to help mom and dad and my biological mom.

Not to mention I missed Void a lot. It'd be nice to spend some time with a cat.

"Hi, Summer!"

I looked over my shoulder and found Layla smiling at me. She was in casualwear, so she must have been clocking out.

"Hello, Layla. How have you been?" I asked.

"I'm great! I am going on a date with my partner today." She was glowing, and hearts were coming out of her eyes. Date. I couldn't remember the last time I had been on a date. "I wanted to ask you if you know about the event next week?"

"Event? No… I don't think so."

She sighed. "It's a bit weird. We have never had a team building event, but I received an email to share ideas about it. Anyway, I'll get going, or I'll get late. Bye!"

I waved at her and watched her step out of the revolving doors of the building. Seeing those doors made me chuckle, remembering how childish Damon and I had been at the charity event I hosted.

"What are you laughing at?"

I smiled at Damon, his gray eyes, and pointed at the revolving doors. "How you suck at being a gentleman sometimes. Remember?"

He scoffed and wrapped his arm around me, even though we were surrounded by employees. "If I remember correctly, I sucked your clit very well a few minutes ago. Remember?"

Color slashed my cheeks, and I pushed him away. "Shutup," I mumbled and hurried away.

His soft chuckle followed me, and I was surprised his driver wasn't present as he opened the passenger door for me.

"So, where are we going?" I asked, strapping on the seat belt as he started the car.

"It's a surprise."

"Fine." I rolled my eyes and looked at the gray skies. "It looks like it might rain today."

"Don't worry, I won't let rain ruin our plans," Damon said, his voice firm.

I believed him. He was stubborn and always got what he wanted.

"Can I ask you something?"

"You already did," he smirked at my poker face and sighed, "Fine, ask away."

"How come you never dated anyone before?" I asked, curious about his answer.

His knuckles turned white as he maneuvered the steering wheel and cleared his throat. "I didn't have time."

"Come on, everyone says that. You must have your reasons."

"If I tell you, you'd have to tell me something too," he said, looking at me before averting his eyes back to the road.

"Deal."

He took a deep breath and said, "I... I had issues with Drake. My dad is—was a porn producer—Don't ask. So, our house was filled with porn stars, and after one after-shoot party, I called it quits and moved here." He swallowed and continued, "My father didn't want to support me since I didn't agree to live with him, and Dorothy didn't know or didn't care where I was. So, I was on my own for a few years."

I laid my palm on his hand that rested on his thigh and squeezed it. "I'm sorry. That must have been very hard for you."

He chuckled, but it was devoid of any emotion, and I wondered how much he had struggled with to be where he was right now. No wonder the death of his mom made him feel angry. He had no one from the beginning.

"It's okay. Remember the deli I took you for lunch?" When I nodded, he said, "The owner, Nina, knew about my situation and helped me. I stayed there with her family for years before I got a job."

"No way! Their baked ziti was so good!" I grinned and shook my head. "I can't imagine grumpy young Damon washing dishes and serving that delicious baked ziti with a scowl on his face."

We both chuckled at that. I smiled, looking at his side profile. I never knew about that, and I was sure Emma didn't either. I always thought Damon Grant was the most mysterious person ever, but I didn't realize he wasn't mysterious. No one ever asked him about stuff and had a decent conversation with him.

"So, you worked hard, opened a sex club, sold it to take care of Moore Beauty, and now you're fake dating the sexiest actress of a trending show. Seems fair," I said with my chin high.

He glanced at me as we stopped in front of a beautiful restaurant. "Mhmm, seems fair."

He opened the door for me and gave the key fob to the valet before we stepped inside. It was a Michelin star restaurant, and it looked empty. I was awed by the golden decor and dark-red wallpaper that gave it a luxurious feel.

"Why is it empty?" I whispered in his ear when the server took us upstairs so we could have a balcony view of the city.

"Because I reserved it for today," Damon replied, like it was the most casual thing ever.

"You booked an entire restaurant for... dinner?" I asked, wondering if he was okay in the head or not.

29

# SHAMELESS

## DAMON

"Yes," I replied, ordering my favorite red wine. "It'd be better to have some privacy from the paparazzi."

Once the server left, I looked at Summer, and she was staring at me with a strange expression. I ignored it. She often had a strange expression on her face, and most of the time it's because she's daydreaming. It was cute. But I'd never ever tell that to her.

"Have you decided what you want to eat?" I asked, already decided what I wanted to have.

"Who the fuck eats a hundred-dollar lasagna?" she asked, checking the price and closed the menu. "I can't. It's giving me anxiety."

I straightened up. "I can decide for you if that's okay?"

Fuck. I didn't want to overwhelm her with choices or anything.

*Did I go overboard?*

*Should I cancel the next reservations for the day?*

"Yes, please order for me," she replied and looked over at the scenery. I sighed internally and watched her gather her hair in a small bun and clip it with a hair accessory, a few of the hairs framing her delicate face.

I swallowed and looked down at the menu. I was glad I had booked the entire restaurant so that no one could see how beautiful Summer Hayes looked in real life.

I ordered our food and enjoyed our wine. I swirled it in the glass and said, "It's my turn to ask a question."

Summer nodded. "Ask away!"

I took a sip of the bittersweet wine and asked, "What happened on the night of your prom when you went to Vixen?"

I saw how a wall came up and she physically pulled away, leaning back on the chair. It must have been something serious that she took a huge gulp of wine before looking at me. "Are you sure you want to know? It'll dull the moment."

"Yes, I want to know."

Summer stared at the candlelight on our table and sighed. "I... well. My prom date was Garrett. He had asked me, and I said yes to him because we were still dating. *Unfortunately.* Anywho, me, Em and Mia dressed up together, went to the school gym, and Garrett was nowhere to be found."

I noticed how the light dimmed in her eyes as she continued, her voice low, as if she was embarrassed. "I went to look for him, and he was in the locker room with his football team and friend. They had snuck in some alcohol and were drinking it." She swallowed and crossed her arms as if she was hugging herself. "I overheard him talking about how I was in bed. That... that I was a bitch in heat, and he was sure I had whored myself to other guys before."

"Jesus, Summer."

She cracked a small smile. "Yeah. He even told them he'd ask me later that night if I wanted to fuck his team, so I left. I couldn't face Emma and Mia because they'd ask about Garrett, and they'd know something happened. I didn't want to go home because my parents would question it while I just wanted to be alone. So, I came to Vixen. A sex club."

She chuckled, trying to hide how vulnerable she felt.

I held her hand and rubbed her knuckles. "I wish you had told me this that night."

"It was nothing."

"It wasn't nothing, Summer," I said, reeling back my anger. I should have punched him in the face when I saw him. "I would have helped you."

"Helped me how?" she teased. "By fucking me?"

I looked at her face and answered honestly, "No, but I would have gladly shown him his place with my words or… fists if it came to that."

"Oh, please." She rolled her eyes. "I don't think you'd beat up a kid over my heartbreak."

"He's not a kid anymore," I reminded her.

She shook her head, not believing me, and I pulled back my hand when they served our dinner. Lobster with sautéed vegetables covered in butter and paprika in white wine sauce.

"It smells and looks delicious," Summer whispered in awe, and I was glad that I at least got the food right.

We both ate the food in silence, looking over the night lights of the city and having a small talk about work, her show, and Void. I showed her the adorable pictures I had taken of the cat while he slept in the weirdest positions. She giggled and *aww*-ed seeing them, telling me how much she missed him.

I wished she would stop being so stubborn and just move in with me and Void.

We ate chocolate tiramisu for dessert, and I had to glare at her when she moaned, taking a bite from it.

"I'll give you better reasons to moan. Tiramisu isn't one of them."

She sputtered and bit her lip. "You're shameless, Damon."

I placed the cloth from my lap on the table and tugged my tie low. "I will show you how shameless I am, kitten." I pulled my tie over my shoulder so it wouldn't get in the way. Her eyes widened when I continued, "I am starving for a particular dessert. Try not to scream."

"Damon!" she hissed, watching me go underneath the table that was covered with a long tablecloth. Even if the server came to us, they wouldn't know I was between her thighs.

I licked my lips seeing her bare legs and I spread them apart, her skin shivering when I leaned closer, tugging up her pencil skirt. Her hand clutched it, and I could imagine her flushed face, freckles standing out.

"Damon, please..." Her soft voice trailed off when I found her glistening entrance and caressed the sensitive nub with my finger. Her gasp made me smirk as I kissed her thigh, inching closer to her pussy.

I hummed when she tried to close her legs, but I pushed them apart with my shoulders, staying on my knees and kissing her pretty pussy. Her soft sigh encouraged me further as I licked her slicked slit, groaning at the sweet, musky taste. She was so fucking delicious. I didn't think I could ever tire of her taste. Of *her*.

Squeezing her thighs, I pulled her closer and dove in. Eating her out for my pleasure and sucking her clit in my mouth before altering to licking her cream. I could hear how hard she was trying to hold back from moaning—

"Ma'am, do you want to order anything else?"

I paused when I heard the server.

"Um, I'd like one more..." I pulled back and when she spoke, I slid two fingers inside her wet pussy. "O-one more tiramisu."

I bit her thigh, curling the pads of my fingers inside her as she stuttered.

"Of course, ma'am." The server must have noticed my empty seat and asked, "Where's Mr. Grant?"

I'm licking my favorite dessert with my face between the most perfect thighs.

"H-he went to washroom," she replied, my fingers fucking her slowly. I was kind enough not to increase the pace, or hearing the wet squelches of her pussy would embarrass her. "Thank you!"

I didn't care if the server left or not and leaned close to wrap my lips around her clit and sucked. Her response was quick with a jerk of her leg, her heel stumbling off as I took it over my shoulder and curled my fingers inside her cunt.

I wasn't expecting her to cum when she let out a small whimper, her hand curling in my hair as her lithe body trembled with the orgasm. I growled and sucked her, prolonging the orgasm and licking her juices. I didn't stop until she tried to weakly push me away. My mouth lowered to her thighs, kissing the soft skin and running my hands down her legs to soothe the tremble. I kissed her knee before sliding out from under the table and sitting on my chair.

Her skin was flushed, and eyes were dazed as she leaned back on the chair. I smirked at her, licking my lips and running a hand through my tousled hair. Her chest heaved up and down as she tried to catch her breath and shook her head.

"You're an insatiable demon."

"You loved it," I replied smugly and licked my fingers clean. I straightened my tie and watched her struggle to fix her skirt and put on her shoe. "By the way, you owe me one punishment."

"What?" She frowned.

"You came without permission."

Summer gaped. "That's not fair! Y-you didn't ask me to ho—"

"It *is* fair, kitten. Don't worry, I'll go easy on you since you were such a good girl being quiet." I hummed and checked my watch. "I'll ask them to pack the tiramisu. We might get late."

"Late for what?" she asked, tapping her lips with the napkin. She missed a spot where the cream was stuck on her upper lip.

"Another secret," I replied, leaning close and wiping it with my thumb. I licked it, ignoring the dirty fantasy of having her spread out in front of me right there as I licked cream off of her sexy body. She was too sensitive for that, and I was too possessive to have anyone but me see her that way.

"Let's go," she said, her voice breathy.

My card was already on the tab, and I thanked the server and dragged Summer away when she tried to split the bill. Like hell I would let her pay for anything while she was with me.

I opened the door of the car for her and strapped her in. We drove in silence, and I ignored her when she kept asking me where we were going. It had taken me two weeks to plan out the dinner and the carnival correctly to match with our schedules. I wasn't going to spoil it for her even when she kept on pouting. Even though she looked adorable.

"We are here," I said, parking the car and making her swap her heels with one of the pairs of sneakers I had bought for her.

"Why am I changing into sneakers?" she asked suspiciously. "I swear to god, Damon, if you are going to make me run, I will murder you."

"Shush, drama queen. No one is making you run. Come

on," I dragged her along and walked her into the darkness, holding her hand.

"This is creepy, but at least we aren't doing cardio."

I rolled my eyes and said, "You are safe with me. You'll see in a minute."

When we had reached the spot, I sent a text to the employee, and they turned on all the lights of the surrounding rides, making us and the entire place lit up.

"Oh my… God," Summer gasped, covering her mouth as she looked around, turning in circles as she looked at all the rides. Carousel, bumper cars, ferris wheel, mechanical bull, rollercoaster, and many more. "This is insane, Damon!"

I slid my hands in my pockets and said, "I'll take it as you liking it."

"Like it?" she asked with a huge grin. "I love it! I can't decide which one I want to try first."

"Take your time," I assured her. "We have the whole night."

"Really?" she asked, her eyes wide as she held my arm.

I nodded and smiled when she squealed and rushed to the nearest ride, which was a carousel with little horses.

I rubbed a spot on my chest to calm myself down. Seeing her happy made something churn inside my chest. I'd need to see a doctor about it. Soon.

30

# RIDE MY THIGH

## SUMMER

I giggled when the merry-go-round moved up and down. Damon was too grumpy to enjoy the ride with me, so he stood in the middle of the carousel, taking pictures.

"I don't remember the last time I went to a carnival," I said, looking around and noticing it's just us two. "Maybe as a kid, but it'd have been better if there were more people."

"I didn't want paparazzi posting more pictures of us and invading our privacy," Damon replied, helping me off the tiny horse as I hummed and looked around the rides.

I had already gone on so many that it started getting dark. But I wanted to try one more.

"Let's go." I held Damon's hand and dragged him to the Ferris wheel. The employee smiled at us, but Damon stopped me.

"I-I don't think I want to go. You go ahead," he said, looking up at the Ferris wheel.

I gaped at him. "Are you scared of it?"

He scoffed, fixing his tie. "Of course not."

"Then come with me." I pulled him along with me and we

both strapped in. I was grinning and taking pictures of the quiet scenery, cold air kissing my bare skin.

"Isn't this fun?" I asked, looking at him, and my smile dropped seeing his pale face. "Oh my god, Damon, are you okay?"

He shook his head and said, "I'm fine."

I held his hand and said, "It's okay, we will be down soon."

He squeezed my hand. I leaned close and kissed his cheek. "Thank you for today. It's the best date I've ever been to."

His pupils dilated and glancing at my lips, he whispered, "Yeah."

"I didn't know you were scared of heights."

"I'm usually not."

I giggled. "Usually?"

He shrugged and kept his eyes on me as the Ferris wheel slowly moved. It was huge, so we were going to be at the top soon.

"I'm scared of planes, too."

I hummed, swaying my legs. "Do you know people who are scared of planes have controlling issues?"

"Excuse me?"

"Mhm, it's because they are not in control."

He narrowed his eyes at me. "Why would I trust two strangers with my life when we are thousands of miles away from the ground in a flying chunk of metal?"

I laughed and his hand tightened around me. "You are such a big baby!"

"Shut up. I'm not."

If one looked closely enough, they would find that Damon Grant, my grumpy boss and fake boyfriend, was pouting.

"Okay, fine, I'll stop teasing you," I said, tucking my hair over my ear, but the wind was too much, and I left it alone.

"Why the fuck has he stopped it?" Damon asked, his

knuckles turning white as he held onto the railing and my hand. "Is it broken? Are we stuck here?"

"Hey, you're okay," I said, cupping his cheek and making him look at me. "They stop it at the top for a few minutes. Don't worry."

He swallowed and nodded. "Keep talking to me."

"Okay, you asked me a question, so it's now my turn." I kept my eyes on him and asked, "Have you ever been in love?"

He rolled his eyes and answered, "No. I don't believe in it."

"Why not?" I frowned. "Emma is in love with Cillian, and Mia loves James. Hell, you love Void. Don't even try to deny it."

Damon thought about it for a while and shook his head. "I don't think romantic love can exist for someone like me."

"What do you mean, someone like you?" I asked, not liking the tone of his voice. It seemed like it was robotic, as if he was saying things that he had heard from someone else.

"That's two questions now." He glanced at me and said, "Do you regret falling in love with the wrong person? Like your exes?"

I hummed. "That's a good question and even though both relationships ended on bad terms... I don't regret loving either of them."

"Not even that douchebag with the stache?" he asked in a dry voice.

I chuckled and shook my head. "No. Not really. I am not scared of being in love because at the end of the day, I opened my heart to someone, and if they broke my trust, then it's on them. Not me."

He sighed and tucked a lock of hair behind my ear. "You're too trusting, Summer. And too optimistic. What if someone takes advantage of that?"

I shrugged, thinking about Carol, my bio mom. "It's okay. I know in my heart that I did the right thing, but the person didn't deserve it, so I moved on. Life is too short not to fall in love."

Damon kept looking at me, and I held my breath when he leaned closer. "Can I kiss you?" he whispered. His stormy gray eyes felt like a whirlwind, and all of a sudden, I felt really shy.

"Yes, kiss me," I replied, squeezing his hand when he closed the distance between us and claimed my lips in a soft kiss.

This kiss was different. Most of our kisses were passionate, hungry and rough. But *this* kiss… He was so gentle. His soft, pliant lips moving against mine with his warm breath caressing my cheek. It felt brilliant.

It felt like lo—

I pulled away and said, "Let's go to your car."

He blinked at me and pulled back enough that I could think. "What happened?"

I swallowed. "I'm just really horny."

He raised our entwined hands to his lips and kissed the back of my hand. "Whatever you wish."

I looked away and blinked when the water dropped on my cheek. Soon showering rain started, but thankfully we reached his car without uttering any words or getting soaked.

Before he could sit in the front, I pulled him on the back seat and straddled his lap, kissing him. I made sure the kiss was rough, passionate and hungry, moaning into his mouth and grinding him.

"Right here?" he asked, inching my dress high and kissing my neck.

"Yes," I gasped when he kissed down my neck to my chest. "Fuck me now, Damon."

He looked at me from his long lashes, his hair damp, and asked, "No role-play?"

I shook my head, and holding his hand, I brought it between my legs. "Make me cum again," I said, my voice breathy when he did what I asked, rubbing my pussy until I was soaking his fingers.

I made a quick work of removing his belt and shoving down his boxers, pulling out his hard cock and lining it against my slit.

"Fuck, Summer," he groaned, holding my waist and pulling me away, so I sat on his thigh. "Calm down."

I scrunched my hands on his shirt, his suit jacket on the car floor as he leaned close and kissed me, slowly. Too slow. He was being too gentle.

He unzipped my dress and tugged it off as rain pattered on the roof of his car. It seemed like we were in our cocoon as he took his time, removing my bra and kissing my breasts. Licking and biting each nipple until I was panting for him, riding his thigh.

"Yeah, does that feel good?" he asked, his voice gravelly, watching me ride his thigh. I was naked while he was fully clothed, his expensive watch shining in the dark. "Ride my thigh hard, love. Make yourself cum."

*Love?*

I squeezed my eyes shut, but he was stubborn and he wrapped his hand around my neck. "No, keep your eyes on me and grind my thigh. Look at me when you cum," he whispered, touching my bottom lip. I bit his thumb before sucking it in my mouth and rode his thigh as he watched me with heady eyes.

I came quickly, trembling in his arms, and before I knew it, he was rubbing the leaking tip of his cock against my sensitive sex and inching inside.

"Fuck." We cursed together when he filled me up, my pussy stretching around his thick girth.

"You feel so fucking good, Summer," he moaned, the sound so euphoric that it made my toes curl.

"You fill me up so good." I whimpered when he moved, raising my hips and slowly riding me on his cock. Topping me from the bottom.

"I know, love," he groaned. "This pussy is made for me. My hands. My mouth. And my cock."

He enunciated each word with thrusts, making me cry out as I clenched him, rocking my hips and arching my back. He grabbed my tits, playing with them, kissing them as I tugged on his hair, getting closer and closer to another orgasm.

"Fuck yeah," he grunted, his voice deep. "Cum on my cock, love. Let me see your pretty face when you cum again."

*Pretty?*

It was too much. My moans turned low as I reached my peak, my abdomen clenching as my entire body tightened up for the upcoming release.

Damon rubbed my clit. "That's it, good girl. That's it." His soft whispers and praise were my undoing.

I came with a soft whimper and quivered when my head went blank. My toes curled as I kept gasping for air, his thrusts slowing as he released inside me with a low grunt, holding me tight.

I felt his warm cum in me, and it felt so good that I melted in his arms. Slowly, our gasps and pants calmed down, and I heard the loud pattering of rain.

*Fuck. Fuck. Fuck.*

"That was so go—*Summer?*" Damon cupped my face as I blinked at him, my vision blurry. "Are you crying?"

"No, I just…" I sniffled, trying to hide my face, but he didn't let me.

"Shh, it's okay," he whispered, wiping away my tears and slowly pulling out of me. "Tell me if it hurts anywhere. Was that too much?"

I shook my head and hid my face in his chest. I didn't want him to think I was so emotional or sensitive that the one time we had vanilla sex, I started crying.

# 31

# GOOD TALK

## DAMON

I cooed sweet words and praise in her ear as I stroked her back. "You were so good. I'm so proud of you. You looked so pretty." But her silent tears kept making my shirt wet, and I didn't want to move until I made sure she was okay.

I knew many people cried during intense orgasm and I tried to explain it to her, but she kept her face hidden.

"Summer, I need to know if you are hurt or not," I said, keeping my voice soft. The last thing she needed was someone like me being stern with her.

She sniffled and pulled back, her eyes swollen, and I didn't know why it made my heart ache. I needed to book an appointment with the cardiologist soon.

"Sorry," she said, wiping her tears. "I don't know why I'm crying so much."

"Hey, don't apologize for it, okay?" I said, taking my handkerchief and wiping her nose. She turned red, but I didn't care. I had made her squirt and eaten her out. The last thing she needed to feel embarrassed about was crying and her snot. "Maybe it was a sub drop or an intense orgasm. Either way, don't feel embarrassed."

Summer didn't meet my eyes, so I helped her get dressed, uncapping a bottle of water for her.

Once we were cleaned up and I had started the car, she spoke, "I didn't like… whatever that was."

I swallowed and after some silence I said, "I know it was overwhelming for you and you were flustered, vulnerable, and most of all, confused by it but… having my partner go through a sub-drop or crying because of an intense orgasm makes me feel very honored." I held her hand and added, "I'm glad that you trust me, Summer."

She hummed, looking out of the window. "I would like to go home, please."

I clenched my jaw but didn't show my irritation and drove her to her place, forcing myself to stop the car at Heather's place, knowing she'd walk back to her own.

"Thanks, I'll see—"

"Summer," I interrupted her. "Do you regret it?"

"What?"

"Regret that one-night stand or whatever we have going on."

She didn't reply, her eyes looking anywhere but at me, and I wished I could stop her and hear her reply, but she got out of the car. "I'm sorry, I have to go."

She left without an umbrella in the thundering rain, leaving me without an answer.

Maybe the silence was her answer after all.

I closed my eyes and laid my head on the steering wheel. It was getting too overwhelming.

Sighing, I changed the gear and reared my car. At least I have a cute black cat to go back home to.

Next morning, I woke up with a small headache and I ignored it as I opened the door to the basement that I had renovated into an in-house gym. Void followed me and sniffed one dumbbell before losing interest and strolling over to his cat tree that I had installed by the windows so he could look at the garden.

"Do you think she's fine?" I asked him after finishing three sets of squats and wiping down my sweat.

Void blinked at me and started cleaning his butt.

"Yeah, I thought so too." I nodded. "Good talk."

I was definitely going crazy if I was talking to my cat about a relationship problem.

I finished my workout and started sprints on the treadmill. Maybe I can call her, ask if she's okay. Or I could text her, to not sound so desperate. What if she didn't make it back home? What if she—

I snapped out of my mind when I realized that the treadmill was too fast while my head was in the clouds. I couldn't stop it in time and I fell off with a loud *thud*. I winced, rubbing my forehead as Void stood up, his eyes wide and staring at me as if I was responsible for waking him up from his nap.

"Sorry, I fell off the treadmill," I replied, sitting up and wiping my hands.

He meowed at me before circling around his warm spot and sitting down.

"Yes, I'll call her," I said, stopping the treadmill and dialing her number. I paced around when it kept ringing and she didn't pick up. I glared at the phone and called her again.

When she didn't pick up on the sixth call, I decided to give up, but finally, she picked up on my seventh call.

"Summer?" I asked.

I heard some shuffling on the other side and a raspy *'Hello?'* Someone coughed, and I checked the caller ID again. I had called Summer.

"Summer, are you okay?" I asked, worried she was sick.

"No," she croaked. "I'm dying."

"What the fuck?" I barked, hurrying to grab my car keys, and stopped. I smelled like sweat and cat hair. If she was sick, being around me would be the last thing she'd want. I threw a random tee shirt and pants, still hearing some shuffling on the other side. "Hello? Summer, are you there?"

"Y-yes. Void. Void will get all my assets," she said, her voice groggy. "Goodbye, cruel world."

"Shut the fuck up and keep breathing. I'll be there in fifteen—*no*, ten."

She had already ended the call. I wanted to call her back and scold her, but there wasn't enough time.

It took me twelve minutes and fifty-seven seconds to reach her place. I stopped by the pharmacy to pick up some medicines, and at the grocery store for some vegetables because I didn't think she'd have any food.

I glared at the mold growing on the entrance of the small building and glared harder at the burly men sitting out in wife beaters. I was sure they were staying there for the shelter of the almost abandoned building, since all the tenants had already left. I walked past them and climbed to the second floor. The wooden stairs were so wobbly that it should have been a living hazard.

I knocked on the door, and when she didn't open it, I barged in since it was unlocked. The place was a mess. The wall was peeling with holes in it, and even though it was unlivable, the owner had decorated it with lots of plants, fake flowers and art prints. Candles were on every surface, and it looked warm and cozy.

Unfortunately, my concern was more than my anger, so I closed the door behind me and took two steps to reach Summer. Who was lying on the... bed? I didn't know what it was, but at least she wasn't sleeping on the floor.

"Summer?" I tried to wake her up, but she didn't move. I

turned her on her back and gently pushed her hair away from her face to check her body temperature. As expected, her forehead was burning.

I sighed and rolled up the sleeves of my shirt. I needed to get to work and make sure she got well soon and moved out of this hellhole.

But first, I needed to cook her something and air out the place.

I stopped when I noticed the familiar white mask on her nightstand table. I picked it up, tracing the feather with a small smile. She kept a memento from that night.

32

# DREAM DAMON

## SUMMER

I don't really remember what happened after Damon dropped me off at Heather's place. I remember walking back to my place, rain hiding my tears and getting completely soaked. My phone rang, and I took it, water droplets falling on my small bathroom as I tried to get out of the soaked clothes.

I remember shouting. And crying. Carol, my biological mother, had called me in a drunken stupor, complaining about her alcoholic boyfriend who didn't love her.

It felt like a fever dream.

Especially when I opened up my heavy lids to the handsome and worried face of Damon, mine inches away from his.

I closed my eyes again, knowing I was dreaming. Damon would never know I lived here or else he'd never stop teasing me. And why would he care?

"Summer?"

I waved him off, my limbs feeling heavy. "Go away. I know it's just a dream." My throat felt scratchy, and I needed water. I snickered. Dream Damon can bring me water though. "Bring me a glass of water."

Dream Summer sat up and hazily blinked at the blur of broad shoulders and a blue shirt moving around in my kitchen. I yawned as Dream Damon brought me a glass of water wearing a cute apron that read: *Hot Stuff Coming Through.* "You're definitely hot alright," I mumbled, sipping the water and smacking my lips.

"How are you feeling?" Dream Damon asked, kneeling beside my bed-slash-couch-slash-desk and touching my forehead.

I frowned and flicked his forehead. It felt very real. "What the fuck?!" I cried out, jumping and spilling water on his shirt as he sighed. "What? This is real? You're here. Why are you here? Are you Damon?"

"You're feeling much better." He took the glass from me and said, "And yes, I'm Damon."

"B-but how?" I asked, taking a tissue in time to sneeze on it. My hair was in a braid, and I hadn't braided my hair for over a year. "Did you braid my hair?"

Very real Damon looked away and replied, "Yes. It was getting in the way."

I clutched my chest. "In the way of what?"

Then I looked around and saw medicines on my small island. There was a bowl of water with a damp cloth beside it. I touched my forehead. He must have tried to cool down the temperature of my body.

"Take this," he ordered, handing me some capsules and a glass of water. "You got cold after getting soaked in the rain. You should have taken my umbrella."

He was scolding me, which was very normal, and I relaxed, taking the meds. "How did you get in?" I asked in a small voice.

His glare hardened. "The door was fucking open, Summer."

I winced. "I must have forgotten—"

"Forgotten to lock your fucking door? You live alone in LA, in the worst neighborhood, and you forgot to lock your door?"

I glared at him. "If you are here to scold me, you can leave."

His eyes turned cold. "Like hell. There are druggies shooting heroin in their arms downstairs. You are moving out, or I'm kidnapping you."

"What?" I asked, feeling dizzy. "I'm too sick to have this conversation right now."

Damon sighed, and I noticed that he hadn't shaved. A sexy five o'clock stubble peppered his sharp jaw. I must be really sick because I said it out loud. "Your stubble looks really sexy."

I was too embarrassed afterward, so I pretended to pass out and flopped back on my pillow, hiding my face with the blanket.

Thankfully, he didn't comment any further and let me sleep.

When I woke up again, I was feeling much better, but I was sweaty and sticky. I needed a shower ASAP. I stretched my limbs and found Damon sleeping by the kitchen island. Seeing him dwarf the kitchen stool made me smile.

He made the tiny apartment look smaller with his enormous frame. I wondered how he found out about my house though.

I brushed my teeth and took a quick shower, changing into another pair of sweats and a baggy tee. I was surprised to find him awake and scrolling through his phone when I walked out, patting my hair dry.

He saw me and pocketed his phone. "Where's the hair

dryer?" he asked, and when I pointed to the small dresser in front of the only mirror in the apartment, he walked to it and made me sit down.

I watched him through the reflection of the small mirror. His face focused as if he was handling fine China and not my hair.

I was glad we were staying quiet and not talking about last night. I didn't know why I couldn't tell him I didn't regret it one bit. Something had stopped me, and I was definitely not in the right mind to talk to him after all the crying.

I had read about sub-drop and even though it looked fucking fabulous on paper, it was exhausting and overwhelming in real life. Even though some part of me loved the orgasm, it was too much.

"Eat the chicken soup that's in the microwave."

I rolled my eyes. "Yes, Dad."

He stared at me while I reheated the soup and ate it. He made sure I finished it and I bit back my tongue from commenting on how delicious it was with fresh vegetables and thick broth. It reminded me of my parents and how my dad would cook the best chicken soup in the entire world whenever I got sick, since my mom couldn't cook.

"Good girl," he praised, and I had to pinch myself to keep from blushing. "Put on your shoes and come with me."

I narrowed my eyes at him and crossed my arms. "I don't trust you."

He raised his brow.

I continued, "You came here, took care of me when I'm sick, cooked me delicious chicken soup, dried my hair, and now you want me to go out with you?"

"You liked the soup?"

"Yeah, the broccoli and—" I snapped at him, "Don't change the subject!"

He gave me a cocky smirk and said, "Sure, darling." He

opened the front door for me and said, "Come on. Don't forget your phone."

I sighed and eyed him. "If you kidnap me, I'll call the cops."

He rolled his eyes, and I sucked in a breath before walking past him in the tiny hallway. He was too big for my apartment.

"Better yet, I'll call James and Cillian."

Damon followed me downstairs. "Why them?"

I looked over my shoulder and said, "Do you know how scary they are when they're angry? They'll beat you up."

He flexed his biceps, opening the passenger door for me and said, "I can take them."

I scoffed. "Yeah, sure, big guy."

I massaged my neck when he started the car, freezing when I saw a moving car stopping in the parking lot. "Who's moving?"

Damon stayed quiet and reversed the car.

"Damon?" I asked suspiciously, and when he didn't reply, I knew what he was doing. "Are you fucking kidding me? What are you doing with my stuff?"

He finally smirked, and I hit him on his fucking massive biceps, hating that I was sick and couldn't punch him in his family jewels. That and I'd definitely get arrested for it.

"I told you, love. You have two choices. Either move into another apartment where your previous tenants relocated, or move in with me."

My nose flared at him. "I'm moving in with them."

He tsked. "Too late, princess. I gave you the choice to choose before." He glanced at me and smiled, a dimple popping on his left cheek. I wanted to smack it off of him. "Now I choose for you, and you're moving in with me."

"I don't want to!"

"Too late."

"You can't do this!" I whined, covering my face. "I'm sure this is some sort of house kidnapping or something."

"Oh, come on, don't be so dramatic," he said. "You'll have your own room, and I won't ask you to pay rent… at least till our contract lasts. And you get to live with a sexy man."

Damon dared to wink at me after saying the last sentence.

At least no rent was a good deal, and if I got to eat delicious food while I lived with him, it would be even better. Not to mention, the media would eat it up that we lived together. It made sense.

*Dang it, he is too smooth.*

I nodded. "Right. I can't wait to cuddle with the sexiest man tonight."

"Really?" He looked so hopeful.

I smiled and batted my lashes. "I'm sure Void missed me as much as I missed him."

He sighed and rolled his eyes. "*Brat.*"

Even though he tried to hide it, there was a small smile tugging at the corner of his lips with a tiny dimple.

3 3

# KNEEL

SUMMER

Damon grew his own vegetables, so when we reached his home, Void, with his big yellow eyes, saw us from the glass doors as Damon nerded about different kinds of chilies, which all looked the same to me. He showed me the different fertilizers he used and showed me a chart where he had written how much water each plant needed. He had made a spreadsheet for his plants.

It was adorable.

I would have never thought that Damon, out of all the people I know, was into gardening and growing his own little farm in his backyard. Void greeted me at the front door, and as soon as I scooped him up in my arms and pressed a million kisses to his chubby face, I was glad that Damon house-kidnapped me.

Unfortunately, Damon got my cold the next day, and I nursed him back to health. He looked even grumpier than before, but he was back on his feet in no time.

Since we had lost precious time, we had to pull our asses at work. Heather occasionally called me to remind me how terrible Damon was and I shouldn't live with him.

"Why the fuck didn't she offer you to be her roommate?" Damon asked one night while we were watching *Mean Girls*. Void was asleep between us on the couch.

I didn't have a reply because I never thought about it. He was right. *Why didn't Heather ask me to move in with her?* After all, I was the reason she got a huge bonus and a raise to purchase that apartment.

I was humming and doing laundry when I found Void's whisker on the floor. I picked it up with a grin and stashed it in a tiny box. It was my personal belief that if you find a cat's whisker on the floor, that day will go great or something lucky will happen.

I hoped it did. I had been ignoring Carol's calls, even though it was making me stressed about her situation. I just hoped she'd move out.

"Whatcha reading about?" I asked, walking into Damon's home office and finding him fumbling around with a book and trying to hide it from me.

I narrowed my eyes when he lied, "Nothing."

I hummed and, swiveling his chair, I straddled him. His eyes darkened, and I smiled, cupping his face and kissing him. I moaned when he kissed me back, his hands lowering to my ass.

We had done nothing the past few days since we were sick or exhausted from the shoot. He didn't have to come with me since he was the CEO, but he wanted to, and I was glad for his moral support. It had also helped clear out my name on the internet, and no one talked about the orgy incident or me having Damon as my sugar daddy anymore.

"Gottem!" I said, pulling away as soon as I got the book he was reading. "*How to Have a Normal Conversation With Your Employees, Family, and Friends?*" I read out the title when he tried to yank it from my hand.

"It's nothing."

I tilted my head when he pulled me off of him, my butt landing on the warm chair as he paced around. "Damon. Are you reading a self-help book about how to socialize?" I asked, biting my lip.

"This is why I didn't want to tell you." He groaned and glared at me. "I knew you'd make fun of me. And thanks for the fake kiss, by the way."

I blinked at him and his angry tone as he walked out of the office, slamming the door behind him. I had never seen him like that before. Vulnerable and shy.

"Do you think he's mad at me?" I asked Void, who was rolled on his back and staring at me upside down.

He meowed, and I nodded. "I think so too." I stood up and told him, "I'll go make up with your dad, okay? Be a good boy and don't interrupt us without knocking."

He meowed again, and I left him in the office, wondering what to do. Running to my room, I opened the closet and grabbed the costume. With an evil giggle, I donned it and twirled around in the sheer skirt that covered nothing. The corset was tight, making my small boobs stick out, but it's comfortable enough to move and... bend in.

Rolling up the stockings, I wore my heels and went to his room. It was the weekend, and I knew he didn't have any plans for the rest of the night.

I knocked on his door. "May I come in, Sir?" I asked in my best sultry tone.

"What do you want, Summer?" Damon replied, opening the door and staring at me with raised brows. He crossed his arms and leaned on the door frame. "What is this?"

I smiled, making sure he saw the bracelet on my hand, looking on the floor and getting into the role. "I was here to clean your room, Sir."

He stayed silent for a while and asked me, "You wanna be my maid, kitten?"

I nodded, clenching the see-through black skirt in my hand.

"Start cleaning the shelves first," he ordered. "I want them spotless."

I grumbled underneath my breath and gasped when he pushed me to the wall, flipping my skirt over my ass and landing a harsh spank on my ass. "Make this entire place shine, or I'll be pissed, kitten," he growled in my ear before leaving me alone in the hallway with a burn on my ass.

*Fuck.* I wanted him pissed.

But by the time I grabbed a duster and started cleaning, I got lost in the book titles. Ever since I had moved in, seeing his leadership and stock books placed beside my paranormal reverse harem books made me smile. The place was already spotless since the housekeeper cleaned everything thoroughly once a week.

I snapped out of my head when Damon cleared his throat. "Did you clean everything well?"

"Clean?" I asked and kept the book down when I realized I was still in the naughty maid costume with my tits spilling out. "Oh my god, I totally forgot I was trying to be a sexy maid for you."

He chuckled, playing with my loose hair. "It's okay."

I pouted and smoothed out the skirt. "I wanted to play out this whole fantasy, but I ruined it."

Damon tugged at the lock of hair, his eyes darkening. "Tell me about this fantasy."

I swallowed and whispered, "I… I am a naughty maid who sneaks into your room and finds your sex toys. And when you find me, you punish me."

He raised his brow. "I don't have any sex toys here."

I sighed. "Yeah, forget it."

"No, let's do something else. I still have to punish you for that day in the restaurant." He leaned down and kissed my cheek. "What's your safe word?"

My heartbeat thundered in my ears. "Red."

"And you promise to use it?" he asked.

"Yes, Sir."

"Good girl." He leaned back and sat down on the couch, spreading his legs wide. My mouth went dry when I eyed him shamelessly. Bare feet with gray sweatpants and a tight tee shirt that showed off his muscles. He looked edible.

"What were you doing in my room, kitten?" he asked, his voice deep.

I blinked. "Nothing."

"*Liar*," he said, looking me up and down. "You were touching your pretty pussy in my bed before I arrived home, weren't you?"

I widened my eyes and looked away, playing into the role. "I... I don't know what you're talking about, Sir."

I jumped when he smacked his thigh. "I hate liars, kitten. Tsk, what should I do with you?"

When I stayed silent, he said, "Kneel."

*Uh oh.*

## 34

# CRAWL TO ME

### DAMON

My hands clenched as Summer slowly kneeled on the carpet. She looked hot as fuck in the tiny maid costume. She didn't even need to wear it. She was practically naked. Her breathing increased when I stayed silent, anticipating what I'd say next.

"Come here," I said, eyeing her perfect tits.

She went to stand up, but I interrupted her, "I did not give you permission to stand." She kneeled again, her wide eyes on me as I said, "Crawl to me."

Her hands pressed on the carpet, and I spread my legs wider when she crawled, her tits spilling out of the corset, making me chuckle. She flushed but stayed kneeling between my legs.

"Tell me," I said, tilting her face towards me by holding her chin, "Whose pussy is it?"

She licked her lips, eyes drooping. "Yours, Sir."

"That's right, it's my cunt. So, you don't touch it unless I tell you to."

"I'm sorry, Sir," she whispered in her sultry voice, sounding not sorry at all. "I just got so horny that I—"

"I don't care. You don't touch it until I say so."

She frowned, her fingers twisting in her lap. "Or what? Would you put me over your knee?"

I chuckled darkly, and leaning closer, I whispered in her ear, "Oh, I will put you over my knee, but you'll have to beg for it."

I pulled away, relishing the way she trembled, clenching her legs together. I slapped her thigh. "Spread your legs."

She did, slowly, teasing me as the sheer skirt pinched high, exposing her soft brown skin. My mouth watered to kiss it, but I held back.

"Show me my pussy," I ordered. "I want to see how wet it is."

Summer lifted her skirt, too shy to meet my eyes, and I tsked. "Not shaved?" I sighed and said, "I prefer all sorts of hair, but I want you bare today. You know why?"

"Why, Sir?"

"So I can punish it properly," I said with a smile, her eyes going wide.

"Come on." I stood up and looked down at her. "Crawl to my room."

"Crawl?" Her face heated. "On the stairs—"

I held her jaw and glared at her. "Count yourself lucky that I'm being gentle with you, kitten. I don't mind putting you in a collar and leash all the time and making you beg for every damn thing. You understand?"

She nodded, and I pulled away. "Be a good fucking girl and keep your back arched, and ass high."

"Yes, Sir." Her voice was soft as she made her way to my room on all fours.

I smirked, seeing her shiver and climb the stairs, looking over my shoulder and quickly looking away. My cock hardened seeing her ass peek over the tiny skirt, her wet juices glistening over her pussy as I followed her, spanking her ass twice.

"On the bed," I said once we reached my room. I spread her legs and removed her stockings. I tied her hands together, looping it through the headboard so she wouldn't move.

"S-Sir?" she asked, her voice breathy, stretching on my bed, with bound hands, in nothing but a skimpy maid outfit with wet pussy.

"What?" I asked, tugging down the corset and making sure she could breathe and move around comfortably. I had some rope, and I wanted to tie her pretty body, so I took it out of the chest. "Do you want something?"

"Y-yes, I… My hands?"

Poor girl was so flustered, trying to close her legs.

"Your hands are fine as they are." I started with her chest, loosening the corset so I could loop ties around her breasts, asking to arch her back as I weaved the black rope from behind her and across her chest up to her neck in a pattern. I tightened it and smiled hearing the sharp intake of breath.

"Good?" I asked, making a knot as she nodded, biting her lip. I wanted her legs free for what I had in mind so I hummed and, taking another bit of rope, I looped it through her stockings and tied hands so every time she tried to squirm or move her hands, the rope around her chest and neck would tighten. Not painful enough to hurt her but definitely uncomfortable. Good thing my kitten was also a rope bunny.

I spread her thighs wider and said, "I'll edge you each time you try to close your legs, so keep them wide, kitten. I'll be right back, so don't try to run away."

I smirked, knowing full well she wouldn't be able to move. I picked up everything I needed from the washroom and walked back to the bedroom to find her squirming, tugging at her bonds.

"You look so pretty when you're tied up," I said, placing everything on the bed and raising her hips by putting pillows underneath her butt.

"What are you doing?"

"Shaving my pretty pussy," I said and paused, staring at her. "We didn't talk about this before. Do you want to say the safe word?"

Summer pursed her lips and shook her head. "I-it's okay."

"Are you sure?"

She nodded. "Just shave and fuck me, please."

I smirked and kissed her knee. I kept her skirt tugged up and made her spread her legs wider. I was glad to see her getting wet and applied the shaving cream for sensitive skin liberally on her pretty pussy. She squirmed and whimpered at the coldness, but she stayed still after one look from me.

I had to control myself from diving in and tasting the sweet nectar.

"Please don't cut me!" she said when I took the razor.

"Don't make me use a gag on you, kitten," I warned her and gently tugging her skin, I made the first scrape of razor. Hair came off, and I repeated my actions, focused on her pussy.

"It tickles," she whispered.

"Stay still," I said, continuing my pace. When I reached her lips, I told her to keep her legs still while I gently shaved them. Her clit was perking up, wanting my attention, but I kept shaving and cleaning the razor in between.

I was done with her pussy, so I raised her legs, but with her hands tied, I didn't think she would be comfortable, so I turned her around on her stomach, pressing her face down on the mattress as I spread her cheeks, applying the sensitive shaving cream.

"This feels embarrassing, Sir," she whimpered when I brought the razor to her skin. I kept my eyes on the ropes, smiling when she struggled, the rope tightening. It was going to leave marks, and I couldn't wait to lick them away once the scene was over.

"So?" I asked, shaving her and spanking her ass each time she tried to squirm away. "Your ass is so perky. A pretty gemstone would look perfect here, hm?"

"W-what?" she asked when I cleaned her up with a wet cloth, making sure I didn't miss any spot or cut her.

"I think you know what I mean, kitten," I said, clearing the bed and removing my shirt. "Maybe a tail plug for my kitten. With matching collar and leash."

"S-stop!" I knew if I saw her face, she'd be flustered. "Can you untie me?"

"No," I said, leaning close and licking her wet slit, splaying my hand on her lower back and pushing her down on the pillows when she jumped. "I like you tied up."

I squirted some lube on my fingers and her puckered hole. She gasped but started moaning when I rubbed her pussy before moving those fingers to her tight hole. She froze when I rubbed my finger around it and asked, "Color?"

"G-green, Sir."

I hummed and slowly slid my finger in. Fucking hell. She was tight as fuck. She groaned when I added another finger, my cock hardening as she clenched me, glistening juices leaking out of her pretty pussy.

"Do you want more, kitten?" I asked, fucking her ass with my fingers, making her ready for more.

"Fuck, please," she moaned when I spread her cheeks and licked her again, lowering and sucking her clit in my mouth. Her toes curled and her legs trembled, but I kept sucking and playing with her clit until she was close. "I'm… Sir, I'm going to cum."

I pulled back and spanked her pussy with my other hand. "No, you're not."

She whined, but it cut off into a moan when I started eating her out again while fucking her ass with my fingers. "Let me cum," she whispered, rocking her hips in my face.

"No, I don't think I will." I smacked her ass and squeezed it. "I love watching you squirm. Do you want to see how swollen and sensitive your pussy gets each time you get close and denied?"

"N-no, please let me cum!"

I chuckled and turned her around. I loosened the stockings from her wrists and cut down the rope attached to her chest. "Spread your legs for me," I said, taking dollops of lube and rubbing it over my cock.

Her chocolaty eyes were wide and full of lust as she spread her legs for me to settle between them. Her hands clutching her thighs and her pussy clenching at nothing. Fucking perfect.

"Good girl," I said and pushed her thighs back, lining myself against her ass. "You know why I'm fucking your ass missionary?"

She shook her head, her eyes wide when I gently slid my tip inside her, a twitch in her brow.

I lowered my hand on her thigh to her clit and slowly rubbed, knowing she was close. "So I can see your pretty cunt throb and leak for me."

She moaned, my cock sliding in deeper as she clenched me, clamping me inside her. I groaned as I went all the way in and stayed still, rubbing her clit as her juices slid down her pussy to where I was joined. The sight was so fucking hot that I was sure I'd cum if I kept staring at her pretty holes.

They were mine.

I fucked her, clenching my teeth and clenching her thigh. "Your holes are mine, kitten."

"Y-yes!" she gasped, squeezing her eyes shut.

I spanked her pussy and fucked her ass. "You are mine."

Her half-lidded eyes stared at me as she nodded. "Yours, Sir."

"Yes, mine," I growled and kept my slow pace. "Look how wet your pussy is when I'm ignoring it and fucking your tight little ass."

She whimpered, her orgasm so close that she started begging, "Please, please, please, I'm so close."

"Cum for me, kitten," I groaned, slamming inside her as she squirted, her pussy twitching and clenching when I kept rubbing her clit, filling up her ass.

"Such a good girl," I murmured as I emptied my balls and slowly slid out of her ass. I stroked her legs and then let her calm down from the high as I quickly cleaned up in the washroom.

When I came back to the bedroom with my sweatpants on, she was still in the same position, her legs stretched out. I snipped the rope binding her and kissed her forehead. "You did so well, pretty girl. I'm proud of you," I said sincerely, massaging the rope markings and kissing them.

Summer hummed and let me take care of her, but she still had lust gleaming in her eyes. I tucked her hair behind her ear and asked, "What is it, kitten?"

She bit her lip, her eyes lowering down my abs to the bulge in my sweatpants. "I want to give you a blowjob," she whispered, her eyes begging.

I froze. I wasn't expecting her to say that. I thought she'd ask me to go down on her, and I'd have gladly done it, but hearing her beg so prettily, I couldn't say no to her.

"Will you make it sloppy?"

"Yes, Sir."

"Will you cry for me, kitten?"

Her eyes snapped at me, and her throat bobbed as she swallowed. "Y-yes, Sir."

## 35

# EAGER GIRL

### SUMMER

y heart pounded in my chest with anticipation when Damon sat on the edge of the bed after making sure my ass wasn't sore. I blushed and said it wasn't. I loved how filthy and gentle he was. His dirty words made me horny and relaxed me. The fact that I squirted and came so hard because of him made me want to please him even more. I had been dying to taste him in my mouth for months.

I was still in the skimpy outfit as I knelt between his legs, licking my lips at the sight of his pretty cock. That was the word I'd use to describe it. Long with thick girth and hard veins all over it. The red mushroom head was already leaking with pre-cum. It was slightly curved, so it was perfect in every position to rub against my G-spot and make me cum.

I looked at him through my lashes. His jaw clenched as I spread my legs and licked my palms before wrapping them around his base. His shaky breath encouraged me as I slowly stroked him, leaning close and licking his pre-cum. He smelled like soap and *male*. The bittersweet taste of his cum made me want to show how hungry I was for his dick.

"*Fuck*," he groaned when I took him in my mouth, sucking it before pulling it out and meeting his eyes as I continued twisting my hands over his base.

"Did you like that, Sir?" I asked, my voice husky as I licked my lips, waiting for his answer. I knew oral sex was off-limits for him, but I wanted to show him how good it could be.

"Yes, take my cock in your mouth again," he ordered, his eyes dark, making me smile.

"Gladly." And I did, moaning as his girth stretched my lips, the head of his cock brushing my throat and triggering my gag reflex.

But I stayed still, tears glistening in my eyes, before I pulled back and repeated my actions. I hummed when he held my hair and caressed my hollowed cheeks. I stroked his balls that were full. He groaned, his hips jerking and making me gag on his cock.

"You're such an eager girl," he grunted when I deep throated him, tears sliding out of my eyes. "So pretty when you cry."

I moaned, my pussy getting wetter at his dirty talk. I pulled away to take a deep breath, a long string of saliva and his cum trailing from the tip of his cock as I licked my lips before diving in again.

"Cry for me," he groaned, gagging me with his cock and slowly fucking my face. I kept my hands on his thighs for if I wanted to use the safe gesture and tap out, but hearing his moans, having him in control was so erotic that I didn't care. I had tears sliding down my cheeks. I was wetter than ever, pleasing him as he kept praising me.

"That's my good girl."

"So gorgeous, with my cock in your mouth."

"Look how cock-drunk and pretty you look."

"Fuck," he cursed, his hips jerking and abs clenching. "Swallow my cum."

I nodded, eager as his hand tightened on my hair. "Don't waste a single drop or I'll make you lick it off the floor," he warned, my eyes turning heady as I sucked him, hollowing my cheeks.

One thrust later he was coming, exploding at the back of my throat as I squeezed my eyes shut and swallowed. His cum was bittersweet, and there was a lot that it escaped my lips and slid down my neck.

"Fuck," he gasped when he pulled out, his pupils dilated as he cupped my cheek and said, "Show me."

I licked my lips and opened my mouth to show him that I had swallowed.

"Good girl," he whispered, surprising me with a kiss.

I had never been kissed after giving a blow job, but he kissed me as if he was grateful. I kissed him back, moaning when he cradled me in his lap, his dick brushing against my inner thigh.

"You were so good, kitten," he whispered, pulling away. I clenched my hands on his shoulders when his eyes turned full of mischief. "You ready to cum for me?"

"Yes, Sir," I said, biting my lip.

I should have said no. Because Damon was an insatiable sex monster and didn't understand the meaning of overstimulation.

"P-please!" I whimpered, tears glistening in my eyes as I tried to twist away from him. But his hold was firm, keeping my legs spread on his lap as I faced the mirror, his chest behind me as he kept rubbing circles on my clit. "I can't take it anymore."

"Shh," he purred, kissing my neck. "I decide what you can and can't take."

I cried out, closing my eyes shut when I came once more. I had lost the count after the third orgasm, and he didn't look like he wanted to stop anytime soon.

He cupped my jaw and made me look at our reflection. "Look how hot you look, kitten," he whispered. "My pretty little slut."

My hair was ruffled, the costume askew as my thighs kept shivering. I felt exposed in the best way possible. His veiny hands manhandling me and his fingers glistening as he kept curling out one orgasm after the other. His eyes were no longer gray but pure obsidian. I could feel his hard cock, but he didn't care. He just wanted me to cum.

"P-please," I gasped, trying to twist away from his touch on my clit.

He sighed and kept his chin on my shoulder. "You want to stop?"

I nodded wordlessly.

"Too bad, I don't want to," he said, kissing my cheek, and he spanked my pussy, making me jump. "If you want to stop, try to run away, kitten. I know how much you love primal play."

I swallowed and turned to look at him. "Promise you'll stop if you don't catch me?"

Damon smiled at me, and that should have been my warning. "Pinky promise."

I nodded, standing up on wobbly legs, and gasped when he spanked my ass. "I'd start running and hide if I were you."

I took his words seriously and ran out of his room. Thankfully, his house was huge and there were lots of places for me to hide in. Adrenaline pumped in my veins as I looked around the living room and kitchen to find a cupboard small enough for me to squeeze into.

"Ready or not, here I come." I trembled at hearing his voice. He was whistling as I heard him walk out of his room.

Fear and anticipation kicked in, and I made my way to the laundry room. The washing machine was on, so he wouldn't be able to hear my breathing. It was small enough for two people, so I could lean on the corner comfortably.

My sheer skirt brushed over my thigh, tickling me as I heard him in the living room. "Where are you, kitten?" He sounded like he was having fun. "Are you hiding here? *No.*" He was opening each cupboard and closing it.

I held my breath when I heard him walk past the laundry room to check the guest room and the office room downstairs. I covered my mouth when I heard nothing.

The machine beeped with its buzzer and then it turned off. My eyes widened when I realized my mistake. I hadn't turned off the lights in the laundry room, and he could see the shadows of my feet. And so could I.

The knob turned and my stomach tightened when he stepped in, looming over me with a smirk. "Found you, kitten."

"D-Damon, please no—*mmgh!*"

36

# BREED ME

## DAMON


Seeing her face full of surprise and shock was euphoric. Seeing her try to fight me was even better.

"D-Damon, please no—*mmgh!*" I held her by the back of her neck and pushed her over the washing machine, bending her over.

"Shh," I said, turning the machine on and spreading her legs. "Be a good kitten."

I chuckled at her failed attempts to fight me. Her skirt was getting in the way, so I ripped off the tiny fabric and pinned her down with my weight.

"Damon?" I crooned, pulling out my cock. "I thought it was Sir, you dirty slut."

"Please, I can't!" she whined, trying to push her back at me, but I kept my hand on her neck, lining my cock against her slit.

"Shut the fuck up and take my cock," I growled, bending her over as the vibrations of the washing machine rumbled through her core. "I warned you not to get caught. Tsk, it's your own fault, kitten."

"Please—no, *ah!*" She begged, but I didn't care until she

said the safe word or did the safe gesture. Even though she was at her limit, Summer wanted more.

I slid inside her in one thrust, her walls clenching me deliciously as I groaned with her. It felt so good. I usually gave her time to accommodate my size, but I didn't feel like being gentle, so I held her wrists behind her back, pinning them with my hand and I retreated before slamming inside her warm cunt.

"You have no idea how amazing you feel on my cock," I growled, her cries of pain and pleasure increasing as I fucked her over the washing machine.

"Too much," she whimpered when I pinned her over the machine, making sure she felt the vibrations on her clit. Fuck, how I wished to overstimulate her with a wand or a vibe and make her nice and sensitive for me.

"Shh, you're taking me so well."

Our harsh breathing bounced in the small room, the air hovering with the scent of sex and her feminine arousal. Sounds of our groans mingled with skin slapping against each other, and the whirr of the machine surrounded us.

My other hand dug into her ass cheek, slapping it from time to time as her moans turned softer and longer, which meant she was close. I kept my pace rough and deep. The sight of my veiny cock covered in her juices entering her sopping pussy was enough to send me over the edge.

Her orgasm came hard and fast, her body turning limp as she came moaning my name.

"Good girl," I whispered in her ear, increasing my thrusts. "Give me one more."

Summer whimpered, staying limp on the machine as I used both my hands to hold her hips to fuck her. I was close, but I wanted her to cum again and make a mess.

"Go on, come for me, good girl. I know you can," I said,

stroking her back and kissing her neck. "You deserve to cum more, love. Give me one more."

She made a small sound as I drove inside her like a man possessed, rubbing her clit faster and applying pressure. She was extremely sensitive, thanks to the previous orgasms, that she came with a low groan, clenching me so hard that I exploded inside her.

"Good girl," I said, feeling the wetness in my hand and knowing she had squirted. I hovered over her, catching my breath as I kissed her hair. "You did so good."

"I can't move," she said in a low voice, and I groaned when she reached down with her hand to where we were united. She groaned. "Fuck, you fill me up so well."

I pulled out and grunted at the sight of my cum sliding out of her pussy. "I want to breed you—without getting you pregnant," I said, sliding my fingers inside her, making sure my cum stayed inside.

She trembled and looked over her shoulder. "Breed me, Sir," she whispered, biting her lip.

"Fuck, Summer," I squeezed my eyes shut. "Give me ten before I can pin you down and breed you."

"N-no." She instantly pulled away, her legs wobbly, so I held her, supporting her against the machine. "T-that's enough for today."

I smirked, wrapping my hands around her waist and kissing her. "Shower together?"

"Only if you promise not to tease me," she pouted.

I kissed her pout. She looked so beautiful in post-coital bliss that I wanted to take a picture. Her brown eyes were bright and shining, face glowing, and her freckles were stark against her blush.

"You know that's never going to happen."

She rolled her eyes and looked down at the mess we both had made. "I'm sorry for... this."

"Don't be. I love making a mess out of you."

Her stomach growled and I chuckled, taking her in my arms and carrying her upstairs to my room. "First shower, and then dinner. Sounds good?"

"*Perfect*!" She beamed, snuggling herself closer to my chest, my heart aching. "By the way, I didn't know having sex over the washing machine can be so… *fun*."

"I'm glad you had fun, kitten," I said, checking the water temperature and helping her out of the costume which I had ripped away. "I'll buy you more naughty outfits for more of our scenes."

"There's more?" Her eyes widened, making me chuckle. "Sheesh, I can barely feel my clit right now. I don't think I can handle more."

I hummed when we were both in the bath, her back against my chest. "If I'm going to breed your hot little body, it's going to take some time," I said, caressing her waist.

I chuckled when she splashed water over my face. "Stop being so dirty. You're on time out. I can't think when you speak so much filth."

I smiled, hugging her close, and pressed a kiss on her cheek. I didn't want the contract to end.

* * *

THE NEXT WEEK, I PREPARED HOW I WOULD ASK MY EMPLOYEES for the event night that was postponed since Summer and I were sick. I had already sent out a notice to meet up at the front of the building on Friday evening.

Seeing them gather around me made me nervous, but Summer and Void liked what I had said the previous night. *Speaking of, where the fuck is she?*

"Is everybody here?" Rahul asked, and they all said yes in unison.

I loosened my tie and cleared my throat. "I know I'm sometimes difficult and demand a lot out of each and every one of you." They all nodded, Rahul covering his mouth to hide his laugh with a cough. "And besides the yearly bonuses, I have never taken the time to thank you properly or acknowledge your talents, so..."

I couldn't find Summer in the crowd, but I had already planned everything, so we needed to be on time. "So, today's night is on me. I, along with my assistant, Rahul, have planned this employee-bonding event, which is just another word for having fun... together."

I cleared my throat, seeing the confused looks on their faces as they whispered to each other.

Thankfully, Rahul stepped in and said with a grin, "What he means by that is we are going to laser tag, and the winning team gets free coupons for Moore Beauty!" They all cheered, clapping, and I sighed in relief. "After the game, we will go for dinner, drinks and end the night at a karaoke bar. Who's ready to empty our boss's pockets? I know I fucking am!" Rahul cheered the loudest, laughing and freezing when he saw my expression and cleared his throat. "I think they like it, Sir," he whispered, stepping back.

"I can see that," I deadpanned and nodded when the employees thanked me before filling the bus I had booked for the night.

"Where the fuck is Summer?" I asked Rahul, and he shrugged.

"Her shoot for the ad finished this afternoon, and I think she left after that."

"Left?" I frowned, checking our messages. She hadn't told me anything about leaving. Where was she?

We waited outside as the excited chatter of my employees wafted through the bus. If it wasn't for Summer, I didn't think I would have done anything to show my genuine gratitude for them. They worked hard and didn't question me when we had to pull some all-nighters during product releases. There was a reason that Moore Beauty was always sold out at Sephora among other beauty stores, and I was glad that my mother had handled her brand well before passing away.

"Hi!" I turned around, ready to scold Summer, but my mouth parted when she walked up to me. "Did you wait for long?"

I was speechless. She looked stunning and...

Wow.

Dressed in sneakers, cute shorts and top with her hair reaching her shoulders, she looked younger than she did before, and adorable. I liked her longer hair, but I loved the short hair on her.

"Damon?" She frowned, blinking at me.

I closed my mouth and looked away, scratching my neck. "You are late."

Summer rolled her eyes and thanked Rahul by hugging him in front of me when he complimented her on her new look.

I glared at him when Summer stepped inside the bus.

"I'm going to kill you," I warned him before entering the bus.

"In laser tag, right?" he asked, following me.

I didn't reply, sitting beside Summer.

# CAPTOR AND CAPTIVE

## SUMMER

Before I got my hair done, I was stopped outside the Moore Beauty building by a man. An old man with white hair and an unkempt beard and clothes. His teeth were yellow as he asked me if I knew Damon.

"What do you want?" I crossed my arms, staring him down. He didn't know I knew him, but I did. The only similarity between him and Damon were their gray eyes.

He chuckled, its sound hoarse and empty. "Then you also know that he's a piece of shit, girl."

I stayed quiet, wanting him to continue, and he did, thinking I was dumb enough to listen to him. "You should be with someone better. Heck," he whistled, looking me up and down, and I knew the guard by the building was getting suspicious. "You should come with me and sign with us. We are a huge entertainment media company, and the pay is good. Work is like pleasure." He ended with a dirty smirk.

My palm itched to slap him. I knew what his entertainment media company was. He was trying to woo me into signing with his porn brand which was so outdated that it had negative reviewers. No wonder he said work was like pleasure.

"If I see you again near me or Damon, I will call the cops." He looked taken aback and stepped back at my harsh, cold tone. I straightened my back and said, "Stay out of your son's life. Stop calling him with empty threats. I know he sends you allowance." I scoffed, looking him up and down like he did me and pushed my hair over my shoulder. "If you want to keep receiving that allowance, you'll heed me. If not, I will tell Damon what you did today. And trust me, I don't think he'd be as kind as me, Robert."

I didn't wait for him to reply before I turned away and blew out the breath I was holding. I knew Robert was mad and disgusted, but I didn't think he'd have the gall to approach me in broad daylight, right outside the building, while Damon was still inside. I wished I had punched him.

* * *

Damon was quiet. Too quiet.

"Do you want to say something?" I asked him. Everyone looked so happy, talking to each other and singing random songs.

He looked at me, at my hair, which was shorter than before, and nodded. "You look... *nice*."

I pursed my lips. "Thanks."

It was Damon, so I didn't question his compliment. It felt so much lighter than before, and the hairdresser had added curtain bangs which framed my face perfectly. I loved my new hair.

"Your hair," Damon said, and I looked at him. "I love your hair."

"Thank you, Damon."

"I can't wait to tug at it when I'm fuck—"

*"Damon."* I slapped my hand on his mouth, my cheeks flushing red. "That's more than enough."

He stayed quiet, and I moved my hand away, hoping no one heard him.

"Are you ready for tomorrow?" he asked when we reached the place. It looked like an arcade, but it was the biggest laser tag in LA.

"You mean our drive?" I asked him as we followed everyone inside. It was dark, and I held my breath when Damon held my hand.

"Yes."

I looked around at the glowing lights as everyone talked about guns and how to shoot well. The air smelled like cheap room freshener, with mist covering the entrance. I was so excited to shoot people when the employee explained how to shoot, where to shoot, and not to cover our sensors. We followed her to the gear room as everyone strapped in their gear.

"I just wish we could bring Void with us," I said to Damon, seeing him remove his suit jacket. I and a few of the girls stopped and gawked as he rolled the sleeves of his shirt, exposing his slutty forearms.

*Focus, Summer.*

"Me too, but I'm sure Rahul will take care of him," he replied, frowning at my chest and walking over to me to tighten the straps for the sensors. "You ready?"

I nodded, too tongue-tied by his exposed arms to think about anything else. We made our way to the hallway and got divided into two teams. I was with Rahul, and Damon was on our enemy team. The game was simple. At the end of the round, whichever team has the most kills wins.

Adrenaline pumped through me as we went to our own sites. I rolled my shoulders back and stretched my legs. I was ready to fight with a toy gun in my hand.

The first five minutes of the game were pure bloodshed. Sounds of screams and laughter surrounded the arena, echoing off the spongy walls bathed in darkness. I crouched when I saw the enemy team and quickly shot one man on his sensor. He pretended to die, making me giggle as I disappeared into another alley, making sure Damon wasn't nearby.

I knew he'd be ruthless and wouldn't leave anyone alive. Even me.

After killing two more people in the game, I heard Rahul cry out, "Hide, Summer! Only Damon's alive, and he's coming your way."

Someone scolded Rahul from the enemy team for giving me such crucial information, and I snuck into a cornered wall, making sure my entire body was in the darkness as I eyed the pillar where Damon should walk in from.

"Found you, kitten."

I squealed, but Damon covered my mouth, towering over me and pressing my back to him. "Shh, be quiet."

"What are you doing?" I asked, eyeing the sensor on his chest. Just one second and I could shoot him and win the game for our team.

"I'm flirting with my fake girlfriend," he said, leaning down to kiss me.

I stopped him and narrowed my eyes at him. "We are enemies right now."

He raised his brow and shook his head. "I'm your captor and you are my hot little captive, Summer."

"Captive?" I snickered, wrapping my arms around his neck.

"Yes," he whispered, running his hand down my back to squeeze my ass. "Can we leave early after dinner? Your ass looks amazing in these shorts, and I'm getting distracted."

I gasped and pushed him away. "Damon, behind you!"

He turned quickly, shielding me with his body. My gun was ready when he turned around, "There's nothing—"

I shot him and cheered. "I won!"

Damon glared at me and said, "That's cheating."

I said cheekily, "All is fair in love and war."

I spanked my ass as I sprung out of the arena, laughing and hugging my team. Before we left, Damon announced that everyone would get free beauty coupons. I was happy to see him talking to others and not be in his cocoon anymore.

"He has changed." I looked beside me at Rahul, who was smiling at his boss. He glanced at me and said, "I'm glad you are here, Summer. Because of you, he is being more of himself, and everyone here can see that."

I got flustered and watched Damon smile at someone's joke. He was smiling. What a surprise!

After the laser tag game, we ate at a really cozy Asian place. We had sushi and drank lots of sake before going to the karaoke bar. I was the first one to grab the mic, since I was tipsy, and chose the corniest Taylor Swift song and cried my heart out.

"Wasn't that good?" I asked, smiling at Damon as I took another shot glass.

He took it away from me and drank it himself. "Yeah, no. We'd be glad if no one sued you for damaging their ears with your vocals."

I thought about dunking a glass of water on him but decided against it in the end. "*Rude*," I mumbled into an empty glass. "I bet I can sing better than you, though, you grumpy ass."

He hummed and walked to the stage. My eyes widened, and I sat up straighter on the bar stool as he sang a Taylor Swift song, making half of the population at the bar swoon. I was pouting when strangers tried to hit on him after his song ended so I walked up to him, wrapping my arms around his waist. Shooting daggers at the women, I told him, "Let's go home."

Unfortunately, I couldn't remember what happened afterwards because I passed out.

* * *

"Are we there yet?" I asked for the umpteenth time, nibbling on sour patches and scrolling through songs on the radio.

"I wish I had brought a ball gag," Damon muttered, running a hand through his hair and keeping his eyes on the road.

"I think it'd suit you," I replied, earning me a glance.

"Not sure about that. Maybe a ring gag for you. So, I can use that bratty mouth of yours whenever I want," he replied, squeezing my bare thigh.

I didn't reply and looked out of the window to hide my flustered face. He was so filthy!

"How much longer?" I asked after a minute. I really tried to stay quiet, but my brain wasn't having it. "I'm getting bored."

He sighed. "We are late because you decided to wake up at noon."

"Not my fault you didn't wake me up—"

"I tried, but you slept like a log. And you were snoring."

I gaped. "I do not snore!"

"Sure thing, love."

I shook my head at his smug face and leaned my head back. Tomorrow we will reach Coral Springs.

38

# ONE BED

## SUMMER

"What do you mean you have only one bed?" Damon demanded. "I booked it online."

The receptionist of the small motel where we had stopped for the night yawned and pointed at the small poster that said that they didn't accept online bookings. "Either stay in the room or leave. We don't care."

Damon's nose flared, and I was surprised that the receptionist hadn't turned to ashes from his glare. "Fine. Then give me a refund. We will go somewhere else."

He pointed to another policy that stated they didn't offer refunds.

Damon scoffed, pulling out his phone. "I can sue you for this—"

I held his arm, stopping him. "Damon, it's fine."

We had sex in the same bed, but we never shared it afterwards. If I was passed out on his bed, he'd sleep in the guest room, or I'd take a shower and go to my room.

"Are you sure?" he asked, frowning.

I nodded. "I'm sure."

Damon picked up our bags, and I took the key to our

room, and admired the small bed in the middle with a dresser to the side. At least there was a small balcony.

"This is ridiculous," he said underneath his breath, and I agreed. Damon would dwarf the bed, but we didn't have any options. Might as well cuddle the grumpy bear for a night, hoping he won't eat me by the morning.

"It's okay." I sat down on the bed, its bed springs creaking. "At least, it's comfortable."

He sighed and closed the door, leaving us both alone in the room. With one bed. I had read too many enemies-to-lovers vampire romances to know what happens if the enemies share one bed for a night.

I changed into my pajamas and brushed my teeth beside Damon, who used an electric toothbrush and eyed me when I tried to make him laugh mid-brushing.

"Are you okay?" He asked, foam on his lips.

I closed my eyes and shook my head. I was glad he was still Damon and hadn't completely changed.

Once I was done with my skincare, I found him hogging more than half of the bed, reading some self-help book. My lips curled in distaste. "You are taking too much space. Move," I ordered, getting underneath the blanket.

"You're tiny. I need more room," he retorted, closing his book and turning off his lights, bathing the room in complete darkness.

I could hear him breathe beside me as I wriggled my leg around him. "I need more room, too. I have long limbs."

I could hear him rolling his eyes, and I yelped when he pressed closer to me, wrapping his arms around me. "Shh. Don't move. The blanket is too small."

It was small.

His hands were large and warm against my stomach.

"Are you planning to hold my breast and sleep?" I asked after a while.

He slid his hand up my stomach to my breast, making me smile.

"Goodnight."

"Night, kitten."

* * *

I WOKE UP WITH A MOAN AND ROUGH HANDS HOLDING MY HIPS.

"Damon?" I mumbled sleepily, prying open my eyes and moaning when I felt him rubbing my clit. "W-what…?"

My question died in my mouth as I looked at his bedhead and handsome face between my legs. My night shirt was open, nipples hard and poking the air, pants missing.

"Don't stop," I said, pulling his head closer and closing my eyes as he ate me out.

It was my fantasy, but I never thought someone would be brave enough to fulfill it. Especially in a motel with a tiny bed and an even tinier blanket.

I whined when he stopped just before I could cum and turned me on my stomach. I stretched my hands out as he slid inside me in a slow thrust. I moaned into the sheets, breathing through the pinch of pain as his girth stretched me.

He fucked me in prone bone, his grunts and growl and morning raspy voice doing terrible things to me. "Going to breed you," he groaned, fucking me hard and deep, tugging at my short hair and kissing my neck. "Tell me you love it."

"No," I moaned, scrunching the sheets. "I hate it."

"Hate it?" he asked, spanking my ass. "You liar."

I pushed him. "I hate it and want to forget it."

He stopped, and I wondered if he took it too seriously. After a second, he chuckled darkly, making my toes curl. I cried out when he pulled me back by my hair, growling in my ear, "You want to forget everything? I'll make you fucking forget."

My lips parted when he slammed inside me with furious thrusts, his hand smacking against my ass from time to time. But I didn't give in until he turned me around and threw my legs over his shoulder.

"Oh, fuck," I gasped when he went deeper than ever before, stretching me out and leaning in closer.

"Tell me you hate me," he rasped, his pubic bone grinding against my clit bringing me closer and closer to the edge. "Tell me."

I looked at his handsome face, his gray eyes and the stubble on his jaw. "I hate you so much."

He nodded, increasing his speed and making me cum on his cock. I was still shaking through the aftershocks when he lifted me up and bent me over the small sink, fucking me again.

I had to keep my hands against the mirror as he thrusted hard and deep. My earrings, which I had forgotten to remove before bed, jingled with each thrust.

"Fucking love how your earrings clang each time I fuck you," he whispered, his eyes pinned on them. I bit my lip from moaning when he raised one of my legs over the sink, fucking me faster.

"Oh my god," I uttered when he came inside me, his warm cum painting the insides of my walls. "Fuck… fuck—*ah!* Fuck fuck fuck."

"What happened?" Damon asked, his eyes wide as pain shot up my leg, which he bent over the sink. I jumped around, naked and cum sliding out on my thigh as the sudden pain made me wobbly.

"*Cramps!*" I gritted through the pain, tears glistening in my eyes. "I got leg cramps."

"Oh, shit." He picked me up and laid me down on the bed,

slowly stretching my right leg. "I'm sorry, love. Just take a deep breath."

I shook my head. "It hurts!"

"Just trust me and do it."

I glared at him and took a deep breath. He pulled at it, and I was about to scream bloody murder when the pain disappeared. I sighed, looking at the ceiling.

"All well?"

"I hate you," I replied. "Bend me like that again and I'm twisting your dick."

"*Ouch.*" Damon winced. "Let me make up for it."

I watched him take my feet in his lap. He gently massaged each toe, his thumb pressing into the arch of my feet, making me sigh and moan.

"To be fair," he said, his sexy hands working magic with my feet. "I thought you'd be more flexible."

"Damon," I said, and when he looked at me, I continued, "Don't make me kick you in the face."

He chuckled and kissed my feet. "Yes, ma'am."

# 39

# REMEMBER THAT

## DAMON

My hand tightened on the steering wheel when we drove through the 'Welcome to Coral Springs!' board. I had accepted Emma's request to look after Moore Beauty in order to escape the small town. I had to escape.

"Are you sure?" Summer said on the phone, glancing at me. "Okay. Yes, yes, mom. Bye, see you soon. Love you."

She ended the call with a sigh and looked at me expectantly.

"What did she say?"

Summer pursed her lips. "My parents are hosting a house dinner, and they have invited everyone. Including you."

I swallowed before replying, "I have some things to do, so I might be late."

"*Oh?*" She raised her brow, expecting me to tell her what things I had to do, but I stayed quiet. I wasn't ready to talk about it to her yet.

"You have product shoots right now?" I asked, changing the subject. "And then I think a magazine shoot?"

She looked down at her lap. "Yeah, I'll be busy."

"Good luck."

We stayed quiet for the rest of the journey as awkward silence hung in the air. It was a first for us for a long time. We had spent nights watching movies, documentaries, listening to her erotic audiobooks and recreating our favorite scenes and even roleplaying at the sex club during an auction event. But we never had been this awkward before.

And I knew I was to blame. But I felt too vulnerable.

It was Dorothy's death anniversary, after all.

I dropped her off at her parent's house. I cupped her cheek and leaned in to kiss her, pressing my lips on her forehead. "Have fun," I muttered, seeing the disappointment in her eyes.

"You too," she replied in a low voice before grabbing her bags and leaving me without a second glance.

I took a deep breath and made my way to the prison. Summer deserved better, but I was a selfish prick, and if I had to get better to have her in my life, then I would.

* * *

"RIGHT THIS WAY," THE OFFICER SAID WHEN I DROPPED MY CELL phone in the tray. The gloomy atmosphere of prison made me on edge. All walls covered in white as prisoners and criminals in orange played basketball inside the fence surrounded by guards holding guns.

"No one has ever requested to meet him before," the chatty officer said, eyeing me over his shoulder. "You a relative?"

"Something like that," I replied, not explaining further.

My hands clenched and unclenched when he showed me a room. Walls were gray and there was a partition in the middle. I sat in the creaking metal chair and held my breath.

The door across from me clicked as he stepped in, his hands cuffed in front with an annoyed look on his face.

The air changed, and I held my breath as I looked into the eyes of my brother's killer. Dominick. I didn't know his last name, and even though I demanded it with an offer of ten grand, the officer didn't give it to me. He was a special prisoner, they said. Someone not to mess with.

"Mr. Dominick," I said, keeping my voice level as he turned his chair around and sat on it, propping his chin on the metal back of the chair. He looked younger than me. Covered in tattoos, with olive skin and soulless eyes.

"What do you want?" he asked, tilting his head. "You seem too posh for me to remember. Did I kill one of your family?"

He chuckled as if it was a joke.

"Yes, you did," I said, leaning close to the partition, my hands on the cold metal.

Dominick smirked. He didn't care that he had murdered someone. Too confident and cocky.

"How much?" I asked, counting down the seconds. Even though I knew I was safe with the guards surrounding us, and there was no way a human could pass through the iron bars in front of him, my body knew that he was a killer and wanted to get away from him.

Secretly, I was glad. So glad that he killed Drake.

"How much what, sunshine?" he drawled.

I closed my eyes and sighed. "How much money do you want for killing my brother?"

"Oh?" His obsidian eyes lit up, his accent coming through. He wasn't American. "I killed your brother. Who was it?"

"Drake Grant." Even saying his name filled me with disgust. "He stalked our half-sister and tried to... tried to harass her. Sexually."

Dominick whistled. "I know that fucker."

He leaned closer, a smile on his lips. The hair on the back of my neck rose. "Do you want to know how I killed him?"

I stayed quiet.

His smile widened, an evil gleam in his eyes. "I hate rapists. So, I chopped off his dick and pinned it to his room before gutting him."

I swallowed, clenching my hands into fists.

"Do you want to know his last words?" he asked, taking out a box of cigarettes and a lighter from his pocket. When I stayed silent, he lit up his cigarette and said, "He said he loved Emma. Tell her I love her."

The look on my face must have told him everything I know as he blew out smoke and tsked. "He was stalking your sister, and what did you do?" he asked, cocking a brow. "Helped him?"

"I got help to protect her," I said in a bitter voice and stood up. "I had paid someone else to kill him, but you got to him before he did."

Dominick chuckled and stood up, taking another drag. He was the same height as me but leaner. *How could someone so young be able to kill?*

"I don't need your money, sunshine," he said, eyeing my Patek Philippe. "I have more than you have."

Somehow, I didn't doubt that.

"Then why are you here?"

He hummed. "Would you believe me if I said I killed a guy with my shoelace so I can have a vacation here?"

I blinked at him. Of course, he did.

Unbuttoning my suit, I pulled out my card holder and pressed it on the metal slab. I slid it through the tiny dome of glass to his side and said, "Call me if you need anything."

He grinned, picking up the card and reading my name, "Damon Grant. Hm." He pocketed it. "You are now insured by the mafia. If you need help, you know where to find me."

*Mafia?*

My eyes widened when he winked at me and walked out of the room. He moved like he was relaxed, as if he was strolling in his home.

I exhaled and left the room, my shoulders more relaxed than before. I didn't care if some mafia or the guy I had paid killed Drake. I was glad he was dead and rotting somewhere.

One more stop before I could go back to Summer.

My heart felt heavy when I reached the cemetery, a bouquet of lilies sitting on the passenger seat. I held it and forced myself to get out of the car. My legs felt like lead as I made my way through the graves, then stopping at the one that said, 'Dorothy Moore. A loving mother and superstar.' I scoffed at how superficial it was.

She was never loving or was ever a mother to either of her children. If she could, she would just be known as a superstar. Not a mother or a wife.

"Hello, Mother," I said, looking around at the empty cemetery, and sighed. "This scene doesn't suit you. I'm sure you'd rather get buried on Hollywood streets than here."

Wind breezed past me, ruffling my tie as I opened the letter she had written for me. I didn't open it when her will was read because I was a selfish bastard who cared more about her assets than what she had to say.

I had thought of burning it or throwing it in the bin without ever opening it, but I had kept it. For *this* day.

I took a deep breath and opened it. Clearing my throat, I started reading it, "Damon, my perfect son. I know you wouldn't believe me when I say this, but… I love you. I always have. It means nothing now, but I'm sorry for abandoning you with those two monsters. You didn't deserve it." Tears blurred my vision as my voice broke. "You didn't deserve what Robert or Drake… what even I put you through. Just know that I never hated you. I don't know why

I'm writing this, but I feel that my end is nearing soon. I hope you will look after yourself and find someone to love other than your work and money. I'm proud of you and I will always be your mother. Love, Dorothy."

I crumpled the paper as the bouquet slipped from my hand and fell on her grave. Tears slid down my face as I glared at her grave through them. I kneeled down, hiding my face and wishing she was alive, just for a moment, so I could both yell at her and hug her.

"*How dare you…,*" I said, wiping the tears and glaring at her. "How dare you write shit like this and let Drake and Lincoln get away with everything?"

My voice increased, and all I felt was anger. "How dare you make Emma go through the same shit I suffered through! Do you know how many times I thought of fucking dying?" I was shouting, blaming her for everything. "How disgusted I felt when Drake forced me for all those years—"

I covered my mouth to stop a sob and paced around, angry tears pooling out of my eyes at the flashback of him entering my room and touching me and telling me that it's what all brothers do. That it was okay.

"You could have listened to me once," I said, much calmer than before. "Just once. That's all I asked, but you didn't. You thought Drake was bullying me and waved it off. And guess what?" I laughed. "He stalked your precious daughter. If you could at least have done something, then only one of us would have gone through the trauma, and Emma would have been fine."

My nose flared and I threw her crumpled letter at her grave. "Keep these fake apologies and doting words to yourself. You couldn't say them to me when you were alive, and they don't mean shit when you are dead. Goodbye, Mom."

I fixed my tie and walked out of the cemetery.

My phone rang as I strapped my seat belt. I picked it up. "What do you want?" I demanded.

"I saw you at your mother's grave," he replied, and I looked around to see there wasn't any other car than mine. "It was very dramatic, you know. Even for you."

I clenched my jaw. "Tell me what—"

"That girl of yours, Summer, eh? She's mighty pretty."

"I told you to forget about her, Father," I said, my hand clenching on the wheel. "I'm warning you to stay away from her and forget about us."

He tsked. "How can I forget such a pretty thing? I thought I should remind you that you're just like me, son."

"I'm not."

"No. You're incapable of loving someone, Damon. Remember that." My hand tightened on the steering wheel, my eyes gleaming when he continued. "I called to say goodbye."

"Goodbye? What? You're going somewhere?"

I was joking, but he stayed quiet. I straightened up.

"I met her, and she's a feisty one." I was about to threaten him and ask him where he was so I could talk to him face to face. "Don't worry, I don't care about used goods. I'll leave you alone. Tell Emma to date someone her age."

He ended the call. Confusion, shock, anger, and relief flooded through me. I slouched in the seat. Did he mean it, or would he wreak havoc again and try to—

My eyes landed on the scrunchie. Bright yellow. Summer had used it to tie her short hair in a ponytail, and I had removed it when she fell asleep on the passenger seat.

I should give it back to her.

40

# A SECRET

## SUMMER

"When's your boy coming over?" my nana asked me for the umpteenth time as I helped stir the secret sauce my mom was making for dinner.

"He's not a boy, nana," I said, knowing how much of a man Damon was. "He said he'll be here. Why are you asking me so much about him?"

"Because she wants to interrogate him," Mom said, coming over to help me and side-eyed Nana, who was sitting at the dining table, looking out of the window so she could see who's coming. "She interviewed your dad when he picked me up on our second date. When I came back home, she told me to marry him."

"Aww," I cooed, giving a side hug to Mom. "I hope I find love like you two."

Mom narrowed her eyes at me. "What do you mean find? I think Damon is a pretty good husband material."

I chuckled and shook my head. They didn't know we were in a fake relationship. It'd be easier to lie and tell them that things didn't work out when the six months were over—now only four months were left.

"He's here!" Nana said, standing up, but I sat her down.

"I'll go talk to him first, okay?" I said as Dad opened the front door and let Damon in.

I swallowed and ran a hand down my dress. Our shoot was done, and I could relax with my friends and family for a few days before we had to go back to LA.

"Hello," Damon said, giving a bottle of wine to Mom and looking at me. "Hey."

His eyes seemed dull and swollen. Something had happened. Even his tie was askew.

"Hey," I said and held his arm to drag him upstairs into my room.

"Keep the door open!" Dad shouted from below, and I groaned, closing the door shut loudly so they could hear it.

"Sorry about that," I said, leaning back on the door. "They like to tease me a lot."

He didn't reply because he was too busy taking in my childhood room. The small queen-size bed with white lace draped around it, a bunch of pictures of my friends and family and an overflowing bookshelf.

Damon looked huge in my room. And I wanted to pinch myself because I couldn't believe that he was actually there. My teenage crush in my teenage bedroom. It felt unreal.

"What happened?" I asked him, his eyes going back to me.

"You look beautiful," he whispered, his voice low. "I... I found this in the car."

I took the scrunchie and thanked him. He was acting strange.

"C-can we..." He paused when I looked at him. "I want to hug you."

"*Oh.*" My eyebrows raised, and I opened my arms. "You don't have to ask me for that."

Damon hugged me, his strong arms wrapping around me as I hid my face in his chest that smelled like lilies, cigarettes and his cologne. I knew something had happened, but I was glad he was in my arms and embracing me so tightly that it was hard to breathe.

"I went to my mother's grave," he said against my ear. I was about to pull away, but he held me close. So I stayed still and let him speak. "She had written a letter to me, and I read it today. It... it was so superficial."

I hugged him tighter, his voice breaking. I rubbed his back when he continued, "I yelled at her. Told her I was done and came here."

My eyes burned, and I kissed his neck. "It's okay," I said, my voice muffled.

"Summer, thank you."

"For what?" I asked, running my hand through his hair, petting him, soothing him.

"For talking to my dad. I know he's a piece of shit and I'm sorry for whatever—"

"Shh." I hugged him tighter. "It's okay."

He sighed as if the weight of the world was lifted from his shoulders. "Yeah."

"How are you feeling now?"

He pulled away and cupped my cheek. I closed my eyes and leaned into him as he kissed me, his soft lips moving against mine. When he pulled away, his eyes were brighter. "I've never been better."

I smiled and before I could kiss him again or have a hot make-out session on my bed, someone knocked on the door. By the sound of a wooden crane, I knew it was Nana.

I squeezed Damon's arm and said, "Nana wants to talk to you. Good luck."

He frowned and nodded, clearing his throat and straightening his tie.

When I left my room, Nana was standing there with a serious look on her face. I left them alone and prayed for Damon.

Mom and Dad were in the kitchen, so I sat on the island stool and asked, "Did Carol call you again?"

Their smiles slipped off. Mom said, "She asked for more money."

I sighed and pinched the bridge of my nose. "She called me too."

"Oh, honey." Dad hugged me. "I'm sorry she's bothering you."

I gave them a forced smile. "It's okay. She's not ashamed to ask her daughter or her own sister for money. I don't expect much from her."

"I asked her to come here. Stay with us until she gets a job, but… you know how she is." Mom sounded so sad.

I knew exactly how she was. She gave birth to me, and her boyfriend disappeared, so she left me with her sister and her husband. She never came back unless she was low on money, and one of her many shitty boyfriends wanted more cash to buy drugs and alcohol. Her calls were persistent ever since I started acting, thinking I was loaded. I was, in a way, really glad that my aunt adopted me legally and took care of me like I was her own daughter. I wished I could repay them in any way possible.

"I'll talk to her," I promised. "I have to tell her to get her act straight, or I'm cutting her off."

"Summer."

I shook my head. "No, Mom. Enough is enough. Either she wants to be in my life—our life—or stay in her abusive relationship. She has to choose."

Our doorbell rang, and I walked away from the kitchen to open it.

"Summer!" Mia squealed as soon as she saw me, jumping

for a hug. I chuckled, wrapping my arms around her and squeezing her. "I missed you so much!"

"I missed you too, M." I hugged her tighter before pulling away to see her gleaming green eyes. "Stop! Don't cry, you goober. Come on in."

"Summer," James, Mia's hot boyfriend, said, nodding at me and giving me a bottle of my favorite whiskey.

"I missed you too, James," I said, giving him a hug.

Behind them, Emma, Cillian, Ivy and Aiden were walking in, so I kept the door open, hugging my best friends and inviting them in.

I was putting all the wine bottles and whiskey on the coffee table when Nana walked down the stairs. Damon followed her and it was hard to gauge Nana's expression when she asked me to lean down to her height.

She whispered in my ear, "Marry him." Before walking away.

My eyes widened as I looked at Damon, who was hugging Emma with a warm, sincere smile on his face.

When he walked up to me, I asked him, "What did you guys talk about?"

He hummed, roving his gaze over me and said, "It's a secret."

# PART IV

"I broke a rule."

41

# PARTICULAR PERSON

## DAMON

When Summer's nana said she wanted to talk to me with her serious face, I thought I knew how it would go. After all, I had watched enough K-Dramas with Emma and Mia to know how this works.

So, before she could say a word, I set my intentions straight even though there wasn't a glass of water or coffee nearby for my parched throat.

"I'm sorry, but I like Summer, and I won't accept any money you offer to break up with her," I said, bowing my head.

There. Nailed it.

"What?" she asked, and I raised my head. "Why would I give you money to break up with my granddaughter?"

I blinked at her, confused. "You don't know? They do this in K-Dramas, but usually the genders are reversed—anyway, I thought you wanted to talk to me because you think I'm too poor or unworthy of her."

"Poor?" She chuckled, eyeing my clothes, and sat down on a chair beside Summer's desk. "You silly boy. I'm here to ask about your intentions for Summer." She sighed as I helped her lean her cane against the desk. "She has loved bad people before, and my sweet girl deserves someone better than them. Are you?"

Her stare was so intense that I had to be honest. "No, ma'am. I am not someone she deserves. *Yet*." I took a deep breath and continued, "But I will be. I am sorry, but I must tell you, I'm selfish and ruthless. And she's too… precious for me to let go."

She nodded, staring at me for a little longer, and said, "Make sure you eat a lot before you go, okay? Too skinny!"

*Huh?* I looked at her with confusion and looked down at my body. She thought I was skinny? I followed her downstairs and met my sister.

Summer's face turned sour when I didn't tell her how weird her nana was. She was glowing as she chatted with her friends, and I wished I could kiss her, but Emma and Cillian knew it was a fake relationship. I hated how her Nana kept praising Cillian and how he was not skinny, despite being covered in tattoos with a scar on his lips.

The dinner was delicious, and I helped Summer's dad in cleaning the plates before loading them in the dishwasher. Watching her smile and laugh freely around her parents made me feel warm.

Since the girls wanted to hang out on their own, we guys decided to play basketball in the nearby park. Aiden and James were wearing shirts and pants while Cillian was in a tee shirt, and I was in a suit. I removed my suit jacket and started dribbling the basketball.

I always thought that I didn't have any friends because I didn't need any, but I'd be lying if I said that it didn't feel great to have small talk with all three of them while we played. Cillian was winning since he was the tallest among us, but James was a close second until I took over, dunking the ball in the basket.

Since Cillian's friend, Sean, was passing by, he joined us too, and he was the most talkative among us, keeping the conversation light.

"Emma has started calling me ah-juicy, and it feels weird," Cillian confessed, making Sean burst into laughter.

"What does that mean?" I asked.

"*Ahujussi* means old man or old uncle in Korean," he deadpanned.

Sean added, "And she's calling him ah-juicy. Which makes it hilarious."

"Har har," Cillian said, grabbing the ball away from him and throwing it in the basket.

When Aiden was nearby, I decided to talk to him about my recent struggle. "My friend is having heart issues."

"I'm a therapist, Damon." He looked at me, his dark eyes narrowing. "Not a cardiologist."

James offered him a water bottle and joined our conversation. "Humor him."

"Right," I said. "He told me his chest aches whenever he thinks of this… particular person."

James and Aiden shared a look as Cillian and Sean joined in our little circle, basketball forgotten.

"Oh?" Cillian smirked, wiping sweat by lifting his tee shirt and showing off his eight-pack abs. I made a mental note to ask him how much he benched later. "I have heard about this before. Does his stomach feel warm?"

I thought about it and nodded. "Yes, it does."

*How could they know about such minor details?*

"Oh, no." Sean frowned at me. "I've heard that the worst thing is that their touch feels electrifying."

"Yes, it feels weird. Like a zap of warmth whenever I—*he* touches her."

"I'm sure this is a serious condition, right, doctor?" James said with a smirk, turning to Aiden.

Aiden pushed his glasses over the bridge of his nose and asked, "Damon?"

"Yes?"

"Your heart is okay. You are falling in love with this *particular* person and need to confess to her before it's too late."

I stared at him as the guys started laughing, slapping my back. I frowned at them. So they knew I was talking about me and kept egging me on.

"*Pricks*," I mumbled as they all went back to playing. James stayed back, staring at me with his blue eyes. "What?"

"I like Summer. She's a good friend of Mia's. So don't fuck it up," he said and whispered, "Because if you do and hurt her…"

He didn't finish the sentence and walked away.

Cillian was the buff ex-detective and veteran, but James was too fucking over-protective.

I checked the location of the bar that Summer and her friends went to and asked the guys if we could join them. They all agreed since there was only so much basketball you could play as one guy kept on winning.

We didn't want to be too obvious that we were interrupting their night, so we blended in the crowd. I felt too overwhelmed by the day, so I started my drink with shots. I watched Summer sitting at the bar through the dancing crowd, laughing with Emma, when a group of guys came up to them.

My vision darkened, and I walked up to her, noticing that Aiden, James and Cillian were also glaring at the guys who were trying to flirt with their wife and girlfriends. Meanwhile, Sean was busy flirting with the bartender and asking for her number.

"You look hot," a beautiful woman sat next to my Summer and her cheeks flushed.

I gaped and pulled Summer towards me. "She's mine!"

"Damon?" Summer looked over her shoulder and back at the woman. "Sorry."

The woman rolled her eyes at me and said to Summer, "Call me if you need someone who knows how to eat pussies."

I scoffed and said, "I eat pussies better than you. Right, Summer?"

"Are you drunk?" she asked, crossing her arms.

"No." I nodded my head. "A little"

Emma was with Cillian, Mia with James and Ivy with Aiden, so Summer took me to a corner when I ordered another set of shots. I pouted when she didn't let me drink them and pulled her over my lap.

"Tell me if I eat your pussy better or not," I ordered.

She giggled, kissing my cheek. "You're so cute when you're drunk."

"Tell me or I'll prove it to you right here."

"Yes, you eat me out really well."

"*Bet*," I said, kissing her lips that tasted sweet from her fruity drink. "You are so beautiful, you know that?"

"Mhmm, I know."

"Good." I forgot what I was thinking when I stared at her, so I asked instead, "Would you rather have a nipple-sized dick or dick-sized nipples?"

Summer burst into laughter, making me smile as I mumbled, "That's my favorite sound."

"What? My snorting laughter?"

"*Yes.*"

She caressed my cheek, and I leaned into it, kissing her palm. She kissed my nose and said, "I'd have dick-sized nipple."

"*Loser*," I replied, hugging her close.

## 42

## MY SILLY GOOSE

### SUMMER

Damon was absolutely adorable when he was drunk. He made jokes, which was surprising, and he laughed more, his dimple making more appearances than ever. I took a couple of pictures of him so I could show him why he should smile more.

Thankfully, Cillian helped me take him to his room in Moore's mansion that belonged to Emma. They both said their goodnights and went to Cillian's place as Caleb, his son, and Emma's ex-boyfriend, was in New York.

I helped Damon brush his teeth and remove his shoes. He was way too heavy, but I managed to unbutton his shirt and remove his belt. He mumbled something when I tried to remove his shirt.

"Stop!" he said, looking at me with half-lidded eyes. He covered his chest and said, "I've a girlfriend. A very hot, smart girlfriend."

I bit my cheek. "Yeah? Tell me about her."

"She is a silly goose," he blurted, making me glare at him, but he smiled foolishly as he continued, his dimple poking his cheek, "She's my silly goose. We adopted a cat together."

"That's really sweet," I said, and gently removed his shirt before tucking him into the bed.

*Should I cuddle him? Or sleep somewhere else?*

"Fuck it," I said to myself and removed my bra before climbing beside him and getting underneath the blanket.

I stared at his handsome face as he slept. I caressed his cheek and kissed him on his temple. As sleep came closer and closer, I thought about Nana's words.

*Marry him.*

I smiled and whispered, "I think I'm in love with you."

I had dozed off and hummed when a pair of strong arms wrapped around my waist, warm, minty breath caressing my cheek. I cuddled closer, feeling his chest on my back. And in my sleep, I heard him whisper,

"I think I'm in love with you, too."

I knew I was dreaming.

* * *

Next day, we video called Rahul and talked to Void, who was busy betraying us and letting Rahul pet him everywhere. Even his stomach.

We had already finished the shoot, and Damon was trusting our marketing team to handle it as we spent our time with our friends. It was surprising to see him drink beer with Cillian as they worked together to grill during our barbecue night.

Things would have been so easy if I were to date him and ask him to ignore the contract or burn it. He was different than before. More open and happy. Laughing at angry James when he scored last in Mario Kart, and helping Mia bake cinnamon rolls for us.

It was perfect, and I never wanted things to end.

Unfortunately, we had to go back to LA too soon, and

with one last promise to Mom and Dad about talking to Carol, I left with Damon. Surprisingly, Heather had stopped calling or texting me ever since we came to Coral Springs.

"Garrett published an article about us," I said on Monday morning, entering his office.

He looked over at me from his computer as I closed the door behind us and showed the article on my phone to him. "He thinks it's a fake relationship, since we don't post anything on social media and my fans haven't seen us together."

I twisted my hands as he read the article, trying my hardest not to ogle because he looked delicious in a black suit. Even with a scowling face.

"Let's change that," he said, calling me over and pulling me onto his lap. I stared at him, confused, when he took a few selfies and handed me my phone. "You can post them and tag him."

"That would be like we are playing his game. I don't want to give him so much power. Besides, I don't care what he thinks."

"Good, you shouldn't." He kissed my cheek. "Have you thought about what I said this morning?"

I rolled my eyes. "Who would want to buy candles, Damon? Especially from someone like me."

He had asked me if I'd like to collaborate with Moore and launch my scented candles. It was a huge deal, and I didn't think I deserved it.

"Someone so smart, talented, and driven?" he asked. When I didn't reply, he pulled back. "Fine, I won't push you. But you should think about it. Talk to others and see if you'd like to do it."

I nodded and when I was about to leave, he pulled me back, noticing the bracelet on my wrist. "What do we have here?" he crooned, rubbing his thumb over my wrist.

"It's n-nothing. I know you are busy, we can do it some—"

"Shh," he hushed me and stared at my skirt. "You can stay here. I have a video conference in a few minutes."

"Okay."

He smirked. "Good girl."

Before I could process what he was doing, he was tugging my skirt and removing my panties. "What are you doing?" I squealed when he lowered his zipper with me on his lap. "I thought you have work to do."

"I can work like this, kitten," he whispered, his hard cock sliding inside me, making me gasp. "Cockwarm me like this, yeah?"

"Cock—*what*?" I whimpered when he pulled me down on his dick, his entire length rubbing against my sensitive spot as he kept me seated on him without moving.

"Cockwarming, kitten," he said, kissing my cheek. "Keep my cock warm in your pretty cunt until I'm finished. Then we can play, yeah?"

I could hear him type on the keyboard while his cock was buried deep inside me, keeping me full. I didn't know how long it had been as he kept me like that, his heart beating at a normal pace while mine was hammering between my ribs. It was so hot, yet embarrassing. Keeping me full and horny while he worked. I had to stifle my moans and whimpers every time he twitched or moved inside me.

"Shh." He pulled back, spanking my butt and squeezing it. "You're making a lot of noise and distracting me."

I could feel my juices running down his length. "I'm horny. Fuck me now."

"Manners, love." He tsked, spanking me again and thrusting inside me, topping me from the bottom. "And I'm busy."

"Then stop t-this. I'm so full," I gasped when he fucked me again. "*Please*."

"You're such a greedy girl," he cooed. "I wish I could have you spread out in my office all the time. You know why?"

"Why?"

He rubbed my bottom lip and said, "So I can look at my pretty toy whenever I want to take a break and use you." I took his thumb in my mouth and sucked it, moaning as he continued, "Breed you like my little slut and continue with the conference while my cum leak out of your pretty holes."

I bit his thumb, his eyes twitching as he pulled back. "Please, fuck me, Sir," I whispered, pressing closer and kissing his neck.

He sighed. "I like the previous idea better."

I ignored him and started grinding myself on him. "Little brat," he groaned, holding my waist and fucking me. My hands clenched on his suit as I bit my lip at the over-whelming sensation of his dick pressing against my G-spot.

Our groans and grunts filled the musky air in his office as he lifted me on the desk and fucked me, throwing my heeled legs over his shoulder and driving inside me like a man possessed.

I came as soon as he touched my clit, moaning his name, that he had to cover my mouth shut and kept fucking me. It was so hot and euphoric that it triggered my second orgasm which lasted longer.

"Such a good fucking girl," he growled when his hand muffled my moan. "So pretty."

Just when he was about to cum, his computer notified him of his video call.

*Fuck.*

43

# I FELL FOR HER

## DAMON

"Fuck," I said, pulling out of her and fixing my shirt. "I have to take this."

She cleared her throat before I could accept the call, looking hot as fuck straightening her blouse and skirt.

"What is it?" I asked, knowing she wanted something by the look in her eyes. I'd have to force my wet dick down and suffer through blue balls the entire meeting.

"Sorry, I had something in my throat," she said, clearing her throat again and eyeing me as if I was a piece of meat. "Unfortunately, it wasn't you."

I raised my brow. "You want to suck my cock, dirty girl?"

She bit her lip and nodded. "I came, but you didn't..."

I sat in my chair and said, "Get to work."

Summer grinned, "Yes, Sir!"

My jaw clenched, seeing her kneel on the floor and get under my desk when I accepted the call.

"Good morning," I said, forcing a smile when her hands wrapped around me, stroking me slowly. "I had to take a call."

One of our managers from Paris said, "It's alright. It must be an important call."

I nodded when Summer sucked me in her mouth, my hand tightening over her hair. "Yes, it was very important."

The call lasted for more than half an hour as we discussed sales numbers and how we were going to market Summer's campaign with us, all while she was sucking my cock like she was dying in a dessert and my cum was the only thing that could quench her thirst. She kept me on edge by teasing me with her hands, lips, and mouth.

"Jesus Christ," I groaned when the call ended, her hot mouth hollowed as she sucked me. I held her hair as I fucked her face. "You're such a good fucking girl."

She moaned, eyes glistening with tears when I increased my pace. "Sucking on your boss's cock like a thirsty slut," I groaned, so close to the edge. "I'm sure you'd love to be tied up here. Forced to cockwarm my cock in your cunt or mouth."

Her moans increased when I went deep in her mouth, deep throating her as I came. "That's a good girl," I moaned as I emptied my balls inside her. "Such a good kitten," I whispered when she swallowed everything and cleaned me up. "Licking all her master's cream, hm?"

Seeing the red flush in her cheeks made me chuckle as I helped her up on my lap. I rubbed her sore knees and kissed her.

"That was really fucking hot, Summer," I said, caressing her body.

"I'm glad you enjoyed it."

"Next time, I'm using a remote-controlled vibrator on you," I promised.

Her eyes lit up. "Next time?"

I nodded. Her thinking face appeared, and I stayed quiet

when she said, "I've been dreading to ask this question for a while…"

"Hm?" It seemed serious.

"What are we…" I held my breath when she continued, "What are we having for dinner tonight?"

*Oh.*

I swallowed and said, "We can go out. Try out the vibrator. What do you say?"

She hid her face in my chest, making me chuckle. I wondered if that was her real question or something else.

Because I wanted to be more. I wanted a real relationship. Not a fake one.

* * *

"Hello sir." I nodded as the man bowed and showed me to the door where the douchebag worked.

"Remember our contract or you know what happens," I said in a cold voice and walked into Garrett's office. It was worse than I had imagined as he munched on chips and scrambled to sit straight upon seeing me.

"What are you doing here?" he asked, his voice high pitched. I looked around at the pile of papers and post-it notes, some of them spelling out Summer's name. He had ruined her prom night and continued to ruin her image for money.

"I'm here to spill some secrets," I started, sitting down on a chair. It creaked with my weight. "You need to post a long article. It's very juicy and filled with details that no one knows."

His eyes lit up as he opened a new document and asked me for the heading.

*What an idiot.*

"I'm not fancy with titles, so you can come up with a

creative one. Start typing," I ordered, crossing my legs. "Hello, I'm Garrett. I was a complete asshole to my ex-girlfriend, Summer Hayes. I lied to her that I loved her to get in her pants, but when she wanted more, I spread false rumors about her being a whore and sharing her with my locker—"

"Hey! What the fuck is this stupid nonsense?" he asked, nose flaring.

I looked at him and he shut up. "That's the fact, isn't it? You continue to spoil her image in the public, hiding behind a screen while you are the real asshole."

"So what?" He shrugged. "Many journalists are—"

I slammed my hand on his desk and stood up, glaring at him. "Post the story. With all the tiny details down to what color dress she was wearing and how she broke up with you. If you don't, I'll make sure you get fired and no one in the entire world hires you. Understood?"

He kept staring at me with wide eyes, leaning back in his chair.

I held his collar and pulled him to my face. "Understood?" I repeated.

He nodded, trying to get away. "Y-yes."

I pushed him back in the chair and buttoned my suit. "Post it by midnight."

I left his office and called Rahul to check the article before he published it. I had already called Heather and threatened her as well, but she was smart and left Summer a resignation email. I had suspected Heather since the beginning since all she cared about was money. Heather was the one who had called paparazzi on the night of Summer's premiere, so she'd get bad PR. Since bad PR was also good PR. Summer had been devastated, but I had found a better agent and even a better agency to support her.

Summer had finally agreed to Moore's collaboration with her candles, and I was thrilled to have her working in her own department in my building. I had found her staying up late in the living room and researching different scents for seasons. She was hardworking, but her impostor syndrome held her back.

"Are you ready for the interview?" she asked as cameras were set up in front of us, people whispering to each other as makeup was kept in front of us on a table.

Since she was getting lots of recognition from her role, and our products were selling out faster than ever, one of the most famous Hollywood editorial companies had reached out to us, asking for an unusual interview.

The concept was 'boyfriend does my makeup', and I had agreed without asking Summer.

I nodded. I was prepared. I didn't know if she was.

When the camera started rolling, the interviewer started with a very simple question. How had we met? Was it love at first sight?

But the catch was, I had to do her makeup while we answered.

"Did you apply sunscreen?" I asked, not knowing if she had.

She smiled and nodded, her short hair pulled back with a cute headband.

I hummed as she answered how we met while I looked for concealer. I wasn't an ignorant boyfriend. I had a sister, the prettiest girlfriend, and I was the CEO of a cosmetic brand. Of course, I knew which makeup product was which.

"Close your eyes, love," I said, applying the concealer which was in her shade around her nose, under her eyes and forehead.

I could hear people swooning as we both answered the questions while I gently dabbed the golden-brown foundation on her skin. She took skincare very seriously, and it showed because her skin looked dewy even without any makeup.

"What's her favorite color?"

"Yellow."

"Favorite cuisine?"

"Italian."

"Weather?"

"Monsoon."

Her eyes were wide as I answered each question correctly.

"How am I doing so far?" I asked her, using the monstrosity that's called eyelash curler.

"Hmm, so far, so good," she replied as I held her chin.

"Just good?" I asked as she opened her eyes. "I'm better."

She giggled and I couldn't help it, I leaned in and kissed her lips. Just for a second. Everyone *aww-ed*, but I ignored them as I smiled at her flustered cheeks.

She looked adorable.

The interviewer continued as I did her eyeshadow with a neutral base and applied some blush. Once I had applied a peachy red lipstick, we were done. Summer loved it and gave me an eight out of ten.

I narrowed my eyes and whispered in her ear, covering my mic, "You're cumming eight times tonight, love."

Her gasp made me smirk as I asked the interviewer if we had answered all the questions or not.

"Now one last question," she replied, smiling brightly at both of us and said, "Who fell in love first and when did it happen?"

Before Summer could reply, I said, "I did. I fell for her first." I held her hand and squeezed it. "I never knew what love was until I met her. I hated her cookies and hated her when she pranked me, making my hair blue." Everyone chuckled as I looked at her and said truthfully, "I have loved you since the beginning, Summer. Even if you vent about the dark lord, which is me, by the way, to my sister, I'll still love you."

I swallowed and looked at the interviewer. "I can't answer when because I didn't wake up one day and realize I loved her. Because I have always loved her."

Her hand went clammy in my hand, but I didn't let go as we cleared the interview, and all the people watching from behind the camera came rushing to thank us and compliment me on my makeup skills.

"Summer?"

She removed her hand from mine and said, "I-I need to go."

*I fell for her first.*

His words rang in my ears as I made my way out of the studio with shaky legs.

"Summer!" Damon called, following me as I hurried my pace. "Summer, wait!"

I turned around, all of a sudden angry at him. "What do you want?"

He looked around at the employees that were in the building and held my hand, dragging me to his private elevator. He pressed the button for the highest floor and asked, "Why did you run away?"

I pulled away and stood as far as I could from him. "I didn't know you could lie so well in front of the camera."

He clenched his jaw. "Don't change the subject. Tell me why you ran away."

"How could you lie about all this?" I asked, hating how inaudible my voice was. "I get it. It's a fake relationship, but—"

He stopped me and held my shoulders. "What if I told you

that I wasn't lying?" he asked, his voice soft. "What if I told you that whatever I said was the truth?"

My eyes widened and lips parted. "W-what?" I shook my head as I stared at him. "It couldn't be. You're just teasing me, right?"

Damon swallowed as he shook his head. "It's the truth, love," he whispered. "I'm yours as long as you'll have me."

I took a sharp intake of breath hearing his words. My heart was pounding in my ears as the doors of the car opened and he pressed the button for the basement.

"But how?" I asked, confused and surprised and angry. "You have the emotional stability of a rock!"

He deadpanned. "Thanks."

I shook my head and paced around the tiny elevator. "I don't understand. What's happening?"

"I broke a rule, Summer."

"What?" I snapped at him. "What rule?"

"I told you not to fall in love with me, but I broke it." He stepped close, and I had nowhere to escape. "I'm sorry for breaking a rule and falling in love with you."

My eyes glistened and vision blurred. I clenched my hands in fists as I asked him, "A-are you sure? You're not pranking me for dying your hair blue, right? Cause if you are, you're the biggest jerk—"

"I'm not, Summer," he said with a firm voice. "And it's okay. I didn't say it because I want to hear you say it back. I just… want you to know how I feel."

I bit my lip, my stomach fluttering with butterflies. I stared up at his gray eyes that were lighter than ever. "You can't take it back," I warned him.

His arms wrapped around my waist. "I won't."

I tipped on my toes and kissed him. He pulled me closer, cupping my cheek and giving me a proper French kiss before pulling away.

"I don't know how to say it yet but…," I said the truth and continued, "I like you. A lot. And I'll get there soon."

He chuckled, and it felt like home. "It's okay, Summer. Lucky for you, I'm not going anywhere."

I smiled and kissed him again. "So, no contract?" I asked him, pulling away mid-kiss.

"Fuck the contract," he growled before kissing me again.

"Damon." I pulled away again and said, "You used pencil eyeliner on my brows instead of eyebrow pencil."

He frowned and stepped back to look at my brows. "Wait really? They all look the same."

I giggled and nodded. I didn't want him to lose the Boyfriend Does My Makeup Challenge.

Someone cleared their throat, and we both turned to look at Rahul. "Someone else uses this elevator too, you know?" he asked, pushing glasses over his nose.

"Take a different elevator," Damon said, pressing a button. "Give us a break."

I chuckled when he turned back to me and pinned me on the wall. "Now, where were we?"

I answered him by wrapping my arms around him and kissing him.

*Who knew I could charm my grumpy boss-slash-best friend's-hot-older-brother-slash-nemesis?*

I definitely didn't.

* * *

"You know," Emma started, sipping on a glass of wine, her engagement ring shining in the bright light of the salon. "I always thought Damon was acting weird. I knew the thing on your neck wasn't a curling iron burn but a hickey. I wondered who you were hiding."

"Right!" Mia said from her chair. "Even Summer was

acting strange. Venting about him all the time. I knew there was something going on!"

I hid my smile as the young girl did my manicure.

After his confession, we both had terminated the contract and signed a different one. To co-parent Void together, and we drove him with us to our new house in Coral Springs. Damon wanted to pay for it all, but I was stubborn since the collaboration with Moore for my candles had done really well.

Garrett's surprising article had made me trend on all the social media for two weeks and the director had approached me personally to cast me as the lead heroine for the next season of *Hate Love*. I was doing really well in my career and relationship.

As promised, I had talked to Carol when she was sober and booked her a ticket to come back home. She had cried seeing me and rambled about how she was going to be a wonderful mother and cut off alcohol. It was hard to accept her as she was since she never cared about me, but Damon was supportive whenever I went to meet her at my parents' house.

"I always had a tiny crush on Damon," I confessed, admiring the black color on my nails. I was sure he'd love it and ask me to show how it'd look better on his dick. Even thinking about it made me blush.

"Crush?"

"Tiny?"

Emma and Mia said in unison.

"Why didn't you tell us?" Emma demanded.

"Because he's your brother, and I felt guilty for having a crush on him. Not to mention, he was an ass."

They both agreed.

"He's still an ass, but he's my hot piece of ass," I said proudly, raising my chin.

"Ew," Emma said, making me chuckle.

"Now you have your own hot older sugar daddy," Mia said with a huge grin. "Just like you wanted!"

I giggled, thinking about it. "You're right." Then I remembered the talk James had with the boys, and one night, Damon had blurted it. "By the way, a little birdie told me that you have rejected James's proposal for the ninth time?"

Emma spluttered on her wine. "Ninth time?"

Mia's cheeks turned red. "It's just... I don't feel ready. I love him to the moon and back, but he has experienced so much and I feel like if I get married, I'll miss out on things."

"Aw, babe." We hugged her as we were done with our manicures. We paid the bill and left a hefty tip to the beauty salon as we walked in the cold, hugging each other.

"I felt the same way when Cillian proposed," Emma confessed. "But he promised me he'd move wherever I wanted, do things I wanted, and if I ever feel weird about our age gap, I should talk to him."

"That's a green flag!" Mia said and stopped walking. "James said the same things, too."

"What's stopping you, M?" I asked her.

"I wonder if I'm holding him back...," she trailed off and shook her head. "I guess we both need to talk before he proposes again."

I chuckled and agreed with her. We all hugged before driving away separately. I smiled as I saw Void peering outside the window, meowing from the house as I parked my car. My legs were attacked with furious body pets and purrs as soon as I stepped in the house.

"I missed you too, baby," I said in Void's stomach, scratching him as I made my way to the kitchen. "It smells delicious."

Damon was cooking red sauce with the same apron he

wore at my place. He kissed Void's head before he got fussy, and I let him sit on the floor.

"How are the girls?" he asked, stirring the pot full of bubbling water and pasta.

"They are well." I pursed my lips, looking at him.

*What's holding me back?*

I stepped closer and hugged him from behind. "Damon?" I whispered into his tee shirt that smelled like our detergent.

"Hm?"

"I love you."

He froze and a moment later relaxed, squeezing my hand. "I love you too."

My smile widened as I hid my face in his back.

**The End**

# EPILOGUE

## SUMMER

"What the fuck are you doing—"

My eyes widened and a small gasp escaped my lips when Damon wrapped his hand around my throat. His stormy gray eyes glared at me, his face dark.

"Shut the fuck up," he said, his eyes lowering to my lips. I licked them. The hand around my throat tightened. "I'm going to kiss you."

Before I could utter another word, his lips captured mine in a hot, fiery kiss. My hands came up to his shoulders to push him away, but when he angled his head to deepen the kiss, all my thoughts of pushing him vanished and instead, I wrapped my arms around his neck.

A small whimper elicited from my throat when he bit my bottom lip. My fingers curled in his hair. He groaned, angling my face to him as I pressed my body against his, feeling his wild heartbeat through the layers of clothes between us.

As if sensing my thoughts, he pulled away, removing his jacket. "Get rid of the dress," he demanded, glaring at it as if it offended him.

If I was able to think and not feel the warmth in my abdomen, I would have attempted a snarky reply. But in my oh-my-fucking-god-Damon-aka-my-hot-boss-just-kissed-me state, I fumbled with the dress zipper.

"Not even a please, Summer?" I taunted, my voice breathy. "I thought you were a gentleman, Damon."

I gasped when he turned me around and yanked down the zipper. "No." His harsh whisper was warm against the shell of my ear. "I'm not a gentleman in bed."

I shivered when his large hands lowered the dress. A sound of approval, a groan came out of his throat.

"But this is not a bedroom," I said, looking over my shoulder to find him staring at my ass. *Who knew that the prim-and-proper boss was an ass man?* "It's an office. Your office."

His pupils dilated and goosebumps erupted all over my body when his hands slid over my back. "Then let me show you how ungentlemanly I am behind closed doors, Summer," he purred, his voice gruff and deep.

My thighs clenched, and I pushed my body back in his arms, wanting him to touch me everywhere. Even though I hated him, I was deeply attracted to the man who confessed his love for me in front of cameras.

My filthy thoughts came to a halt when he pulled away. I instantly missed his hot touch and wanted to order him to hold me again when I heard him say,

"Bend over the desk."

Words died in my throat, my heart pounding in my ears. I wanted to—God, I wanted to so badly. But the brat in me always won.

"Make me, Sir," I said with my chin high.

"Brat," he whispered, turning me around and pinning my face on the cold desk. "Look how pretty you look with your ass in the air."

I gasped when he spanked me, his legs spreading mine before he pressed against me and I felt him. His hard cock rubbed against my panties, making me whimper. He leaned close, his harsh, warm breath caressing the shell of my ear.

"Hard or slow, love?" he asked, his voice deep and raspy, making my toes curl in my heels.

"Hard," I replied. "Fuck me like your slut, Sir."

He kissed my cheek and tightened his hold on my neck. "Greedy slut," he growled, sliding my panties to the side and thrusting inside me. I moaned at the pinch of pain, his thick girth feeling me up so good. "You're so tight. Fuck."

We both groaned when he retreated before slamming inside me again and again. His spanks on my ass made me clench him each time he fucked me. My moans kept getting higher and higher, and I didn't think I could control them.

Damon read my mind and removed his tie. "Use the safe gesture," he reminded me before shoving his tie in my mouth.

I moaned, the sound muffled when he increased his pace. His fingers rubbing tight circles over my clit. I squeezed my eyes shut when he tugged at my hair, my back arching.

"You feel so fucking good, love," he grunted, our skin slapping against each other. "I love fucking you."

I groaned in agreement when I felt closer and closer until I was falling and he was there to hold me. While light blinded me as I came with a moan, his tie fell from my mouth as I moaned his name, trembling in the wake of intense orgasm.

"There we go, love," he whispered, pressing deep inside me and moaning my name as he emptied himself inside me. His warm cum filled me up as I sprawled on his desk, panting for breath.

"I love you," I said when he caressed my body. I loved that he always wanted to touch me after we were done having sex.

He pressed kisses over my back, shoulder, and neck. "I love you too," he said, kissing my forehead before pulling out, making me wince. "Sore?" he asked as he kept my legs spread and cleaned me up, making me blush.

"Mhm, a little." I looked over my shoulder as he threw the tissues in the bin and straightened up. "You were rough in the morning, too."

He zipped up my dress and pulled me onto his lap. "So it's my fault that my slutty little girlfriend wants rough sex all the time?" he asked, taunting me.

I narrowed my eyes at him. "It's not all the time. I asked you for vanilla sex the day before and you made me squirt."

He said smugly, "And you couldn't stop saying you wanted to marry me once you calmed down."

I rolled my eyes. "Whatever."

"You'd look sexy as fuck on our wedding night," he whispered, his hand trialing over my thigh, making me shiver. "In nothing but a little garter."

"Why do you think I'd marry you?" I asked, raising my brow.

"Because I'm never letting you go, kitten," he promised, kissing my cheek. "I'll tie you up with chains in our basement if I have to."

My thighs clenched, and I wriggled my eyebrows at him. He groaned, leaning his head on the chair. "I just gave you an idea for our next role-play, didn't I?"

"You did," I said with a soft laugh. "You can be the hot kidnapper, and I'll be your willing hostage."

He rolled his eyes and squeezed my butt. "Whatever you say, kitten."

I stood up and patted my hair. "Make sure to buy masks and gloves. I want to be surprised."

"Yes, ma'am." He spanked me when I turned around and opened the door of the home office. Void sauntered in, plopping himself on the desk as Damon gave him his attention before looking at me. "Did you invite everyone for Void's birthday?"

"I can forget a lot of things, but I won't forget his birthday." I kissed his black fur and glanced at Damon. "I love both of my boys."

"Damn right you do."

"But I love Void a little bit more."

Damon glared at me, but when Void meowed so sweetly, he chuckled. "That's fair."

**To read Billionaire Boss's Explicit Bonus Scene type this in your browser:** https://BookHip.com/FRPRBZG

# PREVIEW OF DIRTY WILD SULTAN

## NASRIN

Zain chuckled, his laugh devoid of any humor making me shudder. He leaned closer and my eyes widened when his lips went past mine to press against my ear as he whispered, "I don't want to know why you think so lowly of me but I assure you, future *wife...*" A slither of pleasure rolled over my spine hearing his rumbling velvety voice, his lips brushing over the shell of my ear, "That you would be the one begging me to touch you."

He was so right, he had no idea.

I would beg. For him. *Only* him.

My eyes were glazed when they roved over his powerful, lean body, the muscles on his biceps moving when he leaned back on the stool. I pressed my teeth on my bottom lip, the air around us thickening with the steam, exotic oil, his musky cologne.

I met his eyes. "Then I beg you to touch me, Zain." I swallowed the lump in my throat and added in a soft whisper, "Please."

His eyes widened a little with shock, and something darker coursed through them. My heart thudded loudly when I realised what it was. Pure lust. Desire. If I could move back in the bath, I would, because his gaze turned predatory, and I felt like his prey. Naked in the bath, while he was covered in clothes.

I watched when he unbuttoned the top two buttons of his dark shirt, revealing the tan skin underneath. My tongue seeped out to wet my lips. A hint of a smirk grazed his lush lips when he said,

"Spread your legs and show me your cunt, Princess."

# PREVIEW OF DON'T DATE YOUR BEST FRIEND

## KIARA

"If you don't want to kiss me then . . . let's swim."

"Yeah, sure."

"Naked."

"*What?*"

"I always wanted to try skinny dipping." I pursed my lips and said, "And I really want to get out of these clothes."

When I thought about it, I wasn't feeling self-conscious about my body when it came to him. Yes, he had seen in me in bikinis and accidentally walking in when I was busy writing something on my Post-it in my underwear and bra. But I was never self-conscious about what he would think of me or my body. I did have stretch marks, but I wasn't uncomfortable about them. What I was most worried about was *myself*. If he got naked and my hormones spiked up, I didn't know if I would control myself and not jump on him.

Gosh, I sounded so bad in my head. Not to mention, my best friend would be the first guy I would ever see naked. *Way to go, Kiara.*

His voice was strained when he said, "What if someone catches *you* . . . me, both?"

I moved my damp hair over my shoulder. "We will be in the pool, Ethan. And no one can see us from the living room." I smirked when I said, "Unless you want to watch me while I swim, you can stay here."

The thought of Ethan watching me with his intense green-blue eyes while I was swimming naked in the pool sent a delicious shiver down my core.

His eyes darkened and he looked away, probably thinking the same when I noticed red blush creeping up his neck and making his ears and cheeks flush. *Cute.*

I prodded, "Come on, Ethan. Don't be a chicken . . ."

"*Fine.*"

He stood up, his tall frame towering me. I forgot how to breathe when his dark eyes seared me, slowly trailing down my body as if he had all the time in the world. His voice was rough when he said, "Remove that sweater first."

I raised my eyebrow at the sudden change in his demeanour.

Ethan said, "You have an extra piece of clothing than me."

I grinned. "Who said I was wearing any underwear?"

I loved the way his pupils widened in shock, surprise and then they were clouded by scorching desire. Biting my lips, I whispered, "I was messing with you."

Holding the hem of the sweater, I tugged it up and removed it. I straightened my damp hair and shivered. But it wasn't because of the cold air.

His eyes averted down my breasts, which were barely covered by the ivory lace bralette. As it was wet, he could easily notice my hardened nubs, which were begging for his attention.

We were crossing a dangerous line right now. And I knew neither one of us wanted to step back.

"Your turn," I managed to whisper.

# EXCLUSIVE CONTENT

Want more exclusive content? You can sign up for Mahi's Patreon to read exclusive one-shots!

As a supporter, you get access to early drafts, exclusive VIP content, deleted scenes, deleted chapters, cat pictures and YOUR NAME in the Acknowledgements of my books.

www.patreon.com/mahimistry

# ACKNOWLEDGEMENT

In March 2023, I got diagnosed with ADHD and autism. I love to grin and tell people that I'm not only neurodivergent but I'm super neurodivergent! I knew in the back of my mind while writing Tempting Teacher and Bossy Bodyguard that Summer was neurodivergent and has ADHD. I'll take a minute because I wanted to share something.

I remember being thirteen in math class and the teacher picked me to answer the question on the board. I stood up. I stared and started processing the solution. Before I could answer, my silence frustrated her and she said, and I quote, 'Are you from Mars? You can't even answer this?' I stayed quiet, my mind blank as she scolded me for not paying attention while I was trying my best to pay attention to her and not the whirring sound of fan, or the window creaking open and slamming because of the wind, or the students whispering with each other when the teacher basically called me an alien.

It was hard growing up with ADHD and autism. I think

writing Summer's story helped me a lot. It took me visiting two psychiatrists before finding the one who genuinely listened to me and my problems. It's hard to get diagnosed, especially as a woman.

Not everyone knows this but the first chapter, the prologue, of this book is the fourth draft. It was going to be completely different with her dealing with her ADHD but I started it all over again because Summer Hayes is a brilliant, strong person whose story doesn't need to revolve around accepting ADHD. She is not her ADHD and I'm not my ADHD.

I genuinely hope you enjoyed reading Summer and Damon's story. Even though I struggled writing it in the beginning, I love this couple.

Thank you so much for reading Billionaire Boss!

Thank you to my brilliant editor, Jeanie and the best proofreader ever, Edresa. There aren't enough words to convey my gratitude.

Thank you to everyone who accepted the ARC edition of this book and helped me share this book to the world. To all the bloggers and book lovers, bookstagrammers.

If you enjoyed reading this book, please don't forget to leave a review. I would really appreciate it. It helps find more readers like you and they are very important for authors!

Special thanks to the backers who supported the Alluring Rulers of Azmia Kickstarter:

Andie Vargas

Emilie Garneau

Christina-Joy Derrick

Edresa Ramos

Reece Laabs

Jeanie Creech

Danielle Cage
Angelize
Nijeara
Sarah

I adore you all!

# ABOUT THE AUTHOR

Mahi Mistry has been writing since she was in middle school. Soon, she fell in love with writing passionate, steamy romances. Her stories have elements of humor, suspense and character development. Mahi's main purpose in her life is to make one person happy every day, even if that is a stranger reading her book and rooting for the main couple or her cats by giving them extra treats.

She enjoys simple things in life, like spending time with her family and friends, cuddling with her cats, reading and writing drool-worthy characters while sipping on hot chocolate from the wineglass to validate herself that she is actually an adult. She is an avid reader of fantasy, romance and thriller books and thinks writing about yourself in third person is atrocious. She firmly believes that cats rule the world.

www.mahimistry.com